MOSES IN SINAI

Books by Simone Zelitch

Moses in Sinai
Louisa
The Confession of Jack Straw

MOSES IN SINAI

SIMONE ZELITCH

Black Heron Press
Post Office Box 95676
Seattle, Washington 98145
www.blackheronpress.com

Moses in Sinai is a work of fiction. Names, characters, and incidents are either the products of the author's imagination or are used fictitiously.

ISBN 0-930773-59-4

Black Heron Press
Post Office Box 95676
Seattle, Washington 98145
www.blackheronpress.com

For Juan Sebastian, who argued

PART ONE: GOSHEN

One

After the Pharaoh's daughter took baby Moses from the bulrushes, a wise man made him choose between a gold coin and a live coal. "Take the pretty thing," the Princess whispered. "Take the brightest thing." Moses was still damp, and he shivered in her arms. She drew a finger through his hair. "So dark and shining."

The wise man said, "Remember."

"But might I at least have a lock of his hair?"

"You may keep his whole head, Princess," said the wise man, "but if there is some wit in it, he's bound to die."

Princess Bityah curved both hands around Moses' chin and whispered into his hair, "Be witless, witless, witless." In that stone room, the coal gave off the only light and heat, and the Princess pressed him forward. "Take it, take it, take it."

So Moses took the live coal and popped it into his mouth. Bityah shrieked and gave him a violent shake until it flew out, trailing blood.

Holding him, she wept. "Oh, don't cry, Moses. Don't cry."

But Moses wasn't crying. He was choking on his own blisters, and he trembled in Bityah's arms until, drained and exhausted, he thrust his fist in his mouth and sucked. Thus he passed the test and would be permitted to live in Pharaoh's house because he was too witless to do any harm. His eyes closed, but he would not take his fist out of his mouth for all of Bityah's gentle prodding until, at last, he fell asleep.

Around the ridge of his lips there was a line of blisters, and the lower half of his face shook as though the coal still rattled there. If Bityah had called in a physician, he would have ground a paste of aloe, and in a week the burn would have healed into the perfect, blush lip of a child, but Bityah would not leave the side of Moses. Her hand was in his black hair, and her eyes and face were still.

The room she had prepared for Moses felt wrong now, with its copper bedposts and its heavy azure curtains. He should have had a little room, she thought, everything tiny. There was something too rich about that room, too ponderous and haunted. It would make him have bad dreams. Fiercely, she tore the curtains down, but then light fell on his face and he looked blighted, cursed. In the morning, she called the physician, but it was too late to treat the burn properly. For the rest of his days, he would speak with a stutter.

"Well then, you'll be my little monkey," Bityah said to him. "My little taken-from-the-water-Moses-monkey who chatters nonsense and climbs all over me." .

His eyes were deep and warm, and they might have made a beauty of him, but his burnt mouth gaped and made him look perpetually bewildered. This wrenched the heart of Bityah as pure beauty never could, and she trembled to think of how he had come so close to death.

Death had been marked for him because of the Pharaoh's dream. The Pharaoh was not often troubled by dreams, so he was surprised to find himself sitting bolt-upright one morning with his hand on a wildly beating heart. Without rising from bed, he called for the twelve elders of the tribes of Goshen to be brought to his chamber. They kissed the earth between his feet and piled his lap with their rods of judgement.

He said, "A black fish came to me and whispered in my ear that a son would be born who would shorten my life and drive you out of Goshen into the wilderness of Sinai."

Zohar, the elder of the tribe of Reuben, spoke through clenched teeth. "You wound us!" For who in Goshen did not love the Pharaoh?

Hur, the elder of the tribe of Levi, raised his dark brows over a face like whey. "If such a son is born," he said, "we will all die." For in the Sinai even the shadows of the rocks were poisonous, and snakes ate men.

The elders conferred in whispers. There was no love between them, but on this matter they were of one mind. The elder of Ephraim rose on one knee. He was a landed slave, and in appearance he might have passed for an Egyptian, shaved, oiled and weighted with gold.

He said, "All sons belong to the Lord Pharaoh. There will be no sons."

The Pharaoh blessed the elders, and he was so pleased with their wisdom and affection that he ordered their rods of judgement painted gold, and he served them a breakfast of meat and beer before sending them back to their tribes to dispose of newborn sons.

The twelve tribes kept their promise. Before a mother rose from her childbed, the father would take the newborn, swaddle him, stuff his mouth with stone and straw, and bear him in a basket to the wadi where a current would carry him away to the Red Sea.

A daughter might ask, "What was that?"

"It never was," a mother would answer. "Blessed be our Lord Pharaoh who keeps us from death in Sinai."

It was not long after his audience with the elders that the Pharaoh found in his presence, without invitation, Balaam the blind Moabite prophet, resplendent in embroidered banquet robes. He said to the Pharaoh, "You have a newborn son."

"I do," the Pharaoh said. "Merneptah."

"He will make your life a short one," Balaam said.

Sweat ran between the Pharaoh's eyebrows because although blind Balaam had only been in Egypt for a short time, it was well known that his prophecies always came true.

Balaam drew himself up. His strange eyes flashed, his beard parted, and his open hands turned out to hold his song.

> *Above a man's head flows an arc of water.*
> *Whispers and fish gnaw ears.*
> > *Boxes unlock.*
> *Blessed are those I bless.*
> *Cursed are those I curse.*

Balaam laughed unpleasantly and clapped his hands. He said, "Truth speaks through me and I am truth's beloved. In Moab, for such wisdom I would be granted half the kingdom."

"From Moab you were exiled!" cried the Pharaoh. "I will not grant you shelter here! Saddle your ass!"

So Balaam left Goshen that day, riding his white she-ass who could see better than her master.

Merneptah liked to walk along the wadi in the morning. He was a sturdy boy who liked the mud, and he would return with wet feet and a pair of encrusted sandals clenched in his fist. He'd stomp into the small room where his father read his maps and would try to jump on his lap.

"Not now!" the Pharaoh would shout. "You're filthy!" Princess Bityah was the Pharaoh's heart's delight but Merneptah had no more place on a king's lap than a stone. The Pharaoh did not want to add that from the pores of Merneptah's skin came the stench of blood as though he'd waded through dead children.

In fact, Merneptah had walked upstream, far from Goshen's tribes. The walk made his legs limber, and though graceless, he was silent. One morning, he had pushed aside the bulrushes and seen his sister. She was soaked to the waist in mud. Her bright hair fell across her breasts and skimmed the wadi's surface like a net of gold. Merneptah's breath caught, and he grabbed a fistful of bulrushes and dropped his sandals. They splashed, and he could feel her turn to him. Her eyes were soft and deep. She might have seen him then if she had not seen something else.

A basket floated upstream, trailing a line of silver. Bityah told her veiled maidservant Zora to retrieve it, and Zora lifted her heavy skirts and waded through the marsh, taking hold of the basket with reluctance, and she said, "It smells like fish."

"Hush," Bityah said. "I must have what is in the basket or I will die."

At that moment, clouds broke, and it was as though a line of clear water ran between Bityah and the basket, pulling it towards her through the blinding rain.

After that day, Merneptah walked the wadi banks every

morning, hoping to catch sight of his sister. Only once did he speak of her to his father. He was five years old. The sun had set and he had taken his little bow and his quiver full of blue arrows, and in the dark he shot three quails. He made the cook teach him how to pluck and clean the birds, a servant's work, but one he took to with a steady hand. Just as steadily, he thought of Bityah, for as brother and sister they were bound by custom to marry.

The Pharaoh himself had been occupied with thoughts of Bityah. He sat in his map room, eating bread and honey, and he looked at the honey and thought of his daughter and dipped the heel in the pot over and over again.

Merneptah appeared in the doorway, up to his elbows in blood. "Father!" he cried, holding up a yellow carcass. "For you!"

The Pharaoh scrambled to his feet, and the honey pot crashed to the floor.

"Father!" Merneptah said, so single-minded that he could only hear his own voice as he wound his courage right up through his chest and let the words unroll through his broad mouth. "I have two birds here—one for you and one for Bityah!"

When the Pharaoh saw his son raise the two dripping carcasses towards the oil lamp and heard him say the name of Bityah, he grabbed him by the shoulders and slammed him against the wall so hard that the two quails fell from his hands and slapped against the floor.

Merneptah stared up at his father, and his mouth moved back and forth. Sweat dripped between his eyebrows.

The Pharaoh said, "You will never lay a hand on your sister!"

Blinking, Merneptah looked down at the quails and up at his father. Before he could think, he asked, "Why not?"

The Pharaoh could not answer. He turned his back on his son and imagined his daughter sleeping. She would sleep with her pet boy tucked under her arm, and her skin would glow like honey. Nothing could touch his Bityah. Let her sleep in peace.

Indeed, Bityah was sleeping. In the chamber she shared with her Moses, she curled beneath a light blanket, blowing a little into

Moses' hair as she exhaled. Above her stood the handmaid Zora in her heavy veil, staring down at Moses with loathing.

For Zora was from the tribe of Ephraim, a queen of Goshen, a great-great-granddaughter of Joseph the Proud. She wore her veil so that no common Goshenites could see her face. And now she would have to serve a Hebrew.

A Hebrew. In other words, a tribeless one, a homeless, landless, cursed, low thing. Zora could already smell witch on the boy. Who else but a witch could make a basket float upstream? Who else could turn her half-mad with longing?

Zora was almost sure she had seen, that day among the rain-soaked rushes, a girl step out from underneath that hair, a girl as ugly as a toadstool, the notorious Miriam, queen of the witches, cursed be her name.

Two

In those days in the tribe of Levi, witches ruled. Levites were kilnsmen and could only stand the oven's heat by night, so before sundown they dozed in the debatable shade of thorn-trees, chewing petrified figs and blinking away the flies. Hur, Levi's elder, seldom judged. He sat under the broadest of the thorn-trees, chewed the softest of the figs, and poked at flies with his rod of judgement. Thus, Levi was left to witches who scoffed at Pharaoh. They stole, slandered and poisoned as though there was no Lord and no law. The crone and her women would circle the tribe three times a day. Green fire would follow her, and in her wake, kiln after kiln would crack and expel a stench like old guts. Levi was helpless. Who could cross a witch?

The crone never approved of the marriage of the two cousins, Jochebed and Amram. Although they had been betrothed from birth, she forewarned disaster.

She said, "Amram is not like other men."

Rather, Amram was not like other Levites. He shaved his chin and clipped his hair to free himself from lice. Rather than hiding in the shade, he sat in the open, even at noon, and as Jochebed cleaned his feet, he absently carved at a branch of sycamore and stared at the sun.

The crone said, "He'll blind himself."

Yet Amram's eyes never dimmed. Rather, they turned a pale, engaging blue. Jochebed never tired of looking at his eyes or his smooth forehead with its cap of tight, black curls.

The crone said, "He'll tire of looking at you by and by."

"He loves me," said Jochebed. "He gave me a little dog."

"It has your face," said the crone.

Jochebed was plain as a pot. Every year, Amram grew more

beautiful until Jochebed looked at him as though she stood at the verge of a deep well and watched him fall away. Every evening, when Amram left Jochebed to stoke the kiln, she would sit with the puppy on her lap, watch her husband get smaller and smaller, and try not to be afraid he would never return. Every morning, he would settle beside her and say, "Lie with me." When she came to him, he'd ask her, "Why do you always wait until I call?"

"Because I love to hear your voice," Jochebed would answer, but in fact she needed to be sure he was her own Amram and not an imposter conjured by a witch.

The witches had already sent jinns in the shape of Amram to confound Jochebed. They were discovered by Jochebed's dog, who would nip a piece out of their ankles and turn them into a little bit of wet ash. When Jinns failed, the witches lit unholy fires to cloud Amram's mind, or they sent him virgins as he stoked the kiln to wipe away his sweat with their long hair. As husband and wife lay together, a chorus of witches stood before their tent and chanted:

> *When a lion mates with a hound*
> *Milk turns sour and fleece turns brown.*

The fleece of Amram's flock looked like old dung, and one day, the goat's milk in Jochebed's cooking pot thickened and stank. Nine months passed, and she gave birth to Miriam.

The moment Miriam entered the world, she leapt onto her mother's knees with her pink palms turned up and a smile spread across a face as ugly as a toadstool. Jochebed knew a curse, so she threw her into the cooking pot and bore her to the wadi.

The pot should have sunk, but it bobbed three times, and out leapt a black fish without fins or scales which swam upstream into the net of the crone. From that day, Miriam made her home in the crone's red tent.

"We must take our daughter back," Amram said to Jochebed. "No one can grant life and death but the Lord Pharaoh."

"Has the Lord Pharaoh borne a child?" Jochebed asked him. To such blasphemy, she added, "Amram, I want a gift. Give me a son."

To ensure fertility, Jochebed traveled to the tribe of Dan, and she returned with ugly little Hannah, the god-carver's daughter, who rolled a tin cart heaped with amulets.

"Lay them on the bed," said Jochebed.

Hannah poured out the amulets: tiny cats with mica eyes, stone scarabs, little bags of witch bane, and twenty-seven statues of Great Bes. That day, Jochebed and Amram took each other on top of a heap of gods. The two of them rose afterwards, bruised and sweating, and the dog yowled disapproval and slunk towards Jochebed to lick her wounds.

As Amram walked off to the kiln, Jochebed moved her hands along her belly. She imagined that as her husband receded, the son inside her swelled into a second Amram who would belong to her alone.

When her time came, she did not call out for the midwives who were, without exception, witches. Rather, she pushed and pushed. The tearing was sweet and wild, like anger. She must finish before a witch crossed the threshold. Never would they lay a hand on him! The whole world bled around Jochebed's thighs and then turned black and then turned white, and when, at last, her tongue swelled with blood, she could not help but cry out. A midwife came to find her pulling her own son Aaron from between her legs.

Jochebed drew him up. When the midwife reached for him, Jochebed spat in her face. "Too late." she said.

The midwife threw back her hood. It was Miriam, in a coarse red head-rag. Her milk-teeth glittered. She stooped, took something from the ground, and ran. Jochebed clouted gods at Miriam, but it was too late. She had taken Aaron's afterbirth.

Amram came home to find his wife with a pinched face. She would not let him touch her son. "He's mine—he's mine—he's mine—" she said again and again.

Amram, a good Goshenite, answered, "The Lord Pharaoh alone gives and takes away."

"He's mine, and so are you!" Jochebed shouted. In her stringy arms she pressed Amram and Aaron together.

That was when Amram first knew his wife was mad. The dog

howled and howled, circling husband, wife and son three times. Just so, three years passed and Amram edged around his wife as he might around something bottomless. Still, one morning he returned to find her sleeping, with her long face tucked into her elbow and her lank hair spread along the straw, damp with her sweat, and something moved in him, so he said, "Lie with me."

She opened her eyes. There was no madness in them. Rather, he read there grief, exhaustion, and a human need that pulled his heart in two directions. Aaron and the dog looked on as Amram closed his arms around his wife and gave her another child.

Those were the days after the Pharoah had his dream, when sons were fed to the wadi. When Jochebed was in labor, she felt a dark shock run from her belly to her loins and thought: This one is cursed, like Miriam. Then the head appeared, plum-colored, silken, perfect, and she thought, This one is blessed, like Aaron. She teetered between death and life and the effort made her swoon.

So Jochebed did not choose life or death for her child. Amram saw it was a boy and took him to the wadi before his wife would try to cross the Pharaoh's will. He swaddled him, tucked him into a basket, and carried him to the wadi's edge. As he lowered the basket into the bulrushes, he searched for a stone to stop newborn's mouth. The wadi was the color of burnt sugar. Just below the surface, pink, many-fingered algae swayed. A fine stone came to hand, and Amram used it to stop the mouth of his son, yet the stone leapt like a live coal from the boy's mouth, splashed, and sent a sheet of water into Amram's eyes.

Blinded, he rubbed and rubbed those eyes, but water streamed down without ceasing as he stumbled through the reeds and up the bank to the tent of Jochebed. He groped and found his seat, rubbing not just his eyes now, but the whole of his face, the face of a drowning man.

"He weighs me down," Amram said. "I cannot carry him."

Jochebed had recovered now. She'd found her newborn gone and felt a sense of relief she could not understand. She said, "Your hands are empty, Amram."

"He will break my back," Amram said. Then he was silent.

Yet, that evening, when he walked to the kiln, something made him look behind. In each of his footprints lay a little corpse with a stone in his mouth. Another step, another corpse, another step, another. Amram's steps quickened. Then he broke into a run.

Jochebed snatched up little Aaron and followed her husband's trail until the corpses melted into dust and moonlight, and only then did she know he was bound for the Sinai.

Amram's exile was well known, and Jochebed herself became an outcast. She pitched her tent at the edge of the marsh. Winter rain turned earth to stew. She was more sad than she could have possibly imagined, and she wept in the company of her dog and her son, chewed the ends of her long, dusty hair, and steeped herself in mud and misery.

Yet she woke one night to a rush of wind. The tent flap was open. Before she could think, she scrambled to her feet and said, "Amram."

He stood before her, burnt black and covered with dust, so breathless he could barely expel words. "Forgive me."

Then he fell straight on her, his arm slapping against the post of the tent and his feet raising a cloud of ashes in the hearth. Jochebed sparked the oil lamp and took his head in her hands, and though the Sinai had left its mark on him, he was still beautiful enough to break her heart.

Aaron sat on the floor, staring up at his father. His face was as plain and sad as Jochebed's. She drew him towards Amram who turned pale and edged away.

"Your son knows you," Jochebed said. She tried to make her voice full, warm and brave because it felt so good to see him, even if he was a ghost.

But Amram shivered. "There are many sons."

Jochebed grasped his arm and was startled to feel blood pulsing. Suddenly she knew her husband was alive.

"No," he said again. "You must listen." He rose and looked down at Jochebed with a face so fine and so despairing that her heart sank to her toes, and she was silent.

Amram told his tale—how he'd fled Goshen and could not shake the dead sons from the soles of his feet, how his madness drew him even into Sinai to seek his own death. He'd hoisted himself over rocks with his staff of sycamore, gone without water or bread, and before him rose mountains the color of manure, snakes, and thorn bushes, and behind him lay a rank trail of dead sons.

Yet once he'd lost sight of Goshen, he stopped, put down his staff, and knelt to take up the closest corpse in his arms. The corpse's purple head was covered with black down and his slant eyes were set deep.

"I cannot give you life," Amram said to the corpse. "And there is nothing you can give me." Still, he could not bring himself to place the corpse back on the ground, and that night he slept with its head between his hands. When he woke, he felt something crumble in his fingers. It was a yellow loaf.

And at his feet lay not dead sons, but yellow loaves which smelled of coriander and honey. That morning, he whispered to a rock, and water sprang in fountains. He'd filled himself with bread and water and he walked on with sturdy, hopeful steps; behind each footfall lay a fragrant loaf.

In that manner, he walked for months, and he saw many wonders, for Sinai was beautiful when it was empty of death. The birds that feasted on men's flesh circled his head and gave him shade. Snakes shed their skins along his path and from them he worked a pair of handsome boots. There was a pool ringed by seventy palm trees, each greener than the last. There was a mountain that moved from place to place, fleet as a storm.

Every day, Amram asked himself, "Who am I that I am fed and watered in the Sinai?" As time passed, Amram's pride overwhelmed his reason, and he thought, "I will return to Goshen, for I have shaken the dead from the soles of my feet, and I am blessed." And for the first time since he'd entered Sinai, Amram looked back.

Standing in his path was a newborn with a stone in its mouth. It looked at Amram with flat fury, spat out of the stone, and asked, *Why are you a slave?*

Amram fainted. He woke to find the sun blazing and no

bread in sight. Still, he was certain the creature he had seen was some trick of sunlight, and he continued back to Goshen. True, now rocks gave only thick, brown drops of water, but he had months of strength and magic in his blood, enough to carry him through deprivation.

The next time Amram saw the newborn, he had reached the place of the seventy palm trees. It sat on the topmost limb, swinging its thick legs, casting thick, green shadows on the pool.

Drink your fill now, it said to him, *for soon you will be thirsty.*

This time Amram did not faint, but neither did he speak. At once, he thrust his whole head in the pool to find it had turned to dust.

After a day, Amram's legs gave way, and he pulled himself forward with his staff, and then with his arms. Finally, he was unable to grasp even the dry thorn of the Sinai with his fingertips. The snakes who had once given him their skins drew close and nipped the edges of his shoes.

For three days, Amram lay still. He felt his skin rise from his flesh and hang in blackened folds. Small desert rats crept in and tested their fangs on his arms. Yet Amram did not die. When the third day passed, he felt something roll him over, and above him stood the newborn.

Now you know.

This time, Amram replied, though in a croak. "What do I know?"

For the first time, the newborn smiled. Its gums were ridged and there was a bubble of milk on its lips. *Why are you a slave?*

After the newborn had said its piece, he vanished, and Amram found strength enough to rise on his own and to return to Goshen. Thus did he find Jochebed and Aaron in the wadi tent. Jochebed had not taken her eyes from Amram as he'd told his story, and now she was silent as he drank stale water from the basin. Finally, she spoke.

"You're wearing the boots."

Amram nodded. He drew them off and held them towards the lamp, and the black and gold of the snake-skin was just the color of his hair.

Jochebed said, "We could go back together."

Through the tent cloth, gray light filtered. It was sunrise. Amram licked the basin dry and looked at Jochebed for a moment before he shook his head.

Again, Jochebed said, "We could go together. Aaron could come with us. Amram!" Now she threw herself at his bare feet and grasped the ankles with such violence that they cracked. "Don't be a slave! Don't make a slave of your son Aaron! Don't make a slave of me."

"We are all slaves," Amram said. "All of us are slaves." In a voice which sounded with both fear and regret, he said, "I can't go back to Sinai."

"You fear the witches!"

But Amram said, "Not the witches. We have another son."

Jochebed looked up at him with great hot eyes. "We have one son and his name is Aaron."

"We have another son, and I don't fear him," Amram said. "I love him. I cannot turn away from him again. When I held him, he sustained me. How can I fear him if he gave me life?"

"You do fear him," Jochebed said. "You're so afraid of him you're shaking even at the thought of him. Or are you afraid of me?"

Amram replied only, "I repent all the wrong I've done."

"Give me a gift then," Jochebed said.

"I would give you my heart if I could open my breast and tear it with my own hands," said Amram.

"No you wouldn't," Jochebed said. "But I want you to give me your boots."

Outside there was a crackle, as women snuffed the night's kiln fire. Amram did not linger, but he left his boots beside his son Aaron, who lay sleeping, and he walked away.

Three

Aaron loved gold. When merchants passed through Levi, he would beg until they let him play with sacks of it, balancing as many as he could in each hand until he felt his toes press into the mud. Later he followed them to Pti-Ramesses where that gold paid for meat, white cheese, wool and linen. It pained him to see the coins exchanged for such homley things, and before he mastered slave-talk, he could bargain in Egyptian.

He loved Pti-Ramesses itself where Seth, the lord of power, night and chaos, had his temple. It was like death to come back to the tents of Levi and sit in wet muck with his mother. His father and his brother were beautiful, yet he had learned early on that they would not return.

He had heard a rumor that his brother lived in the palace. There was a princess somewhere, and more gold. Any day, Aaron would join them. He knew how it would be, the princess herself coming at sunset, alone in a dainty cart pulled by a chestnut horse with bells all down the reins. She would part the cloth of the tent with her small hand and the red sun would filter through the gold of her shift and girdle. Aaron need only hop into the cart and they would ride away together, far from the tent and the mother and the scrawny, yowling dog.

Expectant, Aaron kohled his eyes and swaggered through Levi's tents like a prince. He passed the listless kilnsmen with a chin turned towards the sun, and at night he never joined the other youths who brought their fathers supper. Rather, he watched them like an overseer, wearing a pair of snakeskin boots so big that they flapped on his feet as he walked and raised a finger-high dust trail behind him. The boots were scuffed, but still so richly woven that it was a great wonder such a prize could have found its way into his mother's tent.

"Little bastard!" the Levite girls called, "Where did you steal those boots?" They called Aaron "little bastard" because he had no father.

Jochebed had told her son the tale of Amram, but he suspected that Amram too lived with the princess, sitting at the Pharaoh's feet and whispering, "Send for my eldest son, that he might delight you."

Jochebed could only storm and squint her rheumy eyes, and cry out, "The witches drove him mad, but he came back from the dead! One day, you'll kill every witch in Goshen!"

When she said such things, Aaron's heart rose to his throat. He was afraid of witches. They carried bad things in their skirts that could turn a man's zabb into a hazelnut. His mother was half-witch herself, with her crazy talk. The worst was Miriam. She would come up behind Aaron and he'd jump.

"*La, la, la*"— she'd croon. "Hail Aaron of the pretty voice."

"Stay clear!" Aaron would shout, and then he would run, for in Miriam's basket was his afterbirth.

For fear Miriam would turn into a black fish, he avoided the wadi. For fear Miriam would leap out of a cooking pot, he made his mother scrub out every basin in the tent again and again. He scraped himself raw with a pumice stone. There would be no witch mark on him when the hour came. Still, seven years passed and not once did the flap of the tent part to reveal cart, horse, and princess.

"Why didn't you give me away like my brother!" Aaron demanded of his mother.

"You have no brother. He never was," Jochebed said evenly, like a good Goshenite, but then she turned perverse again and tried to kiss him until he pushed her away and stomped out of the tent to think. The dog tagged behind. He gave it a kick in the flanks, and it whimpered into the thorn scrub.

Aaron walked bravely, not like a Levite shuffling. If the princess saw him now, she would think him her own-born son. His hair streamed back from high temples and his long face was willful and composed. Too soon, he'd have to stoke the kiln beside Levites with the faces of dogs. Under the moon, the road to Pti-Ramesses glowed. He could make out, far off, the jewel box of the palace.

There was a hand on his shoulder. Aaron jumped, ready to curse his mother, but there stood an Egyptian scribe, one of those who numbered bricks and men.

He addressed Aaron in slave talk. "Where did you get those boots?"

Aaron answered in Egyptian, "From my father."

The scribe stepped back and smiled. He spoke Egyptian now. "They are fine boots."

Aaron said nothing. The scribe had close-cropped down on his head and a baton in his belt. He said:

"I like them, Hebrew. Give them to me."

And it was as though Aaron knew, for the first time, that there would be no cart and no horse. He felt so lost he could barely feel himself slip off the boots and hand them to the man, who took them and walked away without a word.

Aaron didn't move. Behind him were the tents of Levi, where the scribe would go that night to number slaves, and among those slaves would be numbered Aaron the Levite, Jochebed's son.

He returned to the tent where Jochebed was rinsing a stewpot full of lentils and the dog was licking the soiled water from the floor. Both looked up with the same eager, open smiles.

Aaron said, "Mother, they took the boots."

When Jochebed saw Aaron's bare feet, the blood drained from her face, and up her neck crept a red like kiln fire. For the first time in his life, Aaron was afraid of his mother.

His voice lost authority. "They have the right to take them."

"No they don't," said Jochebed. She did not raise her voice. "They belong to me."

Aaron ignored such nonsense. He went on. "He called me a Hebrew."

"Your father gave them to me. They are mine and so are you," Jochebed said. She drew him close; her breath was rotten. "I pulled you from myself! Did Pharaoh pull you from himself? Did he taste blood?"

Aaron wrenched himself free, and he made a show of throwing back his head and laughing. "So you're mad? That's old news! But I'd rather be the Lord Pharaoh's than yours! I'd rather be a slave!"

Without looking back at Jochebed, he turned and left the tent, and he kept laughing because it made him feel strong and wild. He laughed at the frogs' eggs lining the wadi. He laughed at the golden moon. He laughed at the palace. When he'd finished laughing, he crouched at the edge of the road to Pti-Ramesses and was surprised to hear his own voice addressing the Pharaoh.

"Say something. Give me something. I know that I belong to you, and in return, give me proof that you know me, some word, some sign."

Yet nothing was said; the frogs sang to their eggs and the gnats sang to their reeds, but nobody sang to Aaron. The tent cloth of the night sky never parted, and nothing, not so much as moonlight, fell into his hands.

After that night, Aaron dropped his swagger and took his place among the other Levite boys, stoking the kiln. He stared clear through the peppery heat in a way no youth could match. Days, he'd laze under a thorn tree like any other Levite and watch newborns thrust into reed baskets and set in the wadi to drown.

So worthy of trust he seemed that the Egyptian scribe in the snakeskin boots began to send him to Pti-Ramesses on errands. Aaron obeyed hungrily, for though he was without hope, he longed for the tiled walls, the carts brimming with cucumbers and eggs and pomegranates, and most of all for a glimpse of the palace, though it was distant, now, as the moon.

He'd wander, carrying the scribe's bundles, and watch the great boat of the god Seth parade though the city. Slave and freeman pushed their way through narrow alleys to see the boat of Seth borne by his servants. The boat was water-worthy, yet it looked all the more splendid on the bare, strong shoulders of those young men, rocking a little as they walked, looming above the heads of merchants, beggars and slaves. The mast was golden and on the stem and stern were fixed baleful sphinx heads overwhelmed by onyx and gold. Within, wooden figures of oarsmen held gold oars.

Aaron whispered in Egyptian to a neighbor, "I thought this was the boat of the god."

The neighbor had a shaved head, and his white linen marked him as a novice priest. He laughed and asked, "You doubt it?"

"I don't see Seth."

"He cannot be seen," the novice said. "He is in the wooden box."

Aaron searched and found, amidst the gold, a box of wood. Simply, he asked, "Why is he hidden?"

The novice whispered now. "Because Seth is not a thing of wood and stone, but a true god, and if ordinary men see him, they die."

Aaron stared at the box as the boat turned a corner. He looked back at the novice and tried to hide his envy as he asked, "You can see the god plain? He speaks to you?"

"Oh no!" the novice answered at once. "He speaks only to the High Priest."

Aaron wanted to ask more, but the chaplain raced towards them with a censer of turpentine to chase evil spirits away.

That night, Aaron did not go home, but lingered in the streets of Pti-Ramesses. It occurred to him that the novice had not spoken to him as a master speaks to a slave. Aaron's Egyptian was passable, and his manners were a freeman's. He compared himself with every half-drunk Syrian trader he saw wheeling his way down the street, and then he laughed, richly, drunkenly, knowing his mother waited at home, yet letting his fancy and his legs take him too far for returning, past the narrow reedy outskirts to the heart of Pti-Ramesses and the gate of Seth's temple.

And at dawn, within those gates, the High Priest opened up the wooden doors of the tabernacle and let Seth see light. Aaron pressed close and peered within the court. Faintly, he heard the morning hymn:

Thou art risen, thou art in peace.

Rise thou beautifully in peace.
Wake thou, god of this city, to life.
It is thou who breaks the prison of clay
to spread on the earth thy powdered gold.
Thou who rises in the east, then sinks in the west
and sleeps in the temple each day.

Aaron knocked with a full fist on the gate of the temple, his heart full and knocking in his chest. He could make out the steps of stone, broad and ornate, all red with sunrise. The pillars, painted blue and gold, led to a gate, a second gate, a third. From within came the fragrance of bread and roasted meat, food for the god.

That day the gate was opened to Aaron the Levite, who gave a false station and was not questioned, and who took his place as a servant of the temple. They shaved his head and dressed him in a shift of linen, and he was given a place among those who dressed the god.

Jochebed entered the tent of the witches. She expected to find ten green fires blazing around Aaron's afterbirth, but there was no sign of wrongdoing. The crone sat on a cushion, so frail that she seemed little more than a handful of bones around two dark, bruised eyes. She set her dry mouth to a cup held by a smiling Miriam.

For reasons Jochebed could not herself understand, the innocence of the two women made her lose her reason. Heedless of danger, she shouted, "Where is Aaron!"

"That," said the crone, "is not your matter."

"If not mine, whose then? Yours? You have stolen two now! Aaron and Amram—"

"And the other," Miriam added, turning with the cup in her hand."

Jochebed shook her head. "There is no other."

Smiling, Miriam spoke. "*La la,* for all your life and wrath and even your forgetfulness are worth, they are like this." And Miriam turned the cup over and poured a little water onto the floor of the tent. It did not even leave a stain. The crone roused herself to shake her head and laugh.

Jochebed took a raw breath. She made as though to gather her gown to take leave, but from its folds she drew a knife, and she drove it through the crone's heart. Blood and water rushed out, and Jochebed turned to kill her daughter Miriam, but Miriam was gone.

The spot where Miriam had turned the cup of water had risen. It rose and rose, at first sluggish and pink and muddy and then abruptly clear, sharp, white. Jochebed backed away, holding the knife, and through the red cloth of the tent she stumbled, into the pack of Levite men who gazed at the sudden fountain that broke through the tent's peak and streamed in all directions.

She shouted, "I have set you free!" and then she waited for everything she'd lost to spring up from the earth's bottom, her husband, her son, her reason and her peace of mind, but the fountain gave only water. No one noticed Jochebed, for now they had sense enough to gather their posessions so they would not be washed off in the flood.

When they returned, Jochebed lay in the middle of a shallow puddle. The puddle was pink and tasted of blood, and her dog lapped at it with a long, wan tongue. The fountain had become a spring, and the Levites rounded that spring with stones and called it Miriam's Well.

Four

When Miriam fled the tribe of Levi, the rest of the women also disappeared. At first, the men thought they had sought higher ground, and they loosed pigeons to send word that the flood had receded, but weeks passed without an answer. Had they drowned? Had Pharoah claimed them? Had madness overtaken them and driven them to death in Sinai? Jochebed's dog rooted through abandoned sacks of figs and curled up in a dead kiln as Levite men forgot to eat and forgot to work for sorrow and confusion.

The only one who did not seem affected was Hur the elder. He sat in his usual patch of shade, ate clusters of dates, spat out the pits, and said, "They were all witches. Best off gone." The more dates he chewed, the sweeter those words seemed, until he did not want the women to return.

So it came about that Hur dislodged himself from his seat below the thorn tree and walked to the court by the well. He drew his gilt judgement rod from his belt and gestured towards the crone's red tent. "Burn it down!"

Stunned, the Levites obeyed and set to work tearing the thick tent cloth from its posts. They were clumsy, handling the posts as though they were red hot, for they still feared the witches. Hur forced his own son, Izhar, to set the fire. Izhar was just shy of ten, and he could barely see the flint for crying for his mother.

"Steady, son," said Hur, guiding Izhar's hand. "The Pharoah is your mother now."

The cloth ignited at once with such a blast that the Levites fell back and closed their eyes, thinking they'd be struck blind. Only little Izhar stared as patches of scarlet detached themselves from the canvas and floated every which way, like loosed birds. Izhar wondered if he could grab ahold of one of those red birds and fly to his mother.

"Father!" he called to Hur. "Let me jump into the fire!"

Hur struck him upside the head with such a blow that it knocked him down, and ever after he was called Izhar the Simple.

Hur himself was no simpleton. He sent messengers along the wadi banks to spread word that Levi loved the Pharoah so much that it rid itself of women who could bear cursed sons. As a consequence, Levi prospered. The Pharoah presented Hur with two gold neck rings and six lapis jars full of scented wax as well as an enamel tub. To the tribe of Levi, he granted pasture far from the outskirts of the Sinai, and he filled that pasture with lambs from his own flock.

For Levi's pleasure, he sent women from the tribes of Gad and Asher, small-boned, dark girls with sly, slant eyes. The Levites met the girls beside the kiln at dawn, and after they lay with them, they loaded a measure of bricks on their backs to pile into their carts and bear to Pti-Ramesses.

It was from such a girl that the news first came, from a widow named Reeba, a timid scarecrow with a scarred face and a way of tucking her head into her shoulder as she talked so that her voice seemed to come from far away.

Reeba's husband had been the elder of Asher. He had died in a way not uncommon, of exhaustion. So early were the deaths in Asher that the elder had been less than twenty-seven when he died. Forsaken, Reeba lived on wild onions and the milk she sometimes stole from the udders of Judean goats. One night, she climbed over a stone fence with a handful of grass to bribe a goat when someone grabbed her ankle.

Reeba dropped the grass. She was prepared to meet a Judean. Instead, she faced a young black girl with a red rag on her head who smiled up and asked, "*La la*, why are you hungry?"

What could Reeba do but weakly try to shake her ankle free and tell her to mind her own business? Yet the girl did not yield, and with that same friendly and fearless smile, she spoke in the same friendly and fearless voice.

"If you follow me, you will never be hungry again."

"Ah, sirs," Reeba said later, "I was so scared, I jumped straightaway over that fence onto the back of the billy goat, and he gave a cry and out came three big men who gave me the beating of my life!"

She pulled a little of her gown off of her shoulder so they could see the scars.

"She's gone," Reeba said, finally. "Praise Lord Pharoah, Miriam left me for the whipping. Lord Pharoah will provide." But later, almost to herself, she was heard to whisper, "Miriam keeps promises."

So they learned that the flood did not break Miriam. Rather, it freed her from the Levites and gave her wider range and power. Rumor had it that she had been seen as far away as Memphis where even the flowers had different faces. She bewitched women from their tribes. The mothers of Ephraim found their daughter's fine veils cast away. Dan's maidens ran off bearing their father's carving knives. The girls of Benjamin stole braided reins from she-asses and strung them through their own long hair, fleeing through pastures, over fences of stone and fences of wood, to the unknown where they would lose their histories and names. Once Levi alone suffered Miriam; now she haunted every tribe so that an honest woman could not bear her boy-child to the wadi without hearing: "*La la la*. Hail mother of the pretty son."

Thus Miriam pressed a forthright woman until she knocked her bundle to the ground and her newborn cried. Well might that woman call, "There are no sons!" but as she drew the boy up, his cry seeped through the crooks of her arms and her breasts filled with milk.

Miriam sang: "*Follow, follow, follow. You'll never bear children again.*"

Such was Miriam's promise and her song. Sometimes the women would dance to that song until they had no bellies where a son could grow, no need to take a bundle to the wadi, nothing to cast away or to forget.

Miriam was welcomed nowhere. Even the lowest Gaddites would not grant her a night's shelter. Still, she would drift through gates, skim water in the shape of a black fish without fins or scales, slip through the well-springs, leap up into courtyards, set her fires, roast her questionable meats, and spit out the bones.

But she would do none of these things in Levi. Hur swept his judgement rod through the last streak of ash where the tent of the crone had been, and by the Well of Miriam he set his judgement seat.

Hur would feel so cozy and so pleased that he would rest his hand on his son Izhar's curly head and recount a little history. "If I hadn't burnt the tent, we would still be under the rule of the witches."

Izhar did not smile. He looked up at his father with a puzzled, bovine expression. "Why did my mother go away?"

Hur did not answer, and he held back his anger. "We have much to be thankful for, boy. Bless Lord Pharoah every day, and curse Miriam."

At the sound of that name, the Well of Miriam bubbled, and a length of water rose and turned, scouting the courtyard. Finding no prey, it settled down again.

In those days, in the tribe of Reuben, there lived ten brothers. Their mother died when the youngest was born, and no one knew if they had one father or many. They were a scrappy bunch, dark or fair, graceful or slow-footed, yet all shared their mother's strength, famous in the tribe of Reuben. Motherless, the boys ran wild and took what they could take, and the steward saw their strength and made use of them, for he knew that soon enough there would be no more Hebrew sons to train as overseers.

He turned them ruthless and he taught them to use a whip and a baton. In pairs, the brothers worked their way up and down the rows of spindly, sad-faced men and women from the tribes of Gad, Asher and Simeon.

Sometimes workers would fall dead among the corn, and the youngest brothers, Abiram and Hoge, would have to bring the bodies to their tribes. The families would all gather around the corpse, staring at the two overseers with their slant eyes. Abiram was as thick around the flanks as a bull, and it would not take him long to dig a grave at the roadside under the palms. For this service the tribe would pay the brothers in grain and salt, but the mud was unstable and after heavy rain often they would find a bloated body in a puddle. Not even the Gaddites would mate with the brothers, for they were cursed.

"Who cursed us?" Hoge asked Dathan, the eldest, one day, as they set off for the fields.

"The Lord Pharoah," Dathan replied.

"What is the curse?"

"Our strength," Dathan said, and then he'd draw out his whip and strike Hoge, crying, "No more questions!"

As Dathan grew to manhood, he would journey to Pti-Ramesses with an Egyptian party to train to serve the steward. He would return with tablets and a stern expression, and when the brothers asked him about the city, the estates on the way, the beer and the women, he would say nothing. He no longer joined his brothers in the field, and at night, returning, they would see Dathan's lips moving over figures on a slate, scrubbing them with the heel of his hand, figuring them again, a line of concentration carved between his eyesbrows.

One hot day, three weeks into harvest, the corn cutters rose up and took their scythes to the brothers. They hacked Hoge's head from his shoulders, and though the others fought hard and cracked their whips, in the end they were bound with straw and set on fire. Only Abiram escaped, and he ran home and wept in Dathan's arms until Dathan pushed him away.

"What would you do? The two of us can't strike down every master's slave."

"They were our brothers!" Abiram shouted.

"Sit and calm down," Dathan said. "It was bound to happen. We'll find steadier work." Dathan told Abiram how he meant to live his life. He hadn't the wit to be a scribe, but he had strength. "And you," he said to Abiram. "You're already twice my size and still growing. The two of us could live soft."

"Soft?" Abiram stared, wet-eyed.

"Meat in the stew pot, brother, and everywhere women."

"Like Dodi?" Abiram asked, for he had seen the elder's daughter once, or rather spied her bathing in the wadi. She was as white and smooth as cheese.

"Egyptian women," Dathan said, "with round eyes and long legs and mouths like wine."

"Dath," Abiram whispered. "How?"

"Tomorrow," Dathan said to his brother, "we'll start for the steward's house and offer ourselves to him as assassins."

Abiram licked his lips, thinking of the meat and wine. He blew a long note through his teeth. "And he'll like us, brother?"

"Bring your club. I'll take my knife."

The next morning, the two brothers set out for their master's house. The journey took a week because Dathan made them travel by night.

"Who knows who we'll meet on the road," Dathan said. "We could cut a thousand down, but why waste our strength?"

It was then that Abiram knew Dathan feared the field slaves who had burned their brothers. It pained him to think that Dathan was a coward, and he found some consolation in striking the ground hard, often, with his club, thinking: "This is for Hoge! This is for Ramas! This is for Timor! This! This!" He would strike those blows until he could not raise the club again.

Then, soft, close by, he heard Dathan whetting his knife on a rock.

As they walked, Abiram would see his brother's face in the moonlight. It seemed to him, then, that Dathan mourned his brothers, for the face was not a quiet face. Light flickered through his black beard and his eyelashes, and his teeth glinted, grinding his tongue.

When they crossed into the steward's estate, Abiram asked Dathan, "What now?"

"We go through the window," Dathan said.

He led Abiram across a garden hung with palm-wide, waxen flowers, all gray and blue in the dark, and there was a low, stone window. It was unguarded. Abiram wondered how Dathan had known. "I've had plans for a long time now," Dathan whispered.

"Since you trained here?"

"Longer. Quiet. Help me up." The two climbed through the window into wooly darkness. Even in the dark, Dathan knew the way.

Abiram asked, "Where will we go?"

"His room," Dathan whispered. "No more questions!"

They edged along a hallway, Dathan's square, outstretched hand feeling for the doors, and at last he paused and caught his breath.

"Here," he said, very low. "Grab my arm and don't let go."

Together they entered the bedroom of their steward who lay somewhere in the dark asleep.

"Dath—" Abiram began, but Dathan set a hand over his mouth and he blushed and said nothing more, though he wondered how they could find favor with a man confronted in bed by two armed slaves.

Dathan drew out his knife. Abiram pressed his hand to his heart, it beat so strong. That was when Dathan stuffed the steward's mouth with a rag and thrust the knife into the steward's heart over and over again.

Before Abiram could cry out, Dathan stuck the same rag in his mouth and pushed him through the door, driving him ahead, and Abiram's teeth were drenched in the warm spit of the dead steward, his bile rising, his head ringing with fear. Dathan made him give him a leg-up throught he window, and as he stumbled after, the cloth dropped from his mouth, but now he could not speak. Outside, the garden wove a maze and they tore their way through beds of flowers and broke out, at last, into the open. It was only when the two lay by the wadi with their arms around each other that Abiram spoke.

"You could have told me," he said.

"You're slow," Dathan replied. "You'll always be slow. By the time you understood, it would have been too late. Now we're outlaws, and we have no tribe. We're Hebrews. We can't return to our house. We must give ourselves to the first steward as overseers and hope he doesn't know us."

"And then we kill him?" Abiram asked.

"Yes," said Dathan. "That's what we do."

"Why?"

"We're good at it," said Dathan. We've killed men all our lives."

"But we had a boss then, Dath," Abiram said. "Who's our boss now?"

Dathan didn't answer. He looked up the wadi towards the long, pale road that led to Pti-Ramesses and the palace, that white box rimmed with light. He plainly saw what was to come, the flight and the fear and finally, certainly, a sentence to the turquoise mines of Sinai where they would be worked to death, the fate of those who hadn't enough wit to know who they must kill to make life bearable but only strength enough to slay some masters in their sleep and move on and move on again: two homeless Hebrews. Surely they'd be asked: Who ordered you to kill? Who gave his blessing?

Abiram asked again: "Who's our boss? Who tells us what to do?"

Again, Dathan didn't answer.

One more Goshenite was a Hebrew. Everyone who saw him could tell that he had been handsome once, but years of sleeping in the open and eating roots and nuts had set his eyes too deep and made his cheeks too narrow. Still, his face was a good one, open and familiar. Gad's elder filled his hands with spit-weed and offered him his best copper spittoon. Zohar, the elder of Reuben, fed him apples and almonds. Dan's cheiftain, On, made his little daughter Hannah sweep shavings into a bed and place seven carved Baals in a circle around their guest so he would feel at ease. Only lordly Ephraim and Mennasheh closed their gates to him; the other tribes welcomed him for the sake of his stories.

He'd come at dusk and take a mouthful of whatever was in the elder's stewpot, beans, goat meat, or strong cheese, and he would spread his feet before a thick, hot brick, which even the poorest tribes managed to steal from the kiln, and tell his hosts about Abraham and his first born.

"Up the mountain slope he took Isaac," he said, "and in his belt was a knife for sacrifice, as sacrifice was called for. Already he had placed a mighty altar stone and laid his son's head down and raised the knife to strike when he was told to spare his life."

Even the dullest tribes knew those old tales, but it never hurt to hear them again.

"And you," the Hebrew would always ask suddenly, looking up with his light eyes very hot under his eyebrows. "Maybe you can solve my riddle."

Always, the hosts would feel honored that the Hebrew thought they could solve a riddle no one had solved before.

"In this tale," he would say, "Abraham was told to spare his son, and now we slay our own sons willfully." His voice would turn sing-song and lulling, and those listening would move in close and doze with their heads on the laps of their neighbors. The Hebrew would go on. "In those tales, we had one master, and now we have another. Who was our master then? Who is the master now?"

Yawning, the tribal elder, if present, would say, "Abraham was the master, and then Isaac, and then Israel, and now we have Lord Pharoah, Amen— Seleh." Then, they would rub their amulets between comfortable fingers, remembering the grace that kept good Goshenites from wilderness and death.

The Hebrew did not find his answer. He was too good a guest to say as much, but they could tell from his sad smile. His teeth were straight, white, and excellent.

For ten years, the Hebrew had asked elders, wives and children the riddle and had not gotten his answer. Though he had gotten a few offers of marriage and an elder even promised his a seat among his sons, the Hebrew gently told them all that he had sworn to wander until he knew the name of the master who made Abraham spare his son.

He would say, "I must serve him."

Such a statement couldn't be met with anything but laughter. The Hebrew's hosts knew he was a little mad.

"Friend, stay here with us and serve Pharaoh, may he live forever, who gives life order and who treats his servants well."

Yet the Hebrew seldom stayed even the night. He liked the feel of a rock below his head, the wadi to his right, the Goshen palace

at his feet, and a wind passing across his face. At times, he believed
the wind itself would give the riddle's answer, a truer answer than
a slave could find. Yet always, just as the wind seemed to find a
voice, sleep would overtake him, and he distrusted dreams.

He dreamed in riddles. They would rise in neat Egyptian
script on a papyrus scroll:

> *Gird up your loins like a man.*
> *I will question you and you shall declare to me:*
> *Where were you when I laid the*
> *foundation of the earth?*
> > *Tell me if you have understanding.*
> *Who determined its measurements?*
> *Surely you know!*

A dream had been his undoing, a dream of a son who would
cut short the Pharoah's life and drive the tribes from Goshen into
Sinai. Even now, when he would walk downstream, the reeds were
so clogged with smothered newborns that the swamp flooded the
banks and swarmed with flies.

If the slaughter was done in Pharoah's name, it was holy and
right. Amram had killed his own son with the Pharoah's blessing, so
his shoulders shouldn't have ached with the weight of that son; he
shouldn't have been driven mad; he shouldn't have been turned into
a homeless wanderer.

Yet he did wander, and where his feet fell, he had trailed
dead sons. Then something had turned those sons into bread; something had sustained him. Now he asked each of the jealous, dull-
brained, prideful slaves his riddle. "Who does not love death and
wants us to love our sons? Surely you know." As he asked, he kept
his shoulders low, as though he carried something.

Five

"Mo— Mo—" cried young Moses. "Mo— Mo!"

The scribe from the tribe of Menasheh etched out the syllables on papyrus, knotting his mouth in concentration. "I beg you, slower, sir," he said, for he had been ordered to get down every word.

Moses said, "Mo— Mo— Little-poo-little-Moses— Low-mo— MO!" in a rapid stutter, relishing the panic of the scribe who was an ugly, froggy man while he was the most beautiful boy in the world with a mouth like a pink flower lined with dew and shining black hair that the princess would not cut. "Mo-ses! Mo-ses! Moses the Master!"

"Here I am!" Bityah called to him, rushing out from her chamber with a cone full of sweets. "Little monkey, here I am!"

Moses ran to Bityah with a face full of sunlight and a mouth full of his own wonderful name. Bityah stuffed him onto her lap, though he was nearly thirteen now and growing tall. She took from the cone first a honey cake and then a pastry made of rose water, minced meat and pistachio, and she put them in his mouth.

"All day now you've played without your nappy," Bityah said. Oh, hadn't he grown like honey streaming through sunlight? Wasn't his chin like a cup of honey? Weren't his lashes as long as a girl's?

Moses said "Nappy." His pink and white lips touched and opened into that gape of wonder that might as well have been carved into his face. The scars made pearl-like lumps along the place where those lips might have been expressive. His eyes alone marked anger or delight, and now they glazed over like two brown pools clouded with mosquitos.

His day had been well spent, babbling out quick-fire nonsense at the scribe and getting himself all dirty with dust and scented water from the pool full of fishes. Beyond the garden wall there was a pen full of oxen, and when they bellowed, Moses bellowed back, kicking up clots of dirt and tiny blue flowers. Sometimes the oxen bellowed and sometimes they stomped, and a rich scent of dung and charnel wafted over the wall and mingled with perfume.

Moses often dug by the wall and found big bones, and that day, he'd found a thigh bone like a club, and he crashed it down on the surface of the pool until the gold carp flew out every which way. By late afternoon he had worked himself into a state of blissful exhaustion. He curled his long legs under Bityah's knees and whispered, "Today I played and the water broke in two."

Bityah turned pink and she drew her hands above her head to clap, shouting out: "Scribe! Scribe! Write it down!"

The scribe was slow in coming, so Bityah drew out her baton and struck him five times on his left hand as he scribbled with his right, and Moses used his own little baton to strike the right hand, spoiling the line and making him write again.

Then it was nap time. Moses loved to nap. Sleep came easily over him. His down coverlets were piled over a sheet of wafer-thin suede, and they were so warm, light and soft and they would flutter just a little when Zora the Ephraimite would wave her reed fan above him. Moses was bewildered by Zora because although her veil hid her face, he knew she did not love him, but she had to wave the fan, on and on, forever, because she belonged to him.

That day, after Bityah had settled him into his cool little room, he looked up at Zora, who drew up the fan of reeds and drew it down again until if filled with strings of light dragged back by shadow. The fan was heavy above the head of Moses, and Zora's stiff arm flexed and flexed again. Suddenly the light burst and set the reeds on fire.

Zora flew back with a cry, and the flames whipped up her heavy veil until she had to tear it off and stamp on it with both feet. Uncovered, she looked skinny and foolish, with tangled hair and little pig eyes squinting, and Moses laughed until he thought he would split in two.

"Dog!" Zora shouted. She raced towards him, all black with smoke, and she gripped the posts of the bed. "Don't you dare laugh at me!"

Laughing, Moses shouted, "Hebrew!"

"You!" Zora shouted. Through her smudged face, blood burned. "You know why I wear the veil?"

"Your ug-gly face!" Moses said.

"*Your* ugly face," said Zora. "Your ugly, cursed face and your idiot stutter and your open, idiot mouth and your low family who are not worthy to set foot in my father's house. But now I am not worthy, myself, to enter. Now even my own face cannot belong to me."

Even as Zora spoke, she backed away as though from the sound of her own voice, for she did not know why she was saying this to the creature she hated above all others. Yet she was driven to say more.

"You call yourself a master? I should have killed you long ago."

Moses stopped laughing. Yet neither did he call for Bityah. He stared at Zora with his sleepy, long-lashed eyes, and he tried to understand. When he spoke, it was without bothering to be clever. "Why are you a slave?"

"Why are you one? And now I might as well kill myself because you'll tell the princess, and I'll be dead by nightfall."

Moses did not answer. He lay back on his pillow and felt grateful when sleep overtook him and set him at ease.

From that day on, Zora watched Moses carefully, waiting, but she could mark no change in her station. Slowly, she decided that Moses planned to wait until the princess was in a bad temper. When a week passed, Zora found herself thinking like a witch, and when two weeks passed, she walked far from the palace grounds to search for poison.

She moved with the dignity of her tribe, hiding behind her veil the shame of her mission. Her steps were small and her hands were tucked into her cloak; she shouldered her way through reeds, eyes glittering. She had come almost to the wadi when she came upon three wild-haired, black-fingered old women sharing a hunk of bread by a fire.

From beneath her veil, Zora spoke. "What is your tribe?"

They answered all together: "The tribe of Miriam."

Zora shivered, but she praised herself for finding so swiftly what she sought. To her surprise, they produced at once a tiny gold flask shaped like a key.

"This opens," the tallest of them said, winking at Zora with an oily eye.

"A quick death?" Zora asked.

"The quickest," she replied.

Zora tucked the flask into her bosom and returned to the palace in time to draw Bityah's afternoon bath and to scatter the afternoon perfume along the tiles. Later, when Moses settled for his nap, Zora noted that he did not drift to sleep at once. He lay with the suede covers pulled unnaturally high. Zora made her voice gentle above the fan. "You cannot sleep?"

Moses turned over and looked up at Zora with a sharp expression. "No. Not like before."

"I have a potion for such things," Zora said. "Would you like some?"

There was a clean moment when Zora did not lift the fan. The muscles in her arm felt like hot knobs. Moses shifted his head and said, "Yes, please."

The "please" turned Zora pale. He had never said the word before. Still, in her bosom was the flask, and she drew it out, unstopped the mouth, and held it above Moses with a trembling hand. Moses reached out as though to steady her, and out came the liquid in a stream to seep into the skin around his heart.

Zora had planned to flee at once, but she heard herself whisper, "I will sing you to sleep, Moses. I will sing you to sleep."

The tongue of Moses searched his pink and white lips for the potion. He leaned his head into his shoulder like a bird, and above him Zora sang in a language he had never heard before. The words were slave talk, the language Zora had not spoken since she had been taken from her family as a girl. When she was a child, her mother might have sung that song; it might have been a song Joseph himself had sung to his children Ephraim and Menasheh.

> *Behold I have dreamed yet a dream*
> *and behold the sun and moon*
> *and eleven stars bow down to me.*
> *Behold this dreamer cometh.*
> *Come now and let us slay him.*
> *What profit is it if we slay our brother*
> *and conceal his blood?*

"Thatsh a good shung," Moses said around his scars, and then he felt the pillow fall from under his arm and turn to stone.

"Moses?"

Moses looked up at Bityah. The paint around her eyes was smudged. He gazed over her shoulder at a blur of a room, all the while keenly conscious that Bityah was following that gaze and wrenching it back towards her.

"Zora is dead," Bityah said.

"Why?" Moses asked. Slowly he could make out his own chamber which had changed in a way he could not fathom.

"She meant to kill you, my love," Bityah said.

Moses nodded. He did not speak again.

With a single finger, Bityah moved a lock of his hair from his forehead, and she kissed him. "You are a darkling little monkey, and if you had died, I would have died with you."

Moses drew the covers up and swallowed, as though his heart was encased in a fist that gave a squeeze then. There was a thickness in his throat.

"You are safe now," Bityahsaid. "Cuddle tight. Count your fingers and your toes and I'll return with supper."

The princess rose from her seat and drew back a layer of curtain so that a film of very faint sunlight covered the far wall. Moses rolled over and ran his hand across his face, afraid to find it changed.

"Don't worry."

Moses turned back. Above him hung a shadow.

It was a woman's voice, but not Bityah's. With effort, Moses could make out the face, black and weathered, crowned with a red head-rag. The woman sat on the edge of his bed, heavy enough to drag the mattress down. When Moses tried to speak, she put a hand over his mouth.

"*La la*," she said, "I am your sister. I sing. Aaron speaks. You do not have a pretty voice. You listen."

Moses pushed the hand away and tried to pull himself upright, but he found he lacked the strength. He had to look at Miriam from below as he might look at a mountain.

She moved in closer, and with her cold, hard hand she touched his forehead. "Little lump of coal, your fever's broken. So's your Hebrew heart."

Moses sat up before he could think. "He-brew?"

Miriam's eyes sparked. "*La la*—yes! Hebrew, hebrew, hebrew, homeless!" Rocking with those words, her laughter fell like small stones and crunched under her big, bare feet. "Fire-eater and split-heart, *la la la*!"

Moses opened his mouth, but his tongue twisted between his teeth, and indeed his strange heart had divided, pulling in two directions, to the east and to the west, to Bityah's need and to Zora's death, to the shadow and to the window, and from far off came a bellowing that ran through that veiled window like blood from an artery. It was an ox taken from the pen at sunset to be butchered, feet bound with heavy twine, muzzle turned up, neck exposed, and in the wake of that bellow, Moses lost all sense of where he was and who he was. When he surfaced, he was bathed in cold sweat. He gripped his suede cover, felt the stuff of it and knew where it was from, raised his hands, let go. Then he wept.

Later, the princess returned. She moved his head up in her arm and gazed at him with damp concern. "Did my foolish monkey have a bad dream?"

Moses nodded. There was a quiet Ethiopian handmaid who

held a tray. The mouth of Moses was already open, and as Bityah gripped his head, he could not turn his face away when she fed him tiny bits of meat.

Six

In the temple of Seth, Aaron learned the sort of obedience a slave could not know, an obedience he took upon himself. He learned how to rise from his pallet and run to a cold black bath. He learned always to walk with his head bowed; raised eyes could mean a blow. He learned to slip cloth over the shoulders of each of the gods who stood in their corners, to hang their hips with golden girdles and set wands of magic and power in their hands.

In return, he ate roast meat at a long table with a hundred servants his own age. They could not speak to one another, and no drop of gravy could touch their lips, so they shared the meat with fixed concentration. At night, sometimes, they would whisper bed to bed.

"They say even the servants learn a little magic by and by."

Mem, a sharp-faced, clever youth, always had a ready answer. "No—only priests. And not all priests. Since the old High Priest died, no one in Goshen can so much as turn a stone to water."

Winter rains pounded on the stone rooftop and their linen coverlets were far too thin to keep them warm. They doubled the cloth again and again and longed for wool which was forbidden in the temple. Talk, at least, distracted. Faceless, bald and lean under their covers, in a hushed nighttime whisper, they spoke of Throth's temple in Memphis where the goddess Maat the Righteous brought such holiness and power that even the mice in the granaries could work wonders. They spoke of Pharaoh the God who wove magic even in his sleep and could dream life and death on nations between two turns of his head upon the pillow.

"What is he dreaming now?" someone far off asked wistfully. "Is he playing with his son?"

From below a white cover: "His wife has yellow hair."

"Well, she's from far away. She worships Baal."

"Can she work magic too?"

"Everyone across the Sinai is a wizard."

No one spoke as each boy imagined the edge of the world and the kings held back by Pharaoh's wall of chariots. There were names: Midian, Amaleke, Moab where Blind Balaam was born, Canaan, Jericho. Each name was like ice, and they pulled their covers all the way up to their chins and wondered if they would sleep before the dawn.

Yet from the farther corner of the room, there was the voice of Aaron. "You say they work magic," he said. "Yet do any of these wonder workers, even the Pharaoh, hear the voice of Seth?"

A few boys sat up and stared, for Aaron did not open his mouth for weeks at a time, and they had never heard him string so many words together. Aaron himself was obscure, a lump of white linen and a pale head like a smudge. His Egyptian was formal and precise; it made them feel ill at ease. It was sharply that Mem answered: "The Pharaoh is a god himself!"

That should have been the end of the conversation, but Aaron went on. "Have we not seen his servants bring questions for the High Priest to pose to Seth?"

Aaron's words hung above that long, dark room for what seemed like an hour as each of the youths strained to find an answer, for it was true: five times that season a servant of the Pharaoh had passed through the gates of the temple with much ceremony and brought a question for the god.

Finally, Mem said: "It is custom."

For the first time, Mem's answer was not enough. The other boys waited for Aaron to speak again, but he seemed to have run short of words, if not questions, and though they could feel his presence as sharply as the cold, they knew he would not speak again that night.

It was true; Aaron was not short of questions. The questions had been mounting for all his years at the temple. If Pharaoh was a god, why did he fear the sons of slaves? If his wife came from a land beyond the Sinai, how did she cross death's kingdom and live? If there were other kings, might there not be other gods, and might not one of those gods call Aaron's name?

As Aaron sat up at night and thought, or ate and thought, or bathed and thought, he kept his eyes on the images of Seth he came upon everywhere. Seth wore the inward-curving calf horns of Baal, and his handsome greyhound face was long and wise. Here, Aaron thought, is true power. And he ached, for every day he passed the holy of holies where the true god lived, but it might as well lay in another world.

Once Aaron was permitted to sponge the flanks of the Apis calf, the black, long-horned god who lived in the temple court and who was paraded through the streets of Pti-Ramesses during festivals. As Aaron drew the sponge down the side of Apis, the dust on the calf's flanks parted and revealed a blackness as rich and dense as gold.

Aaron thought then: I will not be a servant forever. The premonition was so strong that his skull tingled. In the basin of water flecked with clipped black hairs, he saw his own face, long and grim, eyes sharp as topaz, mouth determined. Then a priest passed, and he dropped his eyes.

After some time, he was apprenticed to Nube, an older servant who showed Aaron how to dress the gods. He had lived in the temple for most of his life, and though he clothed the wood, silver and stone with proper reverence, he did not keep his eyes to the ground, and his face was finely painted. He was lean and dark, and his voice sang like the low string of a harp.

"I ought to teach you how to hold yourself, lad," Nube said to Aaron once. "Humility suits servants, but you tuck your head in like a slave."

Aaron did not show surprise. He took note of the warning, straightened his back, and took even greater care with his Egyptian. Nube showed Aaron how to make his eyes look round and how to darken his skin with almond oil, but he never questioned Aaron deeply. For a time, they shared a bed, though what they did there felt less intimate than their work together. After a time Nube chose to sleep alone, and Aaron trusted him enough to have no fear of reprisal.

"You ought to marry," Nube said to Aaron once. "In a few years, take a wife."

They were dressing the figure of Isis and her son, the infant Horus. It was a tricky job, as Isis held Horus on her knee, and the shift had to hang without a wrinkle. The face of Isis was long and calm. There was a golden sun disc on her head, and she wore a necklace of barrel beads around her shoulders.

Nube stepped back and surveyed their work. "We should have brought the lapis bracelets," he said. "And Horus needs a brighter diadem."

He looked so thoughtful, with his great lower lip pursed out and his brown arms folded, that Aaron was moved to ask him something which had long been on his mind. "Who dresses Seth in the tabernacle?"

Nube looked up and said nothing for a moment. Then he walked straight to Aaron and took him by the shoulders. "You know only the High Priest can look on the god in the holy of holies and live."

Aaron nodded. He knew that was supposed to be the answer, but it was not. If only the High Priest saw the god, did the god's clothing change? Just that morning, Aaron had seen the High Priest pass through yards of gold and clouds of incense, preparing himself to enter to holy of holies. Could he really carry beads and linen on his arm and dress Seth, as though he were a servant? It seemed impossible.

Nube read Aaron's face, and he took him under the chin so his lips brushed his ear. "Lad," he whispered, "I have many duties here and some are known not even to the Pharaoh, whom we worship as a god. Would you know?"

Aaron held back a shudder of joy, and he kept a seemly stillness as he whispered, "I would know."

Nube did not speak again. He touched Aaron's shoulder and motioned him down a corridor painted with blue and red Apis calves and yellow men. There was a pass too narrow for men to walk two abreast, so Nube stepped forward first and Aaron followed. The passage smelled of cobwebs and decay, and the paint on the walls soon gave way to naked stone.

Nube's voice was soft, but distinct. "It will be quite black in a moment. Grab hold of my hand."

Just as Nube spoke, Aaron made out a deep step ahead. He caught Nube's hand and stumbled, but he did not fall. The air felt open and damp. There was a pause as Nube struck flint, and then they stood in torchlight.

They were in a tomb. The walls might have been decorated once, but now they were yellow and streaked with grey. There were a few poor wooden bowls and figures scattered on the floor. Tomb robbers, Aaron thought, shivering. They steal gold and set a soul adrift to wander forever homeless.

Most striking was a mummy. Its case was very fine, and there was still a little gilt around the carving of the border, but the nose of the death mask had been broken and the arms were gone.

Nube had already walked on, and he looked back at Aaron who stood bent over the mummy's case.

"Look at the eyes," said Nube.

Aaron looked; the eyes were slanted.

"Yes, his father was Israel and his sons Menasheh and Ephraim," said Nube. "Once he had power here, and his god blessed him and Goshen during hard times. He was buried in the manner of an Egyptian and given a great tomb, and his children were to carry his bones back to his own country."

Aaron drew out a hand to touch the mummy's face, which looked so like his own in the water basin; he saw his hand was shaking and he was ashamed.

"Come with me," Nube said, and he pressed Aaron on to the edge of the tomb.

There was a little room there, just big enough to fit two men, and those two pressed together; Aaron had to press himself against the clammy wall, and he could feel the heat of the torch and the vibration of Nube's beautiful voice through his chest.

"Do you see this pipe?" Nube asked Aaron, gesturing towards a length of copper dropping from the ceiling and ending in a curve just by their heads. "Let me show you something."

Aaron watched as Nube took the copper pipe in his hands and drew it to his lips. Then he called through: *Hear the words of Seth.*

Aaron stared. Nube's cheeks sank and expanded as though he blew a trumpet, and he lowered his voice and lengthened the notes, singing: *My servant, hear me now. There is a young man who has pleased me.*

"I beg—" Aaron began, but Nube pushed him hard against the wall and went on.

He has pleased me and he will be robed in white and gold and ordained with the novices in the spring.

Nube had more to say, about the rains and the planting, about the fate of this or that landholder, but Aaron barely listened. Nor did he listen when Nube told him afterwards, how, at the appointed time, he spoke through the pipe which went straight to the mouth of the god in the holy of holies, how, in some temples, a servant worked a lever to make the mouth open and close, and how some High Priests knew and some, like their own, did not, and how he'd received bribes which he'd saved in a chest for his retirement.

"When I leave here," Nube said to Aaron, "you will take my place." He set a hand on Aaron's head, but Aaron pulled away roughly and hid his face. "I did not know," Nube said. "You believed?"

Aaron did not answer.

"But you are a Hebrew."

Aaron stiffened at the word, but he did not deny it. Nube went on.

"Your own god failed you. How could I know you had faith in others?"

"My own god?" Aaron's voice was broken now and the Egyptian words he knew felt alien in his mouth. "What god?"

"Forgotten," Nube said. He led Aaron back through the passageway, the torch in his hand, and he lingered for a moment by the tomb. "Lad, they say the man whose bones lay here worked wonders, that his god, whom you've forgotten, gave him the power to understand men's dreams. I am no Hebrew, but maybe if you told me what you dreamed, I would listen."

Aaron looked up at Nube, deeply shamed by his own tears. "You will laugh."

"Maybe," said Nube.

Aaron stumbled, finding it difficult to speak his heart; it was, at once, too strange and too familiar. Yet he tried. He said, "I want to know a true god loves me. I want to enter a holy of holies and be chosen and blessed."

"I am not laughing," said Nube. He kissed Aaron on the forehead. "I am sorry that I took you here because now you will hate Seth and hate your place here and hate me most of all for showing you there is no true god but only the voice of a servant coming through a copper pipe. And the hatred will grow, and you will become hard and vain and prideful. There will be no love in you."

Aaron did not answer. He looked, instead, at the ruin of the tomb which held only forgotten bones. Nube raised the torch, and the casket glittered; then he snuffed it out. Through black corridors, the two walked on.

That spring, Aaron was prepared for consecration in the priesthood of Seth, god of chaos and the dark. The first rite was the rite of circumcision.

Seven

Moses.

Here I am, Moses thought, bolt awake and shivering. His covers lay tangled around his feet, and the voice passed through his open heart.

At first he'd thought: Zora. But Zora was dead and the voice was horribly alive, a sharp, homeless voice flavored with such anger that it might have had teeth. *Moses, Moses, Moses.*

With every syllable, his spine stretched up a notch as though he were climbing something. Was it possible to live without sleep? The nights of Moses stretched like his spine as he sat in bed with a hum in his ears in the wake of that voice: *Moses.*

The Ethiopian handmaid would take him in her arms. She was velvet black with gold rings in her ears, and her skin was cool. Sometimes when she breathed, he could breath too. But then Bityah would appear and everything would fall apart. Her hair would be all stringy in her blurry face, and behind her would come a terrible torch. She would make demands.

"Tell me why you cannot sleep."

He would ask, "You sleep?"

"I cannot sleep! Not while my little monkey suffers."

Moses would ask, "You suffer?"

"I suffer for your sake," she would say, and then she would throw her arms around his neck and weep. There was a raw edge to her voice, and below her eyes, faint lines had bloomed. She made him drink warm milk and honey. She brought in three musicians, and they played harp, flute and drum, a low, sweet rhythm that beyond all sense took the form of the voice that called out: *Moses.*

"Why are you slaves?" Moses asked the musicians.

They did not answer, but continued to play songs of rest and tenderness, and Moses took out his baton and struck the harpist who overturned his harp and fled, and like an echo, Moses heard: *Why are you slaves? Why are you unhappy?*

He began to see things previously invisible. The sound of sweeping during his nap came from a stooped man smaller than the broom he pushed, whose feet dragged and whose creased dark head was vivid with perspiration. A child carried a laden chamber pot. His face was smeared with feces where he rubbed his eyes. There were fleas around those eyes, and the child's fingers crushed them. Those dead fleas too had a voice and knew his name: *Moses.*

Bityah thought a demon had taken possession of his soul. She learned the strong charms of a peasant: "Run out, thou who comest in darkness, who enterest by stealth, her nose behind her, her face turned backward, who loses that for which she came." She gave Moses a magic paste made of Ebu fish.

"Who killed the fish?" Moses asked.

Bityah replied, in tears, "My love, I would give my life for you. Why can't a fish?"

Moses refused the fish. He walked around the garden with fixed eyes, staring at the hot, bright heads of flowers, feeling their terror of the sun even as they were drawn towards it. He dipped his hand into the pool, and golden-yellow carp fled as though they knew him. He knelt there in paralyzed agony until his waterlogged fingers drifted to the surface and he felt a shadow over him. It was the scribe from Menasheh, ready with his papyrus and his stylus. His hands were covered with scars from the batons of Moses and Bityah, and he held his stylus a little crooked, face cocked, all eagerness, as though his hands were not ringing with pain.

With a lurch, Moses knocked the papyrus from his hand. "Why follow me?"

Breathless, the scribe backed up a few steps, staring, his jaw working up and down like a wooden toy, and he stumbled back against the wall through which Moses heard, yet again, the bellowing of oxen. The papyrus crackled under Moses' feet as he approached the scribe in an agony of anger and confusion.

"What do I say? Why write it down? Why are you a slave?"

The scribe scrambled up the wall and toppled over with a cry. There was a horrible crunch. From the far end of that wall came the bellowing which took the form, again, of the voice that entered Moses' heart.

A barber was called in to bind the broken elbow of the scribe. Moses shadowed him, dipping his hands in the plaster and filling the pot with lumps. He asked the barber, "Why are you a slave?"

The barber generally treated the Pharaoh's cats and baboons, and he did not know how to address Moses. He settled for tutting and clicking, which had best suited Bityah's pet shrew. "We'll patch him umpums, yes? Right-o. You want a patchy, baby? I'll make you a new nose."

"Do you make new hearts?" Moses asked the barber.

The barber laughed. "Now what would you want with a new heart? Then you'd have two, and they'd argue like two brothers."

Moses' hands were cloaked with plaster that had to be chipped off with a little knife. The knife drew blood, and Moses rubbed the cuts until they formed thick scars.

"Now I have scarred hands like the scribe," Moses said to Bityah.

"Oh, my love!" Bityah cried. "What will I do if your soul is torn away, if you join demons to walk head-backmost in the dark?"

He did not answer. He slumped off, looking at his hands.

Time passed, and one night, Moses did not cry out. The next, as well, passed without interruption. During the day, Moses gradually lost his restlessness; he kept to the shade with his smooth chin on his knee, leaning his back against the face of the north wall. He was still beautiful, but ragged around the eyes now, and the scars around his lips had stretched as though he had worked his mouth too hard.

So it passes, Bityah thought. He approaches manhood. The muscles in his shoulders and legs were well-formed, and there was dark down on his cheeks. Bityah chewed her finger as the Ethiopian combed through her long hair, and she said to her, "So it passes. Like a good baby, my beloved sleeps through the night."

No answer. The Ethiopian's clever hands were braiding now, and Bityah turned her face up and asked:

"Is he not my good baby?"

"Oh yes, my princess," the Ethiopian said. Her Egyptian was charming and slow, and the gold flecks in her eyes implied intelligence.

"And does he not sleep through the night?"

Now the Ethiopian said, "He does not cry out."

Yet for all of that, Bityah did not discover her Moses spent his nights on the garden wall, watching the cattle being butchered.

He sat with one of his long, downy legs hanging above the fish pool and the other knee pressed to his chest. His face was as still as that water in the pool as he took in what he heard.

The bellow of an ox under the knife. It came from the slaughterhouse beyond the ox pen, a dim box with a little torch light seeping through the cracks. There, Moses knew, the neck of the ox was stretched until its arteries stood, as dark nimble slaves strained to keep its legs bound, and a master butcher slit its throat under the eye of an overseer. The oxen in the pen bellowed in reply, raising a cry so wild and endless that it seemed impossible that anyone could sleep.

Why did they slaughter them at night? Moses had seen the butcher boys by day, hacking the flesh out in the open, blood-streaked boys with ox dung in their hair. Surely the overseer could wring their necks as easily as oxen. Even now, Moses could hear the heavy breathing of those slaves swell and bellow like the voice of another beast, and it called: *Moses*.

Perched, Moses listened for hours. His heart pulled in two directions, to the slaves and to the oxen. He thought: Jump down. He thought: Stay here. He'd loose the oxen. He'd free those slaves. He sat and sat. As Miriam had foretold, indecision split his heart just as the burning coal had split his palate, and that heart stumbled against his knee and called out: *Moses, Moses.*

He had been called. How could he answer? What did it matter? What would it take for Moses to leap down, rush to that slaughterhouse and break open the door? He would throw the overseer to the ground and face those oxen and those slaves, say to them: You know my name. I must know yours. The night was dense, and the faint shack seemed to sparkle, drawing him to the wall's edge until he felt the tendons of his legs stretch. He braced himself to leap.

Then came a blow. Moses reeled sideways and caught himself, gripping the wall. There was an arrow in his armpit. Below him stood a youth holding a bow and a quiver who stared at him with narrow, yellow eyes.

"You're not a quail," he said.

Moses opened his mouth, pain mixing with wonder. He tightened his grip on the wall and stammered out, "I—who—"

"So might I ask you!" said the youth. He took a step towards Moses, shaking his head, eyebrows all tangled up in thought. "No bird, but you were set to fly away. Now can you speak?"

"Oh!" Moses cried, for the youth had plucked the arrow from his armpit, taking with it a hunk of flesh. "I am—"

"You're the coal-eater!" The youth's face cracked into a smile, and he shook the loose flesh from the arrow, threw it to the ground, and reached up to grip the hand of Moses, heedless of the blood gathering at the wrist. "My sister's pet! Well met! Well met! Ha! I'll come up and sit beside you. I'm Merneptah!"

Moses freed his hand and realized that except for Bityah and Zora, he had never known anyone's name before. That name seemed to suit Merneptah, all round and hard. He was the first boy Moses had ever seen, and he was daunting, with his thick arms and his quiver full of arrows. His head was slightly pointed, like a hazel nut, and his yellow eyes glittered below a ridge of bone. Still, for all of that, Merneptah was friendly and delighted. He spoke on and on about how he had searched for years to find the garden, only to be blocked by his father's stooges.

"Mind you," Merneptah said, "it wasn't for your sake. You're with *her*."

Moses looked past him, into the yard, but the slaughterhouse was closed for the night. He felt a tugging in his chest, but Merneptah impatiently turned him toward the garden.

"Paradise," he said. He looked again at Moses, with suspicion and wonder. "She must be very happy there."

"Happy?" Moses said, not sure what he meant.

"Happier than I am," Merneptah said. He drew his knees up and stuck his chin between them. "I saw her only once in my life, but that was enough to make me lose sleep. She's like something made of gold and ivory, and her hair falls down like—like something good to eat!"

Past the pool of fishes and the white flagstones, from the chamber, Moses heard the soft, humming throb of Bityah's heart. That heart lived in a rib cage surrounded by flesh, surrounded by a soft brown hide. He said to Merneptah, "She is sleeping."

"I'm destined to marry her," Merneptah said. "That is why she refuses every suitor." Moses did not answer. Merneptah gripped his shoulders, and his breath boiled in his face as he said, "She isn't happy. You said she isn't happy."

"Why isn't she happy?" Moses asked.

"Because she's locked away," Merneptah said.

Moses asked, "Why is she locked away?"

"Because she is a treasure, and treasures are locked away," Merneptah said. He eased back on the balls of his hands now, looking not at the garden, but at Moses directly. "Because a treasure must be won with sword and fire. And now I'll win her, with your help."

"Why with my help?"

Merneptah all at once broke into such rich, wild laughter that he almost fell off the wall and he had to grasp each edge to keep his balance. "You ask a lot of questions! Ask me anything. I always have an answer."

Dazzled, Moses stared at the shaking, solid, completely alive boy who sat across from him, radiating certainty and warmth. To his right were penned oxen and short grass drenched in blood. To his left was a pool full of stupid fish, and the damning heartbeat of Bityah. How strange it was to sit dead-center in the company of someone who could answer his questions.

"I am the question answerer," Merneptah explained. "It's

because I will be a god one day and also because I stick my head into everything. My father says I'm a battering ram, but I can shoot a straighter arrow and give a straighter answer than any man alive. Look up!" he said to Moses.

Moses looked up, and above him were the moon and stars.

"Now those are real," Merneptah said. "Swear to me by the stars that you will win Bityah to me."

"Why stars?" Moses asked.

"Because they're real and true. They burned there before we were born, and they will go on burning after we pass on."

"Pass on?"

"I don't mean some peasant's superstition," Merneptah said. "I don't mean we'll work together in the fields of Osirus. But friendship outlasts friends. What lies between real brothers goes on burning like those stars. We're brothers?"

Never had Moses heard such certainty, nor had anyone before taken his two hands in such a grip. In that same spirit, Moses said, "We are," though his voice broke a little. The stars spilled across the sky like little bits of dirty plaster, but when Moses looked long enough, they sparked, and he drew his hand to his mouth.

"You chose the coal," Merneptah said to him, "but it wasn't because you were simple-minded. I can tell."

"How can you tell?" Moses asked him.

"Because simple-minded people never leave gardens," Merneptah said. "You are my comrade now, bird, so don't fly away."

Moses asked, "Why are you a slave?"

"This," Merneptah said, "is a very interesting conversation." He swung his legs towards the slaughter yard. "We'll have others. Come back tomorrow and tell me about Bityah." With a curving smile, he added, "Or ask me about Bityah. That seems to be what you do best."

He dropped to his side of the garden wall with his quiver flying behind him. Moses looked after him for a long time. Even when he couldn't see Merneptah, he heard his footsteps pass the closed slaughterhouse where the beef carcasses hung in the cool night air, through the kitchen where he plucked his quail, and down the hall to his own room, the clatter of his bow and quiver as he set them down, the sigh as straw ticking gave way and he fell asleep.

When Merneptah slept, Moses once again tucked his knee up against his chin, and the night closed in around him, obscuring the arrow wound, the shock, the conversation. Once again, he faced the slaughterhouse, but it was dark. Then, something sparkled.

A fire flared in a patch of undergrowth. Two men crouched there. How had they come so close? Surely the palace was guarded. A wind rattled the fire so that it was almost impossible to understand their low, strange voices. There was a tall man holding a basin full of something steaming; there was a shivering boy whom Moses knew from the slaughterhouse, a butcher boy with curly, greasy hair and a gaunt face.

The boy raised a hand, insisting on something, asking, maybe, Who are you? or Why are you feeding me?

The stranger's face hung low, and there was no mistaking his answer. I am feeding you because you are hungry.

This exchange was so simple that it did not need translation. A cloud passed, and the stranger set the basin down, looked up and showed his face, clean-shaven cheeks, cropped hair, and hard, light eyes set deep. Across impossible distance, those eyes met the eyes of Moses.

Breathlessly, Moses scrambled down the wall and splashed across the fish-pool, standing in the middle of a circle of stone and moonlight. He held his head in his hands.

Eight

The Pharaoh sat at breakfast and wondered what he would tell the king who had asked for the hand of his daughter. For twenty years now, messengers had come from as far away as Persia, and behind them rode white asses bearing lion skins or purple cloth or the carved tusks of elephants. For twenty years now, the Pharaoh had brought Bityah before him, and she had looked up at him with her round, sweet eyes; he could not make her go.

"She's all good, my Bityah," the Pharaoh said to the slave who poured out his buttermilk. "Is that not so?"

The slave agreed to everything, yet the Pharaoh was in a bad temper and walked out into the sunshine with his plump hands joined behind his back, and his soft, bare feet dragging on the paving stones. The messenger of Amaleke who had arrived that day ate a rich breakfast of red cheese, leeks, and sheep's head. Amaleke. Once it might have been the prince of an empire, and now it came to Amaleke.

The Pharaoh would meet with the Amalekite before midday. He did not like the man. Strung on the back of his ass were nothing but a few sacks of chunky turquoise, very likely stolen from the mines. In Amaleke, the king lived in a big tent and copulated with a priestess once a year to bless his goats. To fete the messenger of such a bandit, let alone consider giving him his daughter, soured the Pharaoh's stomach and set his head to pounding.

Yet there was Bityah's voice: "Father?" The music of it made the Pharaoh himself again.

"My Bityah!" He opened his arms, and she rushed towards him with her bright hair all in braids and her little feet as light as birds. She smiled up with such sweetness that all anger flew from him, and he kissed the top of her head and said, "Another came for you today."

Bityah stepped back. She looked grave, and she folded her hands below her belly and asked, "Father, would you have me go with him?"

"I would—" the Pharaoh began, and he knew he was about to say he would not let her go, but he checked himself. "It would be good for you to marry."

"Father," Bityah said, "you're wise and a god, and I'm silly and little. I'll do just what you choose, though it means I leave you forever."

As Bityah spoke, her small mouth formed a crescent and revealed teeth like a child's, and she raised her hands and bowed her head.

"I won't send you away," the Pharaoh said.

Bityah looked up, and in her eyes was such gratitude and delight that the Pharaoh felt his breath knocked out of him, and he reeled towards his daughter who burrowed herself between his arms and kissed him all over his face and forehead until he could barely think or speak or see. She rushed out with her arms spread behind her and left him standing in a pool of scented light.

It was then that Merneptah appeared. He was on his way to his morning walk along the wadi. The Pharaoh regained his composure, but when he spoke, his voice was thick. "Do not come to me unless I ask for you."

"I won't again," Merneptah said. That brassy voice, those peasant's manners. Maybe he would trace the wadi to the Red Sea and drown. Yet now Merneptah paused and sniffed the air; his face softened like a rotten fruit. "She's been here," he said.

The Pharaoh turned white and said nothing.

"Where is she now?" Merneptah asked. The Pharaoh turned away but not before he saw Merneptah's mouth pucker into a smile that chilled his blood.

Perhaps Bityah should leave the palace. But not with Amaleke, not with a brigand who hangs trinkets on donkeys. No, the matter was decided. The Pharaoh left his court and had one of his scribes write out the answer on a square of dirty wax. He sent to Amaleke not his steward but the reeking slave boy who emptied the chamber pots, and in that slave's hand was the message that the Amalekite should remove himself before the Lord Pharaoh leveled his king's tent with chariot and sword.

As for Bityah, she left her father's court with the heat of him still on her lips. Her light step slowed. She stopped to rest her hand against the wall. Where was her handmaid? The air itself felt heavy, and she would go no farther without aid, for these days she had been overtaken by a waking sickness that she could not name.

"Here!" she called. "Girl, come!"

The Ethiopian took Bityah up in her arms and carried her back to her quarters, singing under her breath: "*La la la*, he's in the garden. *La la la*, he'll see you soon."

When the princess was laid out in bed and a cold strip of linen was placed on her forehead, she said to her handmaid, "Bring him to me."

Not long after, the handmaid returned, leading by the arm not her baby, but a tall young man with shining hair and eyes softened and abstracted as though he walked in his sleep. Bityah raised a hand to touch the young man's face, and when he drew back, she could not see the light before her eyes.

The open heart of Moses gathered in the sight of Bityah lying, so, in bed, with her hair loose and her long, golden arms reaching out to him. The room was a terrible place; lotus leaves burned to force the fever from the air, and their flames were dirty pink, their smoke like sticky fingers.

"My love," Bityah said to Moses, "why do I look at you and feel as though you're getting smaller and smaller, as though you're not here at all?"

Moses couldn't answer; he was too full. He looked at her and knew that he was the source of her pain, and that words, and even his presence, and also his absence deepened that pain. Vaguely, he sat and looked through Bityah. What was farthest away was clearest to him; what lay before him, he could not bring himself to see.

That night, as on many a night before, Moses sat on the

garden wall with Merneptah to get answers to his questions. He asked him, "Can you be somewhere and not be there at all?"

Merneptah had been chewing cinnamon root, and the stalk dropped from his mouth as he looked at Moses in wonder. "How could you know? I almost saw her today! I missed her by no more than a breath. A breath!"

"Missed," Moses echoed. "But can you miss everything? Can there be so many things, you can't choose?" He was thinking of the butcher slaves, dead oxen, Bityah, the feces-stained child. He was thinking, also, of the man who had fed the hungry slave, the one who had met his eyes.

"You must choose," Merneptah said.

Moses almost asked: Choose what? Instead, he asked: "Why choose?"

"Because," Merneptah said, "That is what makes us men. We must sort out what is false from what is true by what we see, smell, taste, hear, and touch. You should know. You're the only boy alive who's eaten coal."

"Is coal more true than gold?" Moses asked.

Merneptah laughed. "It must be. It saved your skin."

"So truth saves your skin?"

"Now you've got me tied up in knots," Merneptah said, with affection. "Sometimes it does, and sometimes it skins you alive. But the main thing is—you choose. You shoot your arrow. Maybe you hit the wrong thing, like I hit you that night, but at least you don't go mad. Moses, will she go to Amaleke?"

"I don't know," Moses said. He said it sadly, and he added, "Are we mad?"

"No," said Merneptah. "You ask impossible questions."

"Why answer?" Moses asked him.

"Because when I answer your questions, I hit what I don't mean to hit. It interests me," Merneptah said. "Ask me more about Bityah."

"Is she mad?" Moses asked Merneptah.

"Yes," Merneptah said. "All women are mad."

"Does she sleep?"

"No. She's like you. She dreams on her feet. I could tell the day I saw her. Even when she's awake, she's asleep."

"What's sleep?"

"Sleep is when life renews itself, when blood turns into breath and breath to thought and thought to breath and blood again."

Hesitating, Moses considered this line of reasoning. Then he asked, "Why think?"

Overcome, Merneptah grasped the hand of Moses, and said, "You speak with the voice of my own heart. No more thinking. No more sleeping on our feet. I will take my Bityah!"

This was not the first time Merneptah said this, and Moses knew he would not take Bityah. He would proclaim love by the stars, by everything real and true, and his eyebrows would tangle with anxiety and misery, but he would not let go of Moses' hand nor would he lose his balance and actually fall into the forbidden garden. He was a steady young man.

From behind, Moses sensed something else familiar, the butchers closing up the slaughterhouse for the night. The loins and rump would be hung up to cool and the door latched, and maybe the slaves would sleep on bits of flea-infested straw. Yet one by one they would creep into the open, and after a time he would appear: the Hebrew. He might be kneeling in his usual place with that bone-white staff leaning against a gate post. Sometimes he fed the butchers and sometimes the little boy who dumped the chamber pots, and sometimes he sat alone and broiled a few wild onions over embers.

"Brother!" Merneptah cried, "We must stop thinking. We must act."

"Act how?" Moses asked Merneptah.

"Act truthfully. Act according to our five senses and our natures."

Merneptah pulled Moses to his feet and clasped him to his chest so that Moses' face was turned towards the oxen pen and he looked for the Hebrew. He wasn't there.

Instead, Moses saw one of the slaves trying to unlatch the oxen pen. He hid among the shadows of empty basins, was so quiet that the oxen paid him no mind.

Merneptah said, "You know, if you weren't here, maybe I would be mad."

"Mad?" Moses said without thinking about it much.

"When I marry Bityah, you must live with us," Merneptah said. "I'll be king and she'll be queen and you'll be—well, what else could you be? You'll be Moses."

Moses.

The sound made him jump out of his skin. It was a bellow of an ox. The slave had laid hold of some of the flesh around his neck to draw him into the open.

Merneptah didn't notice. "You can be the royal Moses," he said. "A king needs one. A god needs one. Without the Moses close at hand, a god will come to grief."

Again, again, that ox bellowed as the anxious slave forced it forward and hung a length of twine around his neck, losing his composure from sheer terror and almost stumbling over an empty basin. The other oxen joined in until the wall itself began to vibrate.

Over this pandemonium Merneptah yawned, looked up in the sky to gauge the hour, and at last took his leave. He leapt down from the wall onto the short grass of the slaughteryard, landing with strong, flat feet, and running obliviously off to bed where his blood would turn to breath and breath to thought and thought to breath again.

The slave had frozen at the sight of Merneptah bounding past. *Moses.* Why do you feed me? Because you are hungry. Where do you take me? I take you to slaughter. *Moses.* The rhythm of the bellowing should have woken all of Goshen, but it could be that it was heard by no one but Moses. He drew himself to the edge of the wall.

There was a crack, the basin knocked aside. An overseer appeared, whip raised for striking. And Moses jumped.

He landed, leapt out, already hearing the whip cracks on the slave. Something closed on him with a snap, and blind and certain he raised the basin and cracked it on the overseer's head. It slammed down, and he stumbled with the force of it and half-turned before

Moses cracked it down again, and that basin rose and fell, hoisted itself with its own weight, though it was slippery now. The overseer cried out from the gut, but the ears of Moses were too full to hear more than the ringing of that basin on his skull, rising and falling. With a final crack, the basin split in two.

Moses looked at the two halves of the basin. Then he looked past them to the massive body of the overseer with its clotted head. He leaned against the cattle pen and tried to steady himself. The slave was gone. The oxen poked their muzzles through the slats of the pen. Moses stood for a moment, as mist gathered around his ankles and obscured the overseer's body. Then he crouched, gripped the arms of the corpse, and pulled.

It was hard to drag that massive corpse across wet grass. The pen seemed to extend forever, as the oxen sank on their haunches, staring up with gloomy expressions. Moses wiped his forehead on his sleeve; he was covered in blood. Still, he felt something crackle in him, the echo of what had passed through, a snap like flint, hot, bright.

There were pale reeds around him now. In that ghostly place, the body of Moses gave off vivid heat. Everything but him seemed unreal, still. *Go farther. Go on.* Moses made himself pull the dead overseer well past the boundaries of the palace, and the air took on the scent of marsh reeds and wet wood. After a time, Moses gave a final wild tug that threw him into the wadi.

Go farther. Go on. The voice pressed him like a comrade. There was something glittering close at hand, a cloud of sparks. Those sparks hung on the stalks of bulrushes without smoke or fire; they winked like red eyes. Moses drew his hand to his mouth, and slowly, against a tide of fear, he walked towards them. He drew the bulrushes back, and stepped inside.

There was the Hebrew who had fed the slaves, sitting alone by a sputtering fire, roasting wild onions on a stick. He looked up at Moses with surprise and said a few words in a language Moses did not know.

Moses stood looking at him, trying to frame a question. The Hebrew shook his head and turned back to the onions. Their scent thickened and melted together with the smell of burning reeds, damp wool, and milk. Moses' face softened.

The Hebrew asked, in bad Egyptian, "You're hungry?"

Moses nodded, and the man took the onions from the fire, scraped off the ash, and took the hand of Moses in his own.

"Eat," he said, and in that hand he put a roasted onion.

Moses looked at the onion the way he had looked at the Hebrew, with bewilderment, with wonder. Had he been brought here to hide the body of the overseer, or to take part in that exchange, to be hungry and to be fed? He popped the onion in his mouth. It was still hot, and the many layers lined his throat and had to be worked down with such force of concentration that it took a long time before he could speak. Then he asked, "Am I covered with blood?"

The Hebrew looked at Moses for a long time, as though he too was working something down his throat. He did, at last, say, "Yes. You can clean up tomorrow. You look tired." When Moses nodded, he dug with his staff into the dry grasses and prepared them both beds out of reeds.

After they had settled for the night, Moses tucked his legs into his chest and wondered what had made him jump down from the wall at last. It was as though the overseer had called to his anger like the neck of an ox had called to a knife. He had become a knife, almost. Whose knife? Who called him? Someone had called him here as well. He glanced at the Hebrew who lay beside him and he wanted to hear him speak again, so he asked, "Why are you a slave?"

The Hebrew sat up. He did not answer at once, and his cheeks sank into his face so that for a moment he looked like a corpse. Then he said, "I was asked that before. I know the answer now. I am a slave because my heart is pulled in too many directions. I need a master for my heart."

"My heart has a master," Moses said. "He calls me by name: Moses." He urgently wanted to hear that man pronounce that name and so he added: "Moses. I'm called Moses because I was taken from the water."

But if that name meant anything to the Hebrew, he did not show it. Rather, he asked, "What does your master tell you to do?"

"He tells me to kill," Moses said. He did not say more. He was afraid that he would stutter, misspeak himself, and leave room for something to disturb the fragile peace he felt. He rolled onto his side. The hard bed of reeds suited him, and he put his fist in his mouth and sucked a little, as he hadn't done since he was a child.

Amram woke suddenly. Something had passed over him that night, something terrible. Through his mind ran the dream's scroll-work:

> Gird up your loins like a man.
> I will question you and you will declare to me.

It took him a long time to work himself back to sleep.

Nine

The next morning, Amram and Moses set out for the wadi. There Amram pulled up a fistful of bulrushes and scrubbed Moses' back. As the crust of mud and blood came loose, it gave way to a soft brown skin that smelled like almond oil. Amram could not shake what he had felt the night before, and he said to himself: Love a stranger. Who isn't bathed in blood? Isn't there blood on your own hands? Still, when they returned to dry themselves with stones, he was startled to find that the young man had no intention of leaving.

Amram rubbed his eyes and finally said, "What if your master calls you?"

Moses looked up at Amram, and his deep, thick-lashed eyes lengthened. "What if *your* master calls?"

Amram rose up, pulled on his cloak, and raised the hood a little against the sunlight. He wondered where he had seen those eyes before and where he had heard those pointed questions. They walked towards the twelve tribes, as was Amram's custom, and by late morning, they reached the huts of Benjamin where women pounded dough on hot, flat stones. Moses asked Amram, "Are those Hebrews?"

"No," Amram replied. "They have a tribe and a home. Do not call them Hebrews."

When the men returned, Amram was given his usual place at the hearth, though the elder did not seem to know what to do with Moses. In the end, Moses stood among the donkeys as Amram told his stories. There was a palpable silence around the boy who could not understand a word but who seemed to be listening to something else instead.

The elder of Benjamin whispered in Amram's ear: "He is cursed."

"He looks that way," said Amram, "because he doesn't speak our language."

"He looks like you," the elder said. In those words was a sharp note Amram had not heard before. He and Moses ate only a little beans, and by late afternoon, they had moved on past the gated camps of Menasheh where Amram did not go, and all the while, the two did not speak to each other. It seemed to Amram that Moses was lost and in need of comfort, yet Amram had not asked for a shadow, and the way that Moses kept at his heels made him uneasy, so he walked farther than he had intended.

After some time, he gazed across the road. Not far off were the chalk-washed workshops of Dan where amulets hung in clusters from the rafters and short-stringed harps clattered from the doors. Farther lay the gardens of Ephraim and to the north Asher, and then the tents of Levi, Reuben's huts, Naphtali's hearth fires, and the pits of Gad where the wadi turned into a low, rank swamp, and then the Sinai.

It was in the direction of Sinai that Moses stared as they walked on, his mouth in that set, scar-lined gape of wonder, his eyes unfocused. The afternoon sun rounded his shoulders with clean light, and Amram felt what he had felt the night before, a terrible presence. And it came to Amram then that this youth was bound for Sinai, would lead him back to Sinai, even against his will.

The tribe of Naphtali made Amram welcome. They brought out goat's milk, and spread fresh dough on the ashes of the hearth; the bread baked there was black and smelled sour, but when they took it out hot and broke it there was a little meat inside.

"From the palace," said the elder. "Some of our men are there, and they bring home a bit now and then." He had a light brown, open face, and there was something boyish in the way he poked at the hearth to make it glitter. "Meat is a good thing, Hebrew," he said. "And after harvest, sometimes we can glean a little barley and there's beer."

Amram nodded, and passed some of the bread to Moses who sat in a corner of the hut and moved his mouth around the crust as though he was a dumb animal.

The elder noticed Moses for the first time. He spoke to Amram sharply. "Why have you brought that witless boy?"

Amram replied, "They say Isaac was witless." Those gathered recognized the tale of Abraham and Isaac, but this was not a tale Amram had told before. He went on. "They say that when our father, Abraham was asked to sacrifice his son, the knife was stayed, but ever after Isaac was bewildered, full of fear. And late in life, he was blind."

"I'm not blind. I see him standing there," said the elder, shifting, and plainly out of patience.

"And I have a riddle," Amram went on, leaning in towards the fire and holding his bread in both hands. "Who was the master who spared the life of Isaac? Who would have us love our sons?"

"Do you love your son?" the elder asked Amram.

Amram dropped the bread. The question took him by surprise.

"Then hide him, at least. Don't bring anger on him and on us," the elder said. "Our own man came home covered in blood and now he is afraid to show his face. But your son has no shame."

Amram rose but could not speak, and then something made him stumble back and leave the hut without a formal leave-taking, and before he could think, he had broken into a run. He did not know where he was running. Towards the wadi? Towards the palace? He only knew that he had not gone far before cramps doubled him over and he had to brace himself on his staff. Air flapped in his ears like wings.

He sensed Moses beside him and too abruptly, he turned and asked, "How did you get your name?"

"Someone took me from the water," Moses said.

"I put you in the water," Amram said, knowing it now. He stood, leaning hard on his staff as though to root his footsteps in the earth and keep from running off again. Breathing hard, he turned towards the wadi, and that was when he saw the corpse.

It had been drifting for some time towards the Red Sea. Flies twinkled around its eyes and nose, and a bit of a hard leather belt had caught on the root of an acacia tree.

"This is the man you killed?" Amram asked Moses.

Moses nodded, but then he must have read something in Amram's face, because he added: "He sank."

"He surfaced," Amram said bitterly. "Mud is shifty. Wait," he said, and he crouched and loosed the belt from the root. "It will drift on, and everyone will know what you have done. And if I let that happen, your death will be on me a second time."

"Why?" Moses asked, and the bewilderment that had once seemed so tender and so lost to Amram galled him now. With a tug, he pulled the corpse towards shore, and sweat sprang on his forehead. Moses reached out to help, and Amram pushed him back.

"No. It's not for you. I'll carry him."

"You can't," Moses said. It was twilight now and the broad leaves and fuzzy crowns of bulrushes made strange blue shadows over his father and the corpse. He raised his voice. "You can't carry him. He'll break your back!"

"Then my back will break. I've carried worse. I am your father and I've carried you." Amram's words came out in bursts as he gripped those waterlogged gray arms and dug his heels into the mud. Feeling his way down the torso, he gripped the heavy belt and, twisting himself around, took the corpse onto his shoulders.

"You can't!" Moses shouted again, trying to take up the feet of the corpse, but stumbling over Amram's fallen staff. Anger passed over him like a wing of light, but he did not know what to do with it, and he took up the staff and bashed it in the mud, tears in his eyes.

Receding, Amram had sunk calf-deep in the wadi mud, and by the time Moses recovered himself, there was no one there at all.

Bityah lay in her bed and raised her arms. Her Ethiopian handmaid should have stuck a stuffed date in her mouth and set a wet, cold strip of linen on her forehead, but her arms moved through thin air. No leaves burned; no smoke passed over her. When Bityah opened her eyes at last, she gave a strangled cry and shouted: "Girl!"

No answer. Her chamber had grown twice as long and twice as narrow, and a strip of moonlight like a knife of gold cut into her face. She cried:

"Draw the curtain! Draw the curtain!"

Tears gathered in Bityah's eyelashes and drew lines down the light. She tried again.

"Girl—draw the curtain! Girl! Must I do it myself? I'm ill!" Her voice turned frenzied and she gripped her throat with both hands and found that both her hands and throat were shaking.

When at last she made herself rise from the bed, she did not recognize her body; it was the body of an old woman. The stomach underneath her gown was distended and her breasts sagged on her rib cage. She drew them up in her hands, and from the pit of her stomach she cried again:

"Girl! Bring him to me now! Bring my beloved."

And so it was, with her nightdress open, on feet as swift as birds, with her hair loose and her scent sharpened with fear, Bityah rushed into the south garden, headlong into the night.

It was there she heard a strange voice call out: "Moses!"

The voice was rough and lonely, the voice of a young man, carrying from the north wall. Bityah stopped at the edge of the fish pool, shading her eyes with her hand.

A figure stood on the wall, holding arrows and a quiver, pacing a step, and calling again: "Moses! Where are you, Moses!"

Bityah grasped her head in both hands and from the soles of her feet, with a voice like a woman in childbed, she screamed: "Moses!"

It was then Merneptah saw her. He knelt down on his perch above, and could neither breath nor speak. There she was, herself, trembling and sobbing, and he felt as though he had been left disarmed and alone to face a battle. Who knows how long he would have crouched there had not Bityah rushed to the wall, reached for his ankle, and sent him clattering down. She staggered back and glared. "Who are you?"

Merneptah's voice shook and his head filled with blood. "Your brother," he said.

Bityah kicked him over. "Have you killed him?"

He stared up, losing the thread of her questions, losing sight even of Bityah herself as the sky swam overhead.

"Where is he?" she shouted again. She swept back her head and her eyes filled with moonlight. She asked the moon, "Where is he?"

"I don't—" Merneptah said. A knot of desperate unhappiness had formed in his stomach. He was not in pain. He was simply at a loss, and he could not finish what he had began to say. Because he did not know what else to do, he reached for Bityah and she scrambled back, eyes still on the moon.

"I need my husband!" Bityah shouted now.

"Husband?" Merneptah was on his feet now. "You have a husband?"

Bityah only cried again. "I need my husband Moses!"

Merneptah watched with a mouth like a crack as his sister fell to her knees and dashed her head against the paving stones, shouting: "Moses, Moses, Moses!"

He felt for his arrow and quiver and with a ringing head leapt over the north wall, striding across the yard where the bull calves were being slaughtered, and as he walked, he kicked over the bucket of entrails; the cattle bellowed, drowning out Bityah. He went to tell his father that Moses had escaped.

Merneptah was a hunter. By day, he speared fish in the wadi and by night, he shot quail as they flew. He told himself he hunted for his enemy. Behind him marched four guards who'd pledged to bring Bityah's pet home alive, four warriors bred to run like gazelles and to see in the dark like birds of prey.

He knew the broad road with its fringe of reeds: it led to the wadi where the twelve tribes drowned their sons. On familiar ground and with steady purpose, Merneptah was most himself.

He gave orders: "Burn tents. Empty the granaries."

Before his men so much as had the tents in sight, Merneptah shot an arrow through the dark and it struck the tent post of Hur, elder of Levi, and set it reverberating, forcing him out into the open.

"Prince!" Hur shouted. "Prince!" He rushed towards Merneptah, threw himself before him, kissed his feet, and glared up with red, wild eyes. "Prince and Lord, what brings you here?"

"Where is Moses?"

"What is Moses, Lord Prince?"

"A boy like me," Merneptah said, and in spite of himself his words broke in a way that Hur read as frustration.

"There are no boys like you," Hur said. "No women to bear sons—Amen, Seleh! With Pharaoh's blessing—"

"You are not blessed," said Merneptah. "Where is Moses?" His voice was his own now, brassy and ringing. He kicked Hur out of the way and led his men to a well; the guards probed deep but found only water.

"No good here," one said.

"Yet not far," said Merneptah. "Not far. I missed him by a breath, a breath." He knew what went on burning after everything had passed away; it drove him forward to the mud pits of Gad where they found the elder in his scraggly garden. Merneptah broke down the gate, pushed the old man to the ground, and asked, "Where is Moses?"

"Prince, God, you'll find no Moses, but take anything, any-thing—it belongs to you," the elder said. He was a dignified old man with a small, oval face and steady eyes, and he rose to his knees, reaching for the hem of Merneptah's gown as he went on: "We have brass rings, we have black cats, we have white dogs, we have wax beads engraved—"

Merneptah pushed him down again and walked past, steady and sniffing. There was a trail; he knew the shape of the feet, the hesitancy in those bones, and motioning his men to stay back, he pursued through the high reeds, and then his breath caught in his throat.

Moses stood before him at the edge of the wadi with his back to Merneptah; Merneptah did not speak. He placed an arrow. Yet he knew his hand was none too steady, and as he watched Moses crouch down to touch the water with a white staff, something broke in him, and he heard himself say out loud, "Look at me."

Moses turned. Had something changed in his friend's face? His eyes had sparks in them; they had grown hard and strange.

Gripping his bow, Merneptah took a step forward and extended his hand to Moses.

"Why do you put yourself in this place? Why? Did I drive you to this? What do you want?"

"Why ask?" Moses asked, and the question penetrated like a hot stone.

"Why ask? Because your place is with us. With me. Come back, Moses. Bityah is lost without you. And my heart is broken."

"Harden your heart," Moses said.

Merneptah blinked. This stranger glared at him through a face smeared thick with blood and mud, and the big staff in his hand crashed down. "Moses," Merneptah said again, his voice shaking a little, "You aren't yourself. What if I said I was sent here to kill you?"

"Harden your heart," Moses said again. "Lock your heart up."

"I can't," Merneptah said, and to his disgrace he felt tears come. It was well past midnight now. The moon set behind the mud pits of Gad where his own men waited with their bows. He would stand there until dawn, until past dawn, wanting some sign from Moses. "Won't you come back?" he asked, and then: "Where are you going? Can I go with you?"

Then he felt the wind knocked out of him. Moses had cracked that staff into his gut and set out running. Doubled over, Merneptah felt blood come to his mouth, and he rose with difficulty and swallowed that blood, feeling his sense return with it, and he felt for his bow and quiver and set an arrow. He struggled through a cloud of dust and moonlight where his men were waiting and he shouted: "Shoot!"

A snap—a burst of light as they shot those arrows high above the mark. Blind dust whirled until everything was lost, and Merneptah cried out, "Moses! Moses!"

Past the arrows that had carried his name through the darkness came crack after crack, a staff striking at rocks, and the guards followed their prince through those cracks like questions, loosed arrows like answers, and everything went awry until they found themselves at the corridor of stone that bordered Sinai. Merneptah called out: "Moses!" and his voice layered over itself and reverberated, echoed by a crack, and over those red stones Merneptah leapt, landing on hard ground. Not too late now. He aimed an arrow.

A distant call: "Prince, your father said *alive*."

"Fuck Father!" Merneptah shouted. His arrow flew out across the blue, and before he could know if it met its mark, he placed another, then a third, and in his bones he felt the hot, sweet joy of three arrows in Moses' back.

Dust parted. On the stone lay three quails, each speared by an arrow. His men stared as Merneptah moved to pick up the quails, one at a time.

Moses stood on a rock on the border of Sinai, dry-mouthed and sticky. His chest swelled to the point of bursting and he hugged himself; it was very cold. He called: "Father!" Then he said, "Merneptah." No one said his name in return. Though he scouted, he could see no sign of his father or his friend. He had to find them, to tell them that it was terrible to strike, to take life. It was—he could not deny—it was wonderful, like light, like praise, like answers. It was an answer to a call. Red sunlight spilled through Moses' hair; he could feel it through his skull. He picked up the staff he had used as a club and turned in a full circle. Nothing but rock the color of dung.

He felt a shiver like a spasm. He could go back to Goshen, kill every master, free the slaves. Another shiver. He was shivering with joy. But then his heart misspoke itself and divided with such force that he lost his footing and lay breathless on the rubble with his fist clenched tight.

Moses might have lain there until sand buried him. He did not want to rise. Behind him lay Goshen and before him lay the Sinai. In Sinai there were snakes, thorns, acacia and birds of prey. No one could walk there and live. He got to his feet with the aid of the staff and climbed down the rock to the gravel below. He entered Sinai because he was afraid.

PART TWO: SINAI

One

The border of Sinai is lined with goat bones, thorn bushes, or the Red Sea. Deeper in, cliffs of brown stone shelter snakes so poisonous that they could pass over the shadow of a bird and make it fall. It was there Moses walked, and by the end of the first day his little shift of linen had shredded to rags, and he knotted the worst of the rags into stout leggings to support his straining calves, but then the leggings filled with sand until he was hard put to set one foot before the other.

In the space of a week, he had sprouted a beard. At once, the beard was full of sand and mud, rock hard, a home for fleas. His brows grew shaggy and they cloaked his eyes from the sun. Moses moved under a moon that grew fat as he grew lean, and he took direction less from the stars than where his will would not have him go.

He was running away from certainty. He had felt it, the way it streaked up his arm into his breast, extending from his brow like horns of light. Sometimes he would take his staff and strike a rock again and again to force up a little water, and he would feel enough of that blazing unity of purpose to make him strike it even after water flowed. Yet, once, he raised his staff to strike, feeling its weight down to the scar in his armpit, its shadow falling across the face of the rock, Moses felt pity for the rock.

"So I am divided," Moses said to the rock. The sound of his own voice startled him so much that he dropped the staff.

When that staff dropped, the rock trembled and split, and from its cleft sprang a fountain. Moses rubbed his eyes, and the scars around his lips trembled in warning, but he could not help himself. He thrust his face into the cleft and drank and drank.

After he drank his fill, he lay in the mouth of a cave and saw a snake. The snakes of Sinai are so black they look like gold; their eyes are the color of olives. As the snake slid past the bare feet of Moses, it shed its skin and dipped under a stone. Moses took up the snake skin and held it to the sun. It felt hot, fragile and holy. He set the snake's gift in his belt and closed his eyes.

As night fell, Moses thought: it is not the skin of an ox, taken by slaughter, but a skin shed cleanly, left behind. And he thought: it is possible to live without doing harm. It is possible.

Moses tucked his head into his arm, curled in the cavern's mouth, and slept.

He woke and walked another day, without direction and without fear. Then he slept another full night in the mouth of yet another cave, a soft, wooly sleep, dense and satisfying. The next morning, he walked farther yet, in no particular direction now because he no longer felt a pull towards Goshen. The stones gave off a hot, sharp scent that cleared his head, emptied it like a porcelain basin to let light shine through.

If he kept walking, he could live an honest life. He could wean himself from anger in a place where there was nothing to hang anger on. The birds of prey shadowed him; he could be thankful for the birds. The thorns he chewed to a dense, stringy pulp; he could be thankful for the thorns. No longer did the world call to him and make impossible demands; rather he called to the world itself, called everything by name. There were few names in the Sinai; they weren't hard to learn: *bird, snake, rock, thorn, acacia.*

Perhaps his own name had been called with that same simplicity and love. Had the trouble been not with the one who called but with the way Moses had listened? If he had only been as simple as those birds, snakes, rocks, thorns and acacia trees, if he had only had a purpose as self-evident, then the call could have been a kind of praise. *Moses, you are Moses. You act like Moses and do what Moses does. Amen—Seleh!*

Praise, praise, praise, Moses thought, as he walked over hard, reddish-brown stones which were sometimes fuzzy with lichen. The Sinai was enormous, beyond human scale. The farther he walked, the more he felt himself as a slight aspect of the landscape, a pair of legs, a white staff, a trail scratched like a fine thread through the dust. When Moses praised what he passed through, that praise was so expansive that sometimes he would have to stop walking and sit on a rock, too overcome to move.

Sometimes he thought he heard a knocking; it could have been his own heart beating or it could have been the wind. Once, distinctly, he sensed a presence, massive and undeniable; there were men close at hand. His head swam and he grasped his staff until his knuckles ached, letting his fear pass over him, and containing it enough to walk away.

The next night, he camped on a sheltered ridge, a desolate place where not even thorn grew. His skin still prickled with foreboding, but he wrestled with himself, twisting and changing his position, until he had worn himself into a stupor, and at last slept.

He woke to the sound of bells and a bleat that ran up his back and made his head ring. He scrambled to his feet. Somehow the ridge was flooded with water and full of sheep, and men dressed in skins circled those sheep, ringing bells and pushing them towards the sunlight. So many sounds and such a stench of blood, blood on the stone, blood mixed with water, blood in the flanks of the sheep as they struggled away from the men. Moses raised up his staff, and at the same moment one of the men saw him and lurched forward, stepping on the body of a dead sheep with a crunch.

Like two fists, the heart of Moses once again divided, and he closed his eyes, thinking: run, run—yet feeling his arm already straining back to strike. He cracked his staff against the head of the stranger, the force of the blow traveling down his arm and filling him with happiness and confusion, making him sick, pulling him forward to where a battle was going on, where the sheep smacked against his legs and yet more men rang bells and stank of blood.

"Strike me dead!" Moses called out, all the while striking in all directions. "Strike me dead!"

And then he slipped on entrails and knocked his head. He might have passed out, because when he opened his eyes the sun was high and the ridge silent. He could make out feet in slippers and the bottom of a dark red gown.

It was a woman who said something in a language he did not know. She knelt down; she was veiled and held a knife.

Moses muttered in Egyptian: "Will you kill me?"

Then he sat up with a start because somebody else had dribbled water on his head, and it filled his eyes until he could see no more than a blur of red cloth.

He hoisted himself up and blinked the water away. There were two women. One held a bucket on her hip, and the other, the taller of the two, rose with that knife; through their veils, it was impossible to read their faces. Behind them, sheep with blood in their wool clustered and drank in a cleft between two rocks.

Moses opened his mouth; nothing came out. In the silence, the sheep's lips smacked against the rock. At last, the woman with the knife addressed him, first in her own language. When he did not answer, she tried Egyptian. "You come with me."

She stepped forward and took him under the arms with lean, steady hands. Moses didn't resist, even tried to help, because it seemed to him he had met an easy death. The woman smelled of yeast; the scent surprised him, neither sweet like Bityah's nor rank like a slave's. Through her veil he tried to meet her eyes.

The gesture took her aback. She said, "In Midian, women do not show their faces."

Tentatively, Moses asked, "When will you kill me?"

"When you cross me," the woman answered. "Stop shaking like a bag of bones. Here—" she said, pushing him forward. "You've got legs. Walk."

Moses staggered a little, but he had no choice but to stay ahead of the two women. They prodded him from behind, the small one breathing through her mouth; the taller he could not hear breathe at all. They walked some distance to a little glade where palm trees grew, and a circle of dark red tents were pitched around a central tent of blue. The sheep seemed to know their way; they moved, unguided, towards their pen. There was shade there, and a cool silence.

"Egyptian," the tall woman said, at last, "Do you want me to kill you?"

"No," Moses said. He was amazed to find that was the case.

"Then you must meet our father," she said, pushing him towards the round, blue tent; from its post flew a banner embroidered with mysterious characters. It did not seem welcoming, but he had no choice but to enter. The air within was thick with sheep dung and date wine, and he was still finding his bearings when he heard, from nowhere, a voice.

"You are Egyptian?"

Slowly, his eyes adjusted: feet shod in palm-leaf sandals, a thick wool tunic fringed with blue, and a straight-brushed beard flecked with shavings of clay; the face was clay-streaked, the eyes slant and intelligent.

"Yes, yes," the man said. "Egyptian. Balaam lived there. Seek righteousness. Do not slander. Use sound weights and measures. Do not oppress strangers."

Around his seat were piled chunks of clay carved top to bottom with what might have been words, fish or grape vines. Some were stacked against the tent post, others spread around the floor, yet more were half-buried in loose shards.

"Law," he said, gesturing around him at the tablets. "You have law in Egypt."

"Law?" Moses fell into his old habit of questions, and the man drew himself to the edge of his seat, spreading his hands so that his little scribe's knife clattered to the floor.

"Law! Law and prophecy! It was Balaam the Blind who taught me law. Long he stayed with us in Midian with his wonderful she-ass. Truth speaks to him, and so long as he serves truth, he has perfect understanding."

Moses picked up the man's knife and held it out to him, but he stared past him and went on.

"Balaam came from the court of Pharaoh where he found great favor, for he says nothing truth will forbid and so is truth's beloved. He told me I would lose my land and lose my wife and gain the Law and thus redeem myself."

The man set his pale palm flat on his chest and went on in a sing-song voice:

"Hearts falter; laws are firm. Hearts cannot know what will come to pass; laws are like blind Balaam, truth's beloved. Follow laws and you will know evil is met with evil, good met with good. Well am I rid of a wayward heart, having gained law. Egyptian, do you know the song of law?"

And the man raised his own eyes so that only the whites showed, as he sang out:

> *How goodly is justice*
> *which rests upon your door post.*
> *How light is the burden*
> *of men with steady oxen.*

Pulling at his blue fringe, he added:

> *Blessed be all he blesses.*
> *Cursed be all he curses.*

Moses took a step back, for as the old man sang, he felt his blood turn to clay, and his feet crunched on two tablets and cracked them to bits.

Flatly, the man asked, "Are you blind?"

"No," Moses said.

The man seemed to lose interest then; he picked up a tablet of sheep tallow and Moses put the scribe's knife back in his hand. He set to work then, and Moses took that as a sign to go. They had not even told each other their names.

Moses stepped outside; the air was hot, but so clear after the air in the tent that he breathed and breathed as though he were drinking water. He realized that he was in a sheltered garden. The stones below his feet were white and smooth, and a few white flowers bloomed, giving off a faint sharp scent. For the first time since he entered Sinai, he thought of the garden of Goshen and of Bityah and wondered how the world could hold so many gardens, so much madness, and so little peace.

The tall woman appeared. She took Moses' arm, and though he could not say why, the gesture angered him.

He said, "I'm not a prisoner."

The fervor in his voice surprised him, and seemed to surprise her as well. Still, she said nothing. She let him go and swept before him, and her red veil blew sideways enough to define the knife-keen angle of her waist. She led the way to a wooden tub by the sheep hedge and she said, "Take off your rags."

Bitterly, Moses asked, "Why are you a slave?"

"I am not a slave," she answered at once.

The hard tone of her voice puzzled Moses, and he added, more gently, "Won't a slave bathe me then?"

"We have no slaves," she said. "Do I have to pull your clothing off you by force?"

Moses stared, silenced, and he could not explain why he felt so shy and so reluctant to strip in front of this woman.

"If you are an Egyptian," she added, "you would want a bath." She paused and turned aside a little to draw water from a basin. "Bathe. There."

Moses shrugged his fragments of linen free and slowly undid his leggings. Then he laid himself, crusty and naked, into the wooden tub. The woman turned back with a tin bucket of water. More to himself, Moses said, "By rights, that ought to be blood."

"Still you think we ought to kill you?"

Moses shook his head. "The men this morning."

"Oh, they're not dead. They crawled off somewhere with their zabbs between their legs." She poured some of the water over Moses, and it ran down his beard and loosed enough sand to turn him grey.

It was the first bath Moses had taken since the morning at the wadi and Moses felt as though he were emerging from layers of dust and stone. He asked, "Would you kill them if you could?"

"Of course. They want to drive us from this place and take it for their own."

"And have you killed? Without regret?"

"What does regret have to do with anything?" she asked

Moses. "There are seven daughters here, and it is enough to live from day to day without talk of regret."

"Why don't you leave then?" Moses asked her.

She answered, "I don't do that."

"I would," Moses said.

What she made of his answer, he could not say, for he did not look at her then. He sat up a little in that tub and gazed past the white stone garden through pease blossom and black vine, towards the blue tent full of fragile blocks of clay. Even as he watched vague shadows move below the cloth of the tent, he felt as though he sought her face below the veil.

She must have watched him, for she added, "Nothing to shield us but a mad father."

"No other men?" Moses asked her.

She didn't answer for a while. She poured a little more water straight into Moses' lap, and she said, "No one would have us."

"I would," Moses answered, looking straight at her now. "What is your name?"

The woman rose and walked away. Below the film of water, Moses' skin throbbed. He had spoken without thinking. He could rise up now and enter the Sinai, but he would wait in the tub until she returned, and he knew she would return. In that certainty lay a calm weight like an anchor. When she appeared with fresh water, she knelt again to wash him before she said, "You do not ask names here."

Moses rubbed his legs. He could feel the water turn to wet sand, but he did not take his eyes from her as he said, "My name is Moses. My father is Amram."

The woman went on as though she had not heard. "If you know a name, you take hold, and you have the power over life and death. I think you make light promises in Egypt."

"I am not—" Moses began, but she would not let him finish.

"Balaam came from Egypt. He made my father many promises. You have met my father."

"But you do not run away," Moses said.

The woman went on. "Any stranger—"

"I am no stranger," said Moses.

"Aren't you?" Though a veil hid her face, her contempt was clear enough. "You think every hand is turned against you. You think water is blood. In your belt were the skins of deadly snakes. I know poison. I know death. Bandits killed my mother. Our slaves are gone. In Egypt—"

"I am not an Egyptian," Moses said. "I am a Hebrew. And I think it's good you have no slaves. My name is Moses." Now Moses knew he had spoken for a long time and not once had he questioned or faltered. "Moses is my name," he said again. He rose and stepped out of the tub and laid a hand on each of her shoulders, feeling the water soak through the many layers of her gown. She pulled back and went on.

"Do not make promises. You do not know anger."

"I know anger," Moses said. "Anger is wonderful. But I don't care. I don't need anger to know who I am. It will not be my master."

That silenced her at last. They stood together at the edge of the dry garden, the naked Hebrew and the veiled woman with two great damp marks on the shoulders of her dark red gown.

"So that is why you are afraid," she said at last. "You are a slave."

"A slave?" A chill crept up the soles of Moses' feet, but he fought it and said, "I will not be a master or a slave. I will stay here."

Now another daughter headed towards them with a bowl of something steaming. The woman looked behind her, and then she lifted her veil. Her face was long and plain, framed by a straight-parted fall of black hair. She looked at Moses squarely. Her eyes were green. "My name is Zipporah. My father is Jethro," she said. "You will have to marry me now."

Two

The madness of the Pharaoh's daughter meant an end to the parade of suitors. For months on months, she lay in her chamber, and all around, her handmaid set leaves flaming. Over her hung amulets, honey-dipped garlic, and silver trails of bells to chase demons away. The Ethiopian was busy stoking flames, plumping pillows, and whispering comfort in the ear of Bityah, and Bityah herself sometimes woke and sometimes slept, and always whispered in a shivering voice as wild and trailing as the bells.

The court physician came and went. Bityah would not speak to him and refused to let him air out the room. She ate only the dates the Ethiopian kept in a sack between her breasts, and what she drank remained a mystery until the physician suspected that her handmaid suckled her like a child.

Beyond the chamber, the Pharaoh sat in the stone hall on a stone seat, and he ceased to attend to the business of his kingdom and kept to the south wing of the palace, drinking barley wine and keeping his ear to the bolted door, staring nowhere with the whey face of a man with wasting sickness.

When the physician passed each day, the Pharaoh begged for an account of Bityah and asked again: "Will she not have me by her bed?"

The physician, a lean young man with the clear eyes of someone who likes an open window and a plain thought, replied: "You know she will have no one near her but the handmaid. Yet you are free to do what you like."

"I can't cross my daughter. She's all good!" The Pharaoh knocked his head against the wall and wept into his thick hands until his tears ran down his forearms and gathered in pools at his feet.

In his quiet voice, the physician said, "Yet she might not

know her own mind. Maybe she wants to see you."

"I must wait until she asks for me! I know she will!" The Pharaoh looked up at the cool young man, and his eyes blazed.

In those eyes, the physician saw the daughter, and his voice gained a note of urgency as he said: "Order the door open. Look inside. She isn't dead. Open the windows and snuff the fires and make her drink spring water and eat fresh figs. Listen to your son."

In the silence that followed, the Pharaoh's cup fell from his hand and his face dried of all tears. He rose from the stone chair, and every bone in his body turned stone hard and stone cold. The physician stepped back without thinking, as against a blow. But the Pharaoh's voice was absolutely calm when at last he spoke.

"Merneptah speaks of Bityah?"

Through tight lips, the physician answered: "He looks in every day."

"She hasn't called for him," the Pharaoh said.

The physician answered, "She has not."

The Pharaoh said to the physician, "Have Merneptah brought to me at once."

Merneptah was called not to the door beside Bityah's chamber, but to the throne room. His father the Pharaoh sat in the grand seat. On his head was the double crown of the Two Kingdoms and in his hand was the rod of authority. He was hung with every golden ring and lapis brooch and amber girdle in the treasure room. From behind that armor, two round, reddened eyes looked on Merneptah with breathtaking contempt.

Merneptah bowed before his father. He had been found on his way back from the wadi, and his muddy feet left tracks on the floor on the hall.

"You shall not," his father said, "ever see your sister again."

Prepared for this commandment, Merneptah kept his head bowed, but his canny heart hardened all the more.

"You shall not ever speak of her," the Pharaoh said. His voice took on the glint of his belts and bands and rang along the rafters so the slaves moved towards the archway of the hall to see.

Again, Merneptah made no answer.

"Nor shall you listen for her footsteps, smell her scent or taste, in any food before you, anything that brings her name to mind." The Pharaoh caught his breath; words did not come to him easily, and sweat made the trails of gold rings stick to his forehead. Finally, he said, "For you it will be as though she had never been born."

At that, Merneptah lifted his head, and his eyes were as hard as his father's. "I would laugh, had I the inclination."

The Pharaoh didn't answer. He stared, his green-tinged face deepening to dirty brown, and he raised a shaking hand from the arm of his throne and motioned his son towards him. Merneptah, however, stayed put.

"I would laugh," Merneptah said again, and now he did something that chilled even himself; he threw back his head so that his eyes rolled towards the ceiling and let out a "Ho ho ho!" Then he crossed his arms and he addressed his father as though he were a slave. "So you would have her stay in bed and breath in poison? So you hate me so much that you'd let her die rather than let me have her? You will soon see," said Merneptah with a tight smile, "that I will have her even if I do not want her. So curse me all you please. Unless you'd have her die a mad virgin, she will be mine in the end."

Below cheek plates, the mouth of the Pharaoh hung in a dry circle, as slowly what his son said passed into his mind. There it rested for a while as Merneptah shrugged his rough cloak forward on his shoulders and turned to go. But Pharaoh suddenly leapt from the throne and shouted: "It was you who drove her mad! You killed her! You drove the thing she loves away!"

In that manner did Merneptah learn his father's intention, that he would not see Bityah and Merneptah marry and would not move on the matter, though it meant his daughter's death.

Merneptah walked along the wall of the south garden, his shadow close at his heels, carrying with it a chill flood of questions. Upon that wall, once, he had answered the one who'd questioned with the voice of his own heart. An age had passed since he had carried from Sinai's edge the three quails of his hatred, and he'd eaten each down to its fragile bones, but he was still hungry.

Hungry for his friend's blood? Yes, oh yes. Hungry for his friend's voice? Yes. Could he want both at once? All of the bitterness that had filled him in the presence of his father was swept away in that confusing question, one that his friend might have asked: Both at once?

"Both at once?"

Stunned, Merneptah choked on air. Staring down at him was the smooth, sweet-eyed, broad-faced Ethiopian handmaid. She stood before him with her arms crossed and her gold-flecked eyes as wise as two pools of fishes.

"You want both Bityah and the throne at once?" the handmaid asked again.

Merneptah steadied himself and addressed the slave harshly. "What I want is my own concern."

"Ah, maybe, *la la la*," the handmaid sang. "Yet my concern is for my lady and I ask you then: Would both boons suit my prince and master?"

After a pause, during which Merneptah felt his heart jump backwards, he said: "Yes."

From between her breasts, the Ethiopian drew out the bag of dates, and she dug deep within. Between her sticky fingers was a flask shaped like a key. "At night," the Ethiopian whispered then. Her voice seemed changed and harsh, and as she spoke, she pressed in closer to Merneptah, and her scent soured, deepened. "At night, I pour a drop into his ear. Once it was poured amiss and a heart opened, but poured into the ear, it seeps into the brain."

"Stop!" Merneptah pulled back, and he clasped rough wall stones with his hands and turned his back on the handmaid, but his consent had been given and could not be taken away.

The next morning, the Pharaoh was found dead of brain fever. His body was prepared for burial and set in a tomb long readied for the housing of his soul. So were his deeds weighed in the underworld, and so did he join Ra in the holy chariot of the sun.

That same sun burst through Bityah's windows which Merneptah ordered open. Moreover, he cleaned smoke from her room and bells from her bedposts and date juice from her lips, and he had her decked out for a wedding. He wondered if he needed to deal with the Ethiopian, but she had disappeared.

Now Bityah had many handmaids from Ephraim and Menasheh, the queens of Goshen's tribes, painted and tall and veiled and reverent. They loved to fuss with Bityah's bridal robes. They braided her long, golden hair, though it came loose again. They did not mind her madness, which they thought magical, and all through the quiet wedding, they held her still to be sure she wouldn't run away.

The Pharaoh Merneptah proved to have the head of a scribe, and he kept an eye on each of his steward's holdings in a way some felt almost unsuitable. Moreover, he did his best to reverse many of his father's impractical measures. To celebrate the jubilee year of his reign, he ordered an end to the slaughter of the sons of slaves so young men could labor in his fields.

By then, the only Goshen slaves with youth enough to work were women, and the women were trouble. There were too many of them, and they had taken to men's ways without men's dignities. Hannah of Dan toted baals everywhere to trade, without regard for tribe or station, beating down even the doors of Goshen's stewards. Gad and Asher's sowers and reapers endured long hours without complaint but stole whatever grain they could stuff into their aprons. If they were caught, they would shiver and moan and deny everything. Reeba of Asher clung to the ankles of an overseer and begged mercy until he dislodged her with contempt.

"Amen—praise Pharaoh," Reeba called out, "who preserves the innocent." But there were barley grains between her teeth.

Merneptah might have sought advice from Goshen's elders, but they had grown frail and vague, and most of them kept to their tents, rubbing poultices into their wrinkles. Zohar, oldest of all, was tended to by his daughter, Dodi, who pushed the covers over his long beard and stroked his forehead with her chubby hands, crying, "Ah—shoo shoo, papa. Don't mind us little creatures. We're just fine."

It was Dodi now who wrapped herself in twelve embroidered veils and sat in giggling judgement before Reuben's well,
holding a dainty lambchop like a judgement rod.

Zohar said, "It is not right that you should sit before them,
daughter. Take a husband."

"Ah, papa, all the men are old, and they're scrawny to boot!"
Dodi said. She flicked a bit of marrow from her teeth.

Zohar made a good marriage for Dodi with the ancient chief
of the tribal overseers who was so grateful and bewildered that he
died on his wedding night, leaving Dodi with a pen's worth of goats
which she slaughtered and milked and roasted and devoured until
she grew so fat that Zohar could not say if she was with child.

"I give my blessing," Merneptah said. "Let mothers make
me sons."

Yet no sons appeared. The Goshen women shunned Miriam,
praised their Lord, and made a great show of stirring potions,
grinding mandrake roots, and rattling fertility amulets. There were
none who had not known men. Still, daughter after daughter was
pulled from between their legs, and the daughters had their mothers'
natures. It would seem that soon every slave in Goshen would be
dead without a son to claim his sheep and that they would become
an abomination, tribes ruled by women. It was only when all hope
had passed that the first son was born.

His father was Nun the Judean. Nun was a mason who cut
stone with a stone ax, famous for his strength and for his ugliness. He
was a grizzled ogre of ninety when a hag met him at the roadside and
opened her legs. At first he tried to pass her by.

"Am I a rooftop that you will pass me over?" the hag
asked him.

Nun spat and said, "I have no use for women."

"They have a use for you," the hag answered, for she was
crabbed and half-mad and would say anything to men.

Nun gave in, and she took him against the milestone and
thereafter remained in his house until a son was born.

The baby arrived with a stone in his hand which he threw at

his mother.

The hag's forehead spouted blood, but she laughed. "You must name him Joshua."

The midwife brought the newborn to Nun, and when she returned, the hag was dead. So it was that Nun raised Joshua alone, and when Nun died, Joshua was given over to his Aunt Shosha. He was as strong and as ugly as his father, though he never grew taller than Judah's milestone.

In Levi, where there were no women, Izhar, the son of Hur the Elder, one day walked home from the kiln at sunrise and suddenly wanted to dance and leap for joy, though he did not know why. He was a simple man, with his father's nervous eyebrows, and those eyebrows flew up when he found out why he felt so happy. A young girl stepped out from the bulrushes and waved.

, "Izhar— Izhar— I cannot come to you, so you must come to me."

Before he could think, Izhar was waist deep in the wadi, and he splashed and waded to the other side. After they had made love, he asked her, "Why are you afraid to enter Levi? Is it because you are a woman?"

She was quiet for a moment. Then she asked him, "Where will our son drink?"

"Miriam's well," Izhar answered.

"He might as well drink blood," she said, and then she fell silent and gathered herself under her tent of sandy hair, and she said to Izhar: "Come back when I call."

Nine months later, she pulled from between her legs a beautiful boy.

"His name is Korah," she said to Izhar, and she was so happy that she died. Izhar lifted the boy, and he clung to his beard. He took him back to Levi.

From that day on, the two were never parted. Whether Izhar worked at the kiln, slept on his mat, or gossiped by the well, Korah was in his arms or slung across his shoulders. Izhar suckled Korah on a strip of linen dipped in sheep's milk and fed him from his own bowl. When Korah could walk and speak, Izhar dogged his heels to listen.

At three, Korah asked his father for a little tablet of wax. Izhar made one out of sheep tallow, and at once his son began to write like a scribe. At six, Korah could speak Egyptian. He challenged a steward to a game of riddles and got knocked down for his troubles.

One day, he asked his father: "What's wet and red and floats?"

Izhar thought he knew and answered: "Blood?"

But Korah shook his head. "Water-babies," he said, and he tugged at Izhar's beard until he joined him at the wadi bank and helped him pull two baskets from the bulrushes. The newborns looked up with mud-smeared, distrustful faces, and Izhar took the stones out of their mouths, tucked one under each arm, and took them back to Levi.

As the years passed, little Korah pulled basket after basket from the wadi, and found, in each, a boy. They were adopted by the men of Levi. When questioned, the women in the other tribes replied, "There are no sons." To each other, the women said, "The Pharaoh says he wants us to keep them now, but who knows what he'll say tomorrow? Amen—Seleh, our Lord will come to claim them by and by, and who needs trouble?"

So did many more slave sons follow Joshua and Korah into the world, but Bityah, wife of Merneptah, remained barren.

In Midian, Moses and Zipporah were childless for many years, but they were not unhappy. They tended Jethro's sheep, carrying with them a bundle of oat cakes and honey, and together they would sit in the shade of palms and talk.

Never had Moses felt such quiet, wholesome pity for the world. He would not let Jethro's daughters slaughter sheep, though it meant they ate no meat and that the flocks multiplied to no purpose. He silenced complaints by watering and grazing those sheep himself. The sheep would return, quick-stepping, with snow-white coats, and in the belt of Moses' mantle would be tucked new snake skins. He would not kill a snake; he would not so much as crush a sand flea under his fingernail.

To Zipporah, he said, "Do you not even pity the wheat you thresh to make those cakes? It was a seed. It troubled itself to grow. It struggled and suffered."

Zipporah shook out her long hair and laughed.

"Don't laugh at me!" Moses cried out. "Don't laugh."

But Zipporah was laughing with pleasure.

Indeed, he ate the cakes and honey, though he asked pardon of everything from seed to leaf to bee. Indeed, he let Zipporah laugh; her laughter was Zipporah. Through afternoons, they'd watch sheep, argue, kiss and turn their lives into long stories. Moses told Zipporah about his years in Goshen and said to her, "Merneptah always had an answer for every question, but it didn't make him happy."

"Why was he unhappy?" Zipporah asked.

"Because he loved the questions too much. You shouldn't love anything too much. It makes you unhappy."

"I think the sand fleas love you too much, or love that beard," Zipporah said, subdued. She handed him an oat cake and said: "Here."

"Here," Moses said, taking the cake but also hanging on the word. "Here. It isn't hard to do it here, make things happy. I can make fleas happy, or snakes or sheep."

"How can a sheep be happy?" Zipporah asked. With those last words, she rose and brushed dry straw from her knees and saw the sheep had eaten through the hedge. "Now look. They're loose!"

But Moses grabbed her around the waist and cried, "Let them go! Let them go! They know their way!"

"Moses!" Zipporah shouted, pulling away and rushing off, and she called the secret name of every sheep, but even that strong magic failed her as they scattered. Distant, Zipporah looked slight, pale and helpless, with her long arms raised and her alto voice calling and calling.

Moses was moved. He ran to help her, but before he helped, he kissed her. She tasted of sheep's milk and of the names of sheep. Breaking away, he asked, "So you'd have me be a master?"

"No," Zipporah said. "You are not a master or a slave."

When all the sheep had been gathered back into the hedge,

Moses and Zipporah lay together and made their son.

Yet there were nights. Beside Zipporah, Moses feigned sleep. He closed his eyes, and through red lids watched moonlight flutter through the cloth of the tent and heard the wind, heard sheep, heard more. Still.

Zipporah knew. She was awake and listening. Once, before dawn, she got up without so much as a stir and told him she would name their son Gershom.

She said, "The name means Stranger."

Moses put his arm around her shoulders, and for the first time, his voice stumbled, as he asked her, "Why?"

"Because you are a stranger to me." Her voice flattened as she sank back against him. "Our souls are strangers."

"We know each other. We have one—"

"God? The one you hear? The one you say is not your master? The god you fled from? That god lives here too." Zipporah shivered. "I can't hear, but I feel—I feel—" She pulled away and stared at Moses with her sad green eyes. "At night, I feel sometimes you'll break my neck without thinking."

"Without—thinking?" Zipporah's neck, below her sad face, was a reed, and Moses moved to kiss it, saying, "When I'm with you, I draw sense out of myself like water from a well."

Zipporah let him kiss her, but she said, "Your name—you told me once it means the one who is taken from the water. And I loved you when you stepped out of that tub, all muddy and bloody, with that stunned look on your face. I cannot turn from you. But Moses—you have never turned to me. You're not here, Moses!" She lowered her head and cried.

Moses held her. He was no longer young. His hair was thin, and the scars around his mouth extended down his chin and up his cheeks and made his beard sprout in patches. His voice had an old man's break in it as he said, "I'm here. Here I am."

"You're not here!" Zipporah cried again. "Moses!" Moses felt his name trembling through his wife's long throat, and it sounded so much like her laughter that he thought all was well, and he held her at arm's length and smiled.

Zipporah was not smiling. She said. "I know this only. You won't be free of that god until you know its name."

In the turquoise mines of Sinai, prisoners worked chained leg to leg, and slept with a heavy chain across their chests. Some of the prisoners came from Goshen. Others were mixed Asians, and a scattering came from as far away as Nubia or Kush. All bore the prisoner's mark just above their right armpit, and around that scar the stone dust sank so deeply into their skin that after a month no one could tell a Hebrew from an Ethiopian.

Dathan's bright eyes stared out from a face like black cloth. His hands ached at night, and he held them before him as he slept like a begging dog. An overseer, drafted from Amaleke, had broken those hands, though it meant he was no good for anything but hauling stone on his back. It was the punishment for killing another miner.

"He had it coming," Dathan said. "Kept on about his wife and daughters. Blubbered in his sleep."

Dathan knew the other miners agreed in their hearts and were grateful because the less their lives were worth, the less it hurt to lose them in the end. Dathan measured the men around him; some were war prisoners; others, like himself and his brother, were slaves who had turned on masters. Most were sentenced for assault or petty theft. The sentence was a leveler; they all would die, sooner or later, of overwork, on the spears of bandits who raided for turquoise or for slaves, of hunger or recklessness.

Some tried to escape and were borne back on the shoulders of overseers, covered in snake bites or mowed down by Amaleke.

"They get to the oasis in Elim and they fall asleep. That's the end of them," Dathan said to Abiram. "Elim's filthy with scouts from Amaleke. Those shits can't even make it past the palm trees, let alone back home."

"As if you could do better!" a miner called.

"Who says I'd try?" Dathan tugged his chains and said, "If these things broke, you know what I'd do? Stay right here. And pound a fucking hole in the stone big enough to bury you all."

Yet sometimes, after dark, Abiram would find Dathan awake and trying to wrap his hand around a tiny bit of iron which he'd tap against his own irons under the cover of his hunched shoulder. His eyebrows, dark and bristling, would entirely obscure his eyes, and his dun-colored teeth would grind in concentration.

Only once did he say to Abiram, "There was a man I saw a few times. Slept just below this dung heap. So close you could smell him. He had a club with blood stains on it."

"Did you kill him?" Abiram asked.

Dathan didn't answer, but went on. "In the morning, he picked up his club and he used it for walking. Walking. And he walked straight off, free as you please." Something made Dathan's teeth chatter, and Abiram eyed his brother with concern.

"You think he was a scout for Amaleke?"

"He had a scar where we do," Dathan said.

"So he's a miner?"

"He's marked." Dathan spat out the word and sank back, resting against the stone. "No one stopped him. They left him to Sinai."

Abiram nodded. He imagined the man dead of thirst, picked dry by birds of prey, buried so deep in the sand that the overseers would never find his body. Abiram curled up to sleep and prayed to Lord Pharaoh for a more homely death chained to his brother.

After three years in the mines, late one night a Persian who shared Dathan's hole sat up and pulled the rest awake.

"The jinn is here," he said.

Abiram's instinct was to slam the Persian against the floor, roll over, and go back to sleep, but the chains wouldn't let him reach. Another miner spoke up.

"I see her too—she just passed us!"

There was a lot of whispering then, and in spite of himself, Abiram edged as close as he could to listen. He'd never heard of a woman in the mines, and as far as he could hear, this woman had come before, always by choice. She would set fire to a steward's house, throw her legs forward for irons, and walk straight to the mines.

"A woman," Abiram whispered to his brother. "How long since we've had a woman?" He imagined her, naked and smeared with grime, squirming, laughing, rattling her chains, her legs in the air. He asked Dathan, "What if she's ugly?" Dathan didn't speak, so Abiram answered his own question. "Who cares if she's ugly." Collapsing with a smile, he dreamed of women.

But when he saw her the next day, he was caught short. She wasn't ugly. She was big. Not fat, but big, taller than even Abiram, and he could no more imagine those trunk-thick legs in the air than the whole world turned upside down. Her face was empty, her brows heavy, her breasts like flat, dull stones. On her head she wore a filthy rag, and around her ankles were bound double-strength chains such as the Egyptians used on the most powerful of men. When a miner filled her bowl with mush, she drank it in a single gulp and with hard eyes stared through the man who served her. He refilled her bowl.

"That's not a woman," Abiram said to Dathan. "That's Miriam."

Dathan said nothing. He gave Abiram a lingering, chilly glance and drank his own mush slowly with his crooked hands.

To Abiram's sorrow, Miriam was chained with his troop. She worked against rhythm and cut twice as much stone as any of them until the overseer thought they had been had been shirking.

"Little boys," she would say, in a voice surprisingly melodious. "Stripes strengthen backs."

Abiram spat a line of stone dust in her face, but a comrade chained beside him struck him full across the mouth, and before he could strike back, Dathan caught his hand.

The day lasted forever, as Abiram strained to match Miriam, blow for blow, against the stone. His shoulders were raw, his neck strained and burning. At nightfall, as they walked back to their shelter, Miriam followed, and Abiram, in spite of himself, thought: She'll be there with us and we'll have her. But then he looked behind him and saw the way she stomped along, and he knew better.

Once back in their hole, the miners doted on Miriam. The Nubian gave her his bowl of mash. The Persian gathered every bit of straw to make her a bed, and he washed her feet and hands. Miriam settled in, legs stretched out, head back, dozing off, taking it as her due. Only Abiram and Dathan sat alone in a corner, watching with tight, hard faces. Dathan's hands must have pained him that night, for he held them straight out, unnaturally. They made a lumpy shadow on the wall.

Miriam opened her eyes and looked at him. "Young pup," she said. "You beg for what? For mercy?"

Dathan's face turned red under the dust, and he tried to pull his hands back but could not.

"Do you beg for a woman, Dathan-pup?" Miriam laughed and spread herself out on the straw. "*La la*, come here and draw off my gown and lay those begging paws upon my breasts."

"I won't," said Dathan. He sank into the corner.

Abiram stared. Miriam had drawn her legs apart, and her gown split below so that he could see straight to her bush, and what lay glittering there. "Dath," he whispered, without turning to his brother. "She's ready."

But Dathan had drawn his arm over his head and closed his eyes. The others didn't hesitate. One by one they mounted Miriam and had her. Abiram ached to join them, every part of him ached, but without Dathan he couldn't. It wouldn't be right.

Then she called him by name. He had to go to her. Her quick, black hair fell from its cloth and swelled, and white rain fell against the cave and drew straight lines down its mouth and spilled in the straw. Quick and diving, black, like sleep, like paradise, she had no bottom. He surfaced from her and in a wild, full voice called: "Dathan!"

His brother hadn't moved. As each man took a second turn with Miriam and felt her turn to water under their hands, Dathan faced the wall, his hands ringing with pain.

Afterwards, when the miners slept and even Miriam snored on her bed of straw, Abiram, feeling so light and at peace that he could not bear it, laid a hand on his brother's shoulder.

"Dath," he whispered, "Why?"

"Why what?" Dathan mumbled, half-asleep. Then he looked up at Abiram and went on with an edge to his voice. "Why are we slaves? Why did we kill the stewards? Why did the overseer break my hands? Or why didn't I fuck the witch?"

"The last one," Abiram answered.

Dathan propped himself on his elbow and turned his face towards his brother.

"You want to be in pain?"

"I don't take orders," said Dathan. His voice sounded dull and unnatural and seemed to come from deep in his stomach. "Not from anyone."

Abiram didn't understand. He stared at his brother who'd rolled back over to sleep, and then he looked at the snoring mound of Miriam, her legs still damp with sweat and sex. He thought: My brother is mad.

Miriam stayed with them for a year and such was her power that to Abiram the year seemed like an hour: a few hot, hard strikes of his pick against the stone, followed by sex. He grew silly with contentment and helped the other miners wash Miriam's feet and hair. He gave her his own mash. Dathan caught him at it and struck him across the mouth.

"You would cut off your zabb and hang it from your nose if she asked you!" he shouted.

"Yes, and why not? Some of us might as well have no zabbs!" Abiram said.

He waited for another blow, but Dathan only walked off with his hands held out and trembling. Abiram almost laughed.

Then, one morning, they woke to find Miriam gone. Her ankle chains lay empty and the straw was still damp and warm. Abiram and the others went as far as their chains allowed, but they saw no sign of her. They returned to find Dathan had devoured all of their mash, and he sat with the seven bowls scattered at his feet, laughing.

"Ah—she's given me something after all! My belly's full!

And I'll let you dream of the witch on an empty stomach!"

Abiram's limbs turned to water. He was filled with fear and hatred as he studied his brother's mash-smeared face.

"I never gave in to her. I never danced to her tune. You keep your paradise—I've got your mash!"

That afternoon, Dathan managed to escape from his chains. He'd taken the discarded point of a pick and turned it to a knife, and with that knife he slew an overseer. He was returned to the hole after a week, and he shuffled, because they had broken both his ankles. On his face was that same awful smear of a smile, like a stripe of dripping mash.

Later, almost himself again, he whispered to Abiram, "You must have known, witless as you are, I had plans."

Abiram rubbed his brother's feet, trying to help the bones set straight this time. "Plans?"

"I thought it was a test," he said. "I wanted her to see I wasn't anybody's slave, that I was as free as she was. I didn't think she'd leave alone."

Abiram looked up then and asked, "You'd go without me, Dath?"

Grimacing as the bones locked into place, Dathan closed his eyes. "No," he said. "We'd go together."

But then Abiram asked, "Where would she take us? Where could we go?"

Three

Three years after Gershom was born, Moses prepared to leave his wife and son to find fresh pasture for the sheep. It was early spring, and in the cultivated lands the lemon trees were in blossom, and the fields were tinged with green, but in Midian, there were no lemon trees or fields of barley. Winter's stock of straw had long since emptied, and the sheep had turned what pasture Jethro had to dust and stone.

Jethro was near death and anxious. He called Moses into the tent. By now, the clay tablets lay piled so thick against the walls that he sat inside a narrow chimney. His beard was brushed by his daughters who also kept the floor clean of shavings, but no one could help the poor light or steady his hands.

As years passed, Moses had learned to carve the laws. Jethro would rest a cold hand on Moses' hand to be sure it was moving in the right direction. Moses felt the piles of fresh clay press in from all sides, clammy and malleable, as he dug into the tablet with the little brass knife.

Jethro marked a map in clay with the end of a stick and told Moses that if he lost his way the sheep would guide him, for the land he was going to was native to all sheep and they were drawn to it by nature. He said to Moses, "Find the green place, forty days hence. If we have no land, we have nowhere to put my laws. Make me a house of clay where I can rest."

"Rest now," Moses said.

To Zipporah, Moses feigned reluctance, but both of them knew he did not mind the journey. Since Gershom's birth the two, more and more, were strangers to each other. Zipporah remained in their tent to nurse their son, and when Moses returned from a solitary afternoon among the sheep, few words passed between husband and wife.

At night, now, he would not even pretend to sleep. He would sit on a palm-leaf stool with his staff across his knees, and he would feel in the wood dull marks of his father Amram's fingers, and he would pass his hand across them as Jethro had passed his hand over those marked clay tablets, like a blind man trying to make out what he cannot see. Eventually, he left the tent itself and sat on a stone outside, and there Zipporah found him with his legs curled under, his beard caught between his knees, and his ears turned, like cups, towards the bleating sheep.

She said, "No need to watch them now. They're safe, penned in."

"Not for long," Moses replied. He looked up at her with eyes like hot stones. Zipporah felt thunder through the soles of her feet and she wanted to answer but found no words. Later, he added, "There's nothing here for them. They must move on."

"But they have grazed here all of their lives," Zipporah said, and there was a break, a falling, in her voice.

"It's empty now," Moses said. That same day, she packed a palm-leaf basket of sheep's milk cheese, oat cakes, onions and sticky dates, and she bound the food in leaves to keep it fresh. In the spring sunshine, before the door of their tent, she gave Moses his son, Gershom, to kiss.

Moses took his son up under the arms and held him to the light. Gershom was small, with his mother's sad green eyes. He had yet to say a word.

"Won't you kiss him?" Zipporah asked Moses.

Moses kissed his son on the forehead and set him on the ground where he stumbled off to play with twigs and stones.

"Won't you kiss me?" Zipporah asked.

Zipporah, too, Moses kissed on the forehead, but the feel of her blood beating under the skin drew his lips towards her own, and he found himself weak with love and regret.

When at last he let her go, he said to her, "I'll come back and lead you somewhere new."

"You will," Zipporah said. She gave Moses the basket and he

took up the staff and led the sheep away from the hedged pasture, down a rocky northern slope below which lay the Sinai.

For a while, Moses walked without looking back. Below his hood, his head burned, and around him rose the stench and drone of sheep. Forty days seemed an impossible distance, beyond all sense, beyond the edge of the world. Pausing, he drew his gourd of water to his lips. He turned. He could no longer see Midian. The gourd dropped from his fingers and his head went white with fear. Wind, road, sheep, fell away.

Too big, too big, he thought. It is too big for me.

But then he felt water between his toes and he looked down and saw road, sheep, wet feet. Foolish, he thought. As though it mattered that the Sinai was too big.

He walked on, leaving damp footprints behind, conscious suddenly of his own trail in a way that brought him back to something he only half-remembered. His beard grew lank with sweat and his eyebrows bristled to shield his eyes from the sun. At night he rested, and from the three damp palm leaves he pulled bread, cheese, dates and onions, and he spread the cheese with a stalk of wild horseradish and ate the strong and sweet together.

Even that pleasure felt remote, like a memory of pleasure. Something else felt immediate, urgent, advancing on him and forcing everything else to insignificance. The night sky dulled as clouds gathered, and all around him the vast plateau turned into crumpled linen.

"Storm," Moses said, out loud. The sheep did not need telling. They mewed and knocked their heads together, ill at ease. Twilight gathered along the rocky hedges and turned everything gray.

Gray sheep, gray rock, gray thorn, gray sky, gray Moses, a sharp premonition as the world buckled slowly like a basin someone had tipped. Then thunder struck. That basin cracked, broke, and Moses walked on as though into a waiting circumstance, although the sheep strained willfully in the opposite direction.

The storm was closing in, and he began looking for stones to pen sheep. He pried one loose with the staff, which now reverberated in his hands. The sheep pressed him back, eyes brimming with betrayal, and he parted them with that same staff, pitiless and determined. Feeling for rocks, he felt the ground turn up and knew that he was climbing, bracing himself against the staff, wondering if it could be possible, if a few drops of rain actually fell and cracked and dripped down everywhere. How could it rain in Sinai? Or had they already reached the new green land?

Would that green land be a garden? Would it have a pool of fishes and four walls? Would they slaughter oxen there? Would a small boy smeared with feces huddle somewhere out of sight? Climbing the ridge, Moses felt stones shift under his feet, and he progressed foothold to foothold. The rain made the sky close in, and it soaked him through; he shivered. There was a final round stone high above and, raising his staff, he pulled himself into the dark.

He stood there, shading his eyes. What he saw made no sense. It was mid-afternoon, dry, cloudless. Before him stood a few stray goats with thorn stems hanging out of their mouths and they looked at him with olive-colored eyes. Between their yellow teeth, thorn snapped without a sound. Then from somewhere: *Moses.*

The name had been said softly, without urgency. Moses stepped back. The sunlight glinted, and he blinked. From somewhere else came:

Moses.

He knew the voice. It was the voice of his father, Amram, hesitant and forgiving. But when he turned, sparks flew in his eyes and he covered them with his hands. He cried out: "Here I am!"

Moses.

It was not his father. He didn't know the voice at all. It did not hesitate and it did not forgive. Yet there were those reeds on fire where his father had waited for him once, and the voice came from inside, or were the sparks, or were the goats. Everything knew his name. Why shouldn't a mountain know it? Overcome, he covered his head and shielded his eyes, willing himself to listen in a new way, to hear something new.

This is what he heard: *Return to Egypt, so that Israel's children might go out and serve me in the wilderness.*

The words were not spoken in anger. They were direct, probing, the way Moses once had heard the word *Further* the day he killed the overseer and buried him in the wadi. Yet he was asked for something impossible, for he knew he could not return to Egypt. When he remembered Egypt, all he could see was an overseer with a clotted head, a Princess with a broken heart, a father with a broken back, a friend betrayed. And then there were the slaves and what they made him do, what he must not do because of the trail of consequences. He forced himself to speak, though he stammered badly. "I cannot return. The slaves—"

I will free them.

Moses felt his staff turn in his hand. In the wake of the voice, he leapt back, and his heart pulled and pulled and leapt and leapt like those goats who leapt through the burning bush but emerged to leap again. He asked, "How will you free them?"

With a strong hand I will free them, and they will serve me.

"I cannot return," Moses said again, but he spoke less in despair than in bewilderment, and the dry heat and white light burned away indecision; he would return.

Why would he return? He would return to free them. How would he free them? With a strong hand. Not his own hand. He would free them with a hand that would not falter. The questions came now, of themselves, like gifts offered. "How will I speak to them?" he asked.

Find your brother. He has a voice.

"Who are you?" Moses asked.

I am the one who answers.

"What is your name?" Moses asked. The air trembled, and he stood on a wet rock in the rain, but his voice echoed back: "your name, your name, your name." And Moses answered his own question in a voice so thick and ragged it might have been thunder: "Here I am, here I am, here I am!"

And from below, sheep's cries, wind and raindrops.

Moses looked out through parting clouds, through fog, and he could see the road to Goshen. Brown-red seeped back into the rocks, and taking up his staff, Moses started down the mountain.

As ever, the vastness of the wilderness opened before him, but now he could not take the time to wonder, to fear, to feel at home, to feel displaced, to feel anything but himself, called by name. If once he had surrendered to the Sinai, now he saw it only as something he must pass over as a hand passes over a table to reach for something no one else can see. He walked at such a pace that by mid-day, he was close to Midian. He might have passed it by without a thought, but in his path stood Zipporah.

"Where are the sheep?" she asked him.

Moses did not reply. He moved to go, but still, she blocked his way.

"We're coming with you," Zipporah said to Moses.

With her stood Gershom, still unspeaking, and he let go of Zipporah's hand and clung to the legs of his father. Moses tried to shake him loose and somehow found the boy in his arms. In a confusion of fear and anger, he stuttered out: "I cannot—"

"You can," Zipporah said. "You will." Her face did not soften, but she added, "We will."

"It is not your place," Moses said, as Gershom burrowed himself into his beard.

"Then we have no place," Zipporah said. She put her hand over his own, upon the staff, and though the impact of that touch showed in his eyes, she did not take her hand away. "We are not as simple as sheep. We are bound to you. How do I pledge myself to your god? Must we die like those sheep you left behind?"

Quickly, Moses said in Amram's words, "He does not love death."

"That is good news," said Zipporah, "for I must love what he loves, so that I might not be parted from you."

She spoke formally, but Moses knew how to read her face, and he saw a great fierceness there and was afraid for her. "All right," he said at last. He set Gershom on the ground and they walked on together.

Zipporah did not touch her husband, but she fell along beside him, and Moses found himself slowing his pace to be sure little Gershom could keep up. Day gave way to evening. Night brought more rain. Moses found a cave where they could take shelter, and there Zipporah tucked Gershom onto her lap, and by very faint moonlight, combed sand from his hair.

It was then that Moses emptied his heart. He told Zipporah all that had befallen him, and she listened with their son on her lap. Her quiet face did not stir. Finally, she said, "So you will not lead us to a green place?"

"Not you," said Moses. "Every Hebrew will be freed, and they will not go to a green place. They are not sheep either." Speaking to his wife again, the thickness left his voice and he felt the urge to take her feet, which had walked so far that day, and to rub them slowly between his hands.

"So where will you lead them?"

"I will set them free."

"But to where?"

"To our god, who loves them."

"And how is he served?"

Well of clear water, wife, Moses thought, and he was full of love as he replied, "By answering suffering with justice. By a people who will not be masters or slaves."

Zipporah shook the sand from Gershom's comb and then she began to laugh.

Moses cried out, "Don't laugh. Don't laugh at me!"

But Zipporah was laughing with pleasure. She kissed Gershom's soft head and smiled at Moses. Then she said, "You're burnt black and covered with sand and fleas. Why shouldn't I laugh at you?"

Then she tucked herself and her son into her husband's arm, under the frayed sleeve of his mantle, and fell asleep. Moses felt them there, warm and frail, their low breath humming. They loved him; their love did not make him stronger, nor did it make his life a simple one. With his free hand he took up the staff his father had carved, and he drew a line through the wet dust, and thought: I do not know what to do with them. If they were sheep, he could water them. If they were fleas, they could rest in his beard. If they were slaves, he could free them. But Zipporah and Gershom were none of those things, and Moses was confounded. He knocked the staff against the stone absently, rubbing it dry, and so completely did these thoughts consume him that he did not notice that the staff caught fire.

"Moses!" Zipporah cried out, scrambling to her feet, "Husband! Where are you!"

For Moses was cloaked in flame, and Zipporah pushed Gershom out of the mouth of the cave and felt her way through flying ash until she caught fast to the white-hot flesh of Moses and threw him into the rain. He kept on burning. Zipporah backed some distance off, as Gershom leaned against her legs and looked at his father. They waited for him to be quenched by the rain, but he blazed and blazed and finally Zipporah called, as from the far end of a canyon:

"Moses! What must I do?"

Moses wanted to say, You must not be. He could not speak at all.

Zipporah drew Gershom forward towards the burning Moses and asked, "What consecrates a priest to gods in Egypt?"

She set Gershom on her knee, and from her belt she drew her knife. With one hand she held their son still, and with the other she cut off his foreskin. Blood mixed with water on her lap and ran down her knees, and her hands filled with blood. She poured the blood onto her husband's feet.

She said, "You have been a bridegroom of blood to me."

Where the blood touched his feet, it quenched the fire there, and slowly the figure of Moses emerged, wreathed in smoke; he was scarred from head to foot now, beard half-ash, eyes bloodshot, and he looked at Gershom, who was screaming, with his hands clamped between his legs, screaming as though he would die. Blood still poured out from him and glistened in the rain.

Zipporah asked Moses, "Does he hear?"

Moses had lost all language. He was unable even to weep.

"Ask the god. Does he hear? Will that do?"

You will not be, Moses wished again. You and the son must

not be or I must not be. No more delay. He turned and started down the road.

Zipporah called after him. "Do you hear me, Moses?"

He walked on, half-stumbling, leaving a trail of blood and ash. He walked into his task as he might walk into a wind, and then, slowly and without a moment when he marked a change, the wind was to his back, and he was borne forward over rocks and over mountains. He was bound for Pti-Ramesses, where he would find his brother, Aaron. By the third day, the feet of Moses were clean; the blood had worn away.

Four

Goshen land is fertile. Sometimes spring rain can wash away a few huts built too close to the wadi, but the silt left behind is like brown gold, and by harvest, the temple granaries overflow. Such was the spring the year that Aaron, son of Amram, took a wife. She was the daughter of a small landholder, a broad-browed girl with a bloodline stretching back to Pharaohs and gods. Her round eyes were shallow and she was aptly named for Hathora, the cow-goddess. Hathora was a good wife. She kept a fine house not far from the temple, and Aaron visited twice monthly to lie with her and balance accounts. She bore him four sons as brown as princes.

Every spring in Aaron's life, thereafter, was a bounty. The temple garden filled with pomegranates. Figs hung in purple clumps. Aaron had his own room in the temple where he slept between white sheets in his white chamber, and at dawn he rose to burn meat and grain for the gods. Some days, he went down to the catacombs and listened, as Nube spoke through the mouth of Seth.

Nube aged like wood, darkening to a glowing black that hardened at the mouth and softened at the eyes. He lost no grace or strength, leading Aaron down the hazardous passageway and smoothing his voice to music through the copper pipe. Aaron watched with care, and once Nube stepped aside and Aaron took his place and finished. No one noticed.

The many new priests ordained with Aaron tried their hand at magic. They burnt the oils of palm, olive, and lotus, and mixed hard barley and soft in the basins of bronze and basins of gold. Above the smoke, they whispered every holy word they knew. There was talk of great wonders—dark turned into light, staff turned into snake, rain turned into fire. More, there was talk of spirits of the dead.

"All ghosts," Nube often said to Aaron, "are light streaming through dust, and memory. Just as dark turns to light when you sneeze. Just as a staff slithers when your hand perspires. Just as moonlight can turn rain to fire."

Aaron watched his colleagues' demonstrations without praise or blame, and did not try his own hand at working wonders. Hathora observed Aaron's career with disappointment. She begged him to work just one simple wonder where her friends could see, to make a basket of lotus blossoms into a jug of wine or to turn bread into meat or meat into bread, but Aaron only shook his head and said, "You have meat, bread and wine enough."

After the birth of Aaron's third son, Eleazar, Nube retired, and before he could leave the temple, he took fever. He was only a minor servant, and his deathbed stood at the end of a long row of beds where men lay dying. Aaron drew on a dark cloak and visited Nube there, leaning close to kiss him. Old age had stripped Nube's face to black, raw bone. He raised that face toward Aaron's own, and feathery, he whispered: "Do not let them throw me in a pit, lad. House my soul."

Aaron stepped back so suddenly his hood fell from his head, and for a moment he could not speak. Then he leaned close and began: "You who have made fools of Pharaohs, high priests—"

"Do not let me wander," Nube said, and like two shutters, his eyes closed.

Thereafter, Aaron used his influence to see that Nube's body lay properly entombed. The next day, Aaron became the voice of Seth.

His life was full. Now, as he swung the censer and burned meat and oil and grain, he listened to every rumor and sorted out good sense so that Seth's words might be words of reason. His voice, a twin of Nube's, brought those words to the ears of the High Priest.

Aaron soon learned that his duties were known to some. He would find bags of gold or land titles by his pillow, attached to notes that read: "There are mines in Kush ready for purchase" or "Tell my husband I am true." Aaron left bribes where he found them. He had all he needed to live in comfort, and wanted to do his job responsibly,

without joy or remorse. Sometimes his prophecies came true; sometimes they did not. In the damp room where the pipe loomed up to
the holy of holies, Aaron's face was dry and serious, and his throat
pulsed as rhythmically as a toad's.

Thus went the life of Aaron for many years. He had made
peace with himself. Another spring came, another storehouse full of
barley, another garden stuffed with blossoms. His first two sons,
Nadab and Abihu, lay in their own quarters in the temple. Eleazar
and Ithamar slept in their mother's house where slaves poured oil
for their bath. Just before dawn, Aaron woke. A moment more and
his servant, the grandson of Mem, would come and help him out of
bed and dress him for the morning prayer. The servant was slow that
day, and Aaron was impatient. He sparked the wick of the lamp
himself so the boy could see his face. Better, let the boy see him on his
feet. He probed the floor for his slippers and his hand brushed
against a pair of boots.

Another bribe, he thought, and a mean one. He made to fling
them aside without a glance, but instead he found himself raising
them to the lamp; they were made of snakeskin.

He turned them, and his hand shook just enough to make the
skins unbraid themselves and slither across the floor in all directions. Their tails flickered; their olive eyes blinked; they converged,
sliding up and over the windowsill, into the court below.

Aaron pulled himself from bed and unsteadily moved towards the window. He looked outside. In the court was a stranger
leaning on a staff. He had his back to Aaron.

Aaron heard himself call like a cook's boy: "Over here!"

Such shame, weakness and confusion overtook him then that
he thought: It is my death out there; I am calling to my death.

From the east came gray light, and the man turned to Aaron;
Aaron saw his own father.

Or not his father, for Amram had been handsome and this
creature was a ruin. His mantle was little more than black rags and
his face was burnt, stunned, fringed with a beard like ashy swamp
grass. Still, there were the eyes set deep, eyes Aaron remembered,
the eyes that drove his mother to madness, lush and searching,

looking at something no one else could see.

A door closed somewhere. Aaron turned and leaned against the wall, waxen and sweating coldly. His hands opened and closed around the air where the boots should have been, and plain gold slippers clattered to the floor.

The servant rushed over and picked up the slippers, a pair like any other that shod the feet of Aaron every day. Aaron cursed himself for dreaming. It was unwise to dream of one's own death. The servant put the slippers aside and lowered his eyes.

Had he heard Aaron call out the window? If he spoke of it, then it would be no dream. He rubbed Aaron's body with oil, and shaved him clean, and he set around Aaron's shoulders first the shift of linen and then the mantle of purple and then the ephod. In Aaron's belt was the rod of authority, and on his neck lay gold band after gold band so that his shoulders rang like bells. Finally, the servant lifted, with a linen handkerchief, the holy cap of gold, and he climbed a silver footstool to set that cap on Aaron's head. Not once, from the moment he picked up the slippers to the moment he bowed to take his leave, did he ask Aaron whom he had called.

Yet would a servant dare? The question nagged at Aaron through the morning sacrifice. As he stood between Abihu and Nadab, waving their censers, singing, eating their portion of the god's meat set aside for priests, he thought: those eyes, that forehead. Souls are light, dust and memory. All wander. Homeless. Hebrew, Aaron thought at last, with such force that he dropped his bread.

"Father," Nadab whispered, picking up the bread from the floor, "Are you overcome?"

Aaron threw the bread back on the floor. "Must I repeat myself? Leave those jobs for servants!"

Nadab turned his eyes back to his plate and did not speak again. Abihu's thick lips turned up, more of a smirk than a smile; his bread was all the sweeter for his brother's shame. He chewed with slow dignity, careful to imitate his father.

Aaron made some attempt to love his sons, as it was expected, but he found himself watching them as from a distance and finding them wanting. Abihu would be a competent priest, but he was too plodding to go far. As for Nadab, he was as delicate and pious as a woman. Yet both were superior to his younger sons. Young Ithamar was a simpleton and Eleazar was less priest than merchant; once Aaron had caught him chattering to some money-lender in slave talk. Granted, Eleazar had his uses. He was a crafty spy and gave his father useful information. He alone, of Aaron's sons, knew where his father disappeared some afternoons.

Light, dust and memory followed Aaron as he walked through the catacombs. Light drifted down the stairway. The dust, leavened with Joseph's dust, rose from the broken case and mixed with such uneasy memory that Aaron wished, with all his heart, that such true horrors were replaced with anything as homely as a ghost. Fear crowded out what Seth would say. The messenger of the Pharaoh had come now and the high priest would ask the old question: Would Bityah bear a son? The god's answer must feed the Pharaoh's pride and not bring to mind the madness of his wife. It must bring riches to the temple. Delicate, cunning wit, Aaron told himself, is the only true magic in the world, as the only true power is gold.

Yet before he entered the chamber, his hand passed half-consciously over the casket and the broken face of Joseph. Joseph interpreted dreams; what would he make of the man in the court?

The answer: It was himself as he might have been had he remained in Levi.

Aaron raised his hand to strike away the plumes of dust, and at last he stepped into the room below the holy of holies, feeling the chill through his skull.

Upstairs was all pomp, music, sweetness, sunlight, chanting. The High Priest was approaching the tabernacle. Aaron felt only envy. Would that their places were exchanged! The High Priest was too young and too fat, and he spent whole winters dining at estates until he had wine for blood.

To that fool, Seth would speak. Aaron readied his voice silently, drawing the pipe close to his lips. Its ridge was worn smooth from years against his mouth; it tasted slightly of dust.

Above him, the doors of the tabernacle opened; Aaron knew

well the music of the hinge. The horned god sat with his long hands resting on his thighs, and his mouth was open, ready. Alone with the god, the High Priest trembled, no doubt, the pious fool. Aaron was tempted to turn him away without an answer, something he'd done more than once before.

In spiteful silence, Aaron made to laugh, but something cut through. The pipe filled with slave talk. *She will bear a son.*

He threw himself against the wall, shaking, head jelly, pipe reverberating. Slave talk! Slave talk! Had he gone mad? He hadn't spoken slave talk since he had left Levi.

It wasn't his own voice, couldn't be. He struggled forward and grasped the pipe as though to wrench it free, but then he drew it to his lips, thinking he might yet save himself and frame something in Egyptian. No doubt the High Priest couldn't understand enough to think the first much more than babble. Yet the throat of Aaron closed, and he found his teeth clamped down so hard they bent the pipe.

The chamber closed in around him, and he pressed a hand against the wall. It came back wet. The place was strange to him, and cold crawled up his arm and with it a terrible thought. There were gods, real gods. There were gods who hated him. His anguish pushed him forward until he hung from the hook of the pipe like a strip of meat and all around him was something that would tear him from that hook and swallow him alive.

Whispering through his swollen tongue in slave talk, the language he'd forsaken long ago, Aaron asked: "Who are you?"

The answer came in Egyptian. "Is there light?"

No answer from Aaron, who was too overcome to hear the scrape of the flint. Then, hot light. Aaron's cold head, weighed down by the golden cap, rose up. There was the man he had seen that morning.

His face was red in the torch, the beard red, the nose damp. He carried a staff that was deeply familiar. His voice issued from his mouth a little behind the movement of his lips. "You know me?"

Aaron said, "You are my father."

"No," said the man.

"Then you are my death."

The hand that did not hold the staff moved towards Aaron's shoulder and pulled him from that copper pipe. "The Hebrew god sent me. I am your brother."

Aaron stared. He had last seen Moses when he had been carried off by their father. There was no explanation for the sudden pulse of feeling that raced through him, relief, wonder, tenderness and loss, as though while falling down an abyss he had caught a glimpse of something he could not have but was glad that he had seen. He threw his arms around his brother and embraced him.

Moses felt frail, and he stank of sheep. The fleas in his beard crawled down Aaron's shoulders and nested among gold rings. He said, "You come with me."

Aaron answered in a rush of tears and slave talk. "You must understand that it's all over. We're homeless and betrayed and so we die together but—"

Moses answered in unpracticed, hesitant Egyptian. "I don't speak—you speak for the god to Hebrews."

Aaron's face burned, and stiffly, he too returned to Egyptian. "God? Which god?"

"The one who will set them free."

"Free? Free from what, brother?" But then, behind them came a rumbling and he leapt from his skin.

Yet Moses took Aaron's arm and started towards Joseph's tomb, saying, "This way."

"No, Moses, no," Aaron begged him, yet Moses moved towards danger with such certainty that Aaron had no choice but to follow, against all sense, through the catacombs into the open, and straight into the path of a guard.

The guard's sword was unsheathed, his face silly with fear. Clearly, he thought the place cursed and his mission unholy. His eyes passed over Moses without notice and when he caught sight of Aaron, a full priest, he scrambled backwards as far as he could, gave a deep bow and said, "Forgiveness, forgiveness, I was ordered here."

Aaron found himself standing stock-straight, and he drew

from his belt his rod of authority. Careful to frame his reply in coldest Egyptian, he asked, "From whom cometh commands?"

The guard shook so hard that his sword dropped from his hands. He said, "Don't strike me dead."

Aaron felt his potency; he had not lost it yet. He said, "I shall not strike you dead, but you must tell me who has sent you here to desecrate a holy place."

The guard's sword kept slipping from his grasp like a fish, and he fumbled for the hilt as he blurted out: "They said a slave—"

"My slave," Aaron said.

It was then that Moses knelt and put his hand on the hilt of the guard's sword until it lay still.

The guard's gaze fell on Moses, and he picked up the sword and frowned, finding suddenly that he could stand up and speak without fear. He addressed Aaron. "Who is this slave?"

"A family servant," Aaron said, suddenly flushed.

"And in the temple? He's awfully dirty," the guard said. He wiped off the hilt where the hand of Moses had touched it, and again he studied Moses' face, with its gaping mouth and strange eyes. He gained courage. "You'd both better come with me."

The guard turned to open the door of the catacombs. In streamed spring sunlight and the smell of burning oil, and Aaron looked at Moses and looked at the guard in whom suspicion fermented with sunlight, and finally Aaron raised his voice until it rang as though through copper.

"Know you shall not touch us!"

It was by voice alone that Aaron hoped to free himself and his brother from death, and by the rod of authority in his hand. He held that rod towards the sun, and the moment the light fell on it, it burst into blossom.

Aaron stood, warm with sun, the heavy stuff of his rings and cap and mantle anchoring him to the earth as he drove towards the sky the flowering rod. Eyes full of tears, he spoke slave talk, from the heart.

"There is a true god, and I speak for him. In the open, I speak for him."

Blindly, he reached for his brother who took his arm and led him through the court. The two men left the temple together.

Five

For some days, the tribes of Goshen had been distracted by signs. Gardens yielded twice the harvest twice as early, so Mennasheh and Ephraim gathered squash and lettuce noon and night. In Dan, On the god carver was found dead with a knife pressed through a stone baal's heart, and his daughter Hannah hawked that baal from tribe to tribe and sold it for a sack of gold. Judean masons hoisted stones as light as straw so that they piled a week's work on their backs and finished a steward's house in the space of one spring afternoon. Four Benjaminite ass breeders turned to find their Egyptian overseers transformed into speckled asses, and at once each woman mounted an ass and rode in all directions, spreading word of miracles.

Chains fell from ankles, coal turned into gold, black bread into white, white bread into cake, and cake into meat which filled so many stewpots that all of Goshen gorged until it burst. The women of Benjamin could not read or write, but they found Korah the Levite who carved word of the miracles on two clay tablets, and so they brought him tales from every tribe until he'd carved the clay so thick with wonders that no one could tell where one wonder ended and the next began.

"What do they mean?" Korah asked the Benjaminites, and the saddle-dizzy women shook their heads, so he posed the same question to his father, Izhar, who was a simpleton and could not answer. That night, father and son worked together in the kiln, and when young Korah stoked the coals, they found themselves blown off their feet by a blast so wild they flew over the tents, clear into the wadi. They rose with swamp grass in their mouths, looked at each other, and laughed.

Korah was twelve years old, and his triangular face was

thoughtful even when it was covered with mud. "Father," he said to Izhar, "what flies and has no wings?"

Rather than answering, Izhar drew Korah up in his muddy arms and took him from the wadi so they could return to the kiln before the overseer gave them a thrashing.

Korah and Izhar both were thick with scars from the whip. Even when Korah was silent he had a way of measuring an overseer with his gray eyes, and Izhar had a way of breaking the whip stroke with his own back. Moreover, Korah was under suspicion as chief of all the Levite water babies who had grown into mongrel boys. He called them out from under their thorn bushes and marched them around Miriam's well, waving a mottled, scarlet flag he'd found somewhere and shouting: "Here's our banner! Let's go find your mothers!"

Their mothers could have been from any tribe. Ezzi had Dannish kinked hair, Jonah the dough face of a Reubenite, Nam the delicate chin of Mennasheh, Hazzan Issachar's dour nature. It was Jonah, the tallest and the fattest, who was the least anxious for adventure. He would always shiver and say, "We can't get too close to Sinai. There are snakes there."

"Here's a riddle," Korah would shout. "What do a snake and a staff and a zabb all have in common?"

"You tell us, wise one," Ezzi would reply.

"They've all got skins!" Korah would sweep up the red flag again and shout: "Let's go to Sinai!"

All of the boys would tire of the game, except for Korah, who would remain alone, staring past the verge of Levite tents, into the wilderness.

For there was talk of a wonder beyond all wonders, of a man who'd come from Sinai. Rumor had it he was not a ghost. No ghost would raise such dust with his staff or stink so profoundly of sheep. The women of Gad dogged his steps and flung rotten onions at his head, but nothing could stop him as he made straight for Pti-Ramesses.

Not long afterwards, he was seen again, but now he had a priest of Seth beside him. Already, they had troubled three tribes. In

Reuben, Zohar the elder, the oldest man in Goshen, permitted them into his presence only to hear such evil tales that fat Dodi, his daughter, squealed and shooed them through the orchards of Ephraim. In Ephraim, Raban made the nomad wait outside, and feted the priest, only to find the nomad breaking down the acacia gate with his staff. Hannah the Dannite knocked two baals together for an auspice, and what she read caused her to drive them eastward behind a rain of stones.

When the two reached Asher, word spread, and as there was no elder in the tribe, everyone gathered to meet them. Ancient men pulled themselves out from under their blankets, and mothers and slight young maidens ran out from the fields, still muddy to the hips. Yet all made way for Reeba who was so old and scarred and stringy that she looked as though she should have died years ago. Let Reeba meet the two men first and die; it would be no great loss.

No one knew what they would be: a snake demon and a wizard? A horned Seth and his servant? They watched the two approach through a film of dust, and then they saw the priest and everything changed.

Such stature! Such a scent! Such a golden cap and a silver rod! They didn't know whether to close themselves up in their tents or fall at his feet!

Yet this priest addressed them. He said, "You have been summoned by a true god."

The air tightened. He had spoken slave talk. So unexpected was this turn that at first no one understood. Reeba was the first to answer, crying out, also in slave talk: "Amen—Seleh! Bless Lord Pharaoh!" and she threw herself in the dust before him so suddenly that he almost lost his balance. Every soul in Asher wept for joy, for his words could only mean one thing, that they could leave hard field work for good and live as servants in Seth's temple.

Aaron, too, seemed overwhelmed. His voice gained strength. "This man," he said, "my brother Moses, has spoken with that true and mighty god."

He gestured towards someone they hadn't noticed before, the nomad, and when that nomad felt the attention of the whole of

Asher, he turned his remarkably ugly face towards them and stared. "Who's that?" Reeba raised her head and her mouth twitched. "Lord, that's just some dirty Hebrew."

"He brings good news. A great god will have you serve him."

"We serve the great god Pharaoh, Amen—Seleh," Reeba said. She raised herself, knocking a little dust from her dress. "My Lord Priest, once my husband was elder here and, Praise Pharaoh, in his name I will receive blessing."

"Our god," the priest said, "would have you serve him in the Sinai."

No answer. A low wind came up from behind the two strangers and mingled scent and filth together into an ill-omened cloud. The nomad gaped; his teeth were brown. He leaned heavily on a staff they faintly recognized as carrying a curse.

Aaron's voice wavered now as he said to the tribe of Asher, "Will you not come when your god calls you?"

"What manner of god is this, Lord Priest?" Reeba asked.

"The true god," said Aaron.

Reeba's forehead beetled. "Our true god would not have us dead." Slowly, the fieldhands raised their scythes. She said, "You'd best move on."

"I speak for my brother who has heard the voice of that god," said Aaron.

"Your brother is a demon and your god is a demon and you are bewitched," said Reeba. "We've got troubles enough. Move on."

Aaron caught his breath and cried out: "Listen to me. You're chosen and blessed—chosen and blessed! Follow us to Sinai!"

At the name of Sinai, all of Asher rushed at Aaron and Moses, beating them back with staffs and clubs and cooking pots and stones until the two men shielded their heads and escaped into open country. Aaron wept, grasping his rod of authority from which all of the blossoms had fallen long ago. In the end, both men sat in the middle of the road.

Moses raised himself from the dust and passed his hand across his eyes. "They are slaves," he said in his bad Egyptian.

Aaron's eyes were still stinging with dust and tears. "Will

the god make another wonder?"

Moses replied, "The god said: *with a mighty hand*," but his expression of perpetual bewilderment did not ease Aaron's heart.

He bowed his head. "They will never go to Sinai. They'll die first."

"He does not love death," Moses replied. He sparked a small fire then and roasted a few wild onions he had found.

"We will have to go to the Pharaoh," Aaron said. He rubbed his bald head in his hands, imagining the two of them before the proudest of men, and very faintly he said, "If slaves do not hear us, what hope do we have before Merneptah?"

Moses dropped the onions into the fire. "Merneptah?"

"A man with a clear head," Aaron said, "and a proud heart."

Moses stared through sparks which rose over the reeds, as Aaron fumbled with a stick for the charred onions. Then Moses asked, "How could that be? Merneptah?"

"Did this god not tell you everything?" Aaron asked, and now he pressed, as he had many times before. "There is danger ahead. Brother, let us gain the blessing of the god. We will make a sacrifice."

Moses raised his onion in unsteady hands. "Merneptah will have an answer."

"He will," Aaron said. He picked nervously at his supper. Neither noticed, watching from the rushes, Korah, who could understand Egyptian and who was awake and curious enough to take in everything, the sheen of moonlight on Aaron's bald head, the sand in the eyebrows of Moses, the riddle of their conversation spoken between mouthfuls of their roasted onions for as long as it took them to finish and move on.

Six

The Pharaoh Merneptah had aged well. Morning walks along the wadi banks kept his flesh firm and clear, and his round head was smooth, save for a crease between his eyebrows. Most days he sat with his maps, a scribe on either hand. Most nights before he went to bed, he shot quail in the dark, and even at an age when the eyes of men grow weak, Merneptah never missed his mark. His cooks were hard-put to roast all the game, and so grew tales of pots which never emptied and feather coverlets piled to the sky.

For Merneptah was also a wizard, a sage and a holy man. Never had a more pious Pharaoh sat in Goshen. His tomb made his father's look like a footstool. He laid such bounty at the temple doors that they seemed made more of gold than stone. Around his throne were ten wise men from Thebes, Memphis and Persia, and there had not been such men since the beginning of the world. Each stood seven feet tall, and it was said that a single blink of their eyes could shut the sky like a window. Yet none of those men could cure the queen's madness, or open her closed womb.

Bityah had been mad since time remembered. Her white hair spilled across her shoulders as quickly as her slaves could bind it up again, and her hands rattled and twitched. She had tried to take her own life ten times. Yet for all of that, she was still impossibly beautiful. These days, she kept a silence which made her seem less a woman than a shaft of light. When Bityah sat on her throne, it quivered as with pleasure. When she lay beside the pool in the south garden, the orange fish would surface and draw their round eyes over the rim of the water. Merneptah's advisers often said: Take a younger wife, one who will bear a child. Yet Merneptah would not forsake Bityah, and on that matter he would not be crossed.

One day, the handmaid who held Bityah still to bind her gown found that it was tight across the bosom. When three months had passed, all the court wondered at her belly; it was round as a ball, and she held it with trembling hands as though she was afraid it would roll off her frame and out the door.

In secret, some spoke of artifice; she was too big for three months' time. In deeper secrecy yet, in the tiny painted room where he kept his maps, Merneptah conferred with the only man in the world he trusted, the Greek physician, and he said, "It isn't possible."

"You," the physician said, his wry face turned off towards the window, "the most pious of men, don't believe in the power of your sacred seed?"

"Shut up!" Merneptah snapped. He cracked his hands against his knees in a gesture of anger and bewilderment. "It's a tumor."

"Very likely," the physician said at last. He set his hand upon Merneptah's and said, "It would be a mercy, you must know."

"It's a tumor," Merneptah repeated, as though he had not heard, and then he bowed his head and studied a map of the sea which flowed off the world's edge, until the physician let him be.

He read until nightfall made the map too dark to see, and then he paced out into a court swimming in moonlight, followed by his long, strong shadow. Most nights, he slept soundly enough, but that night, as many years before, restlessness kept him strutting back and forth with his arrow and quiver strung across his back, and his shoulder aching like any old man's.

As a youth, he had climbed the wall of that forbidden garden where Bityah had kept a pet who asked a lot of questions. That pet had haunted the wall's summit, not on guard but waiting. Waiting for him, he'd thought. Now no one waited. Now the garden was just another garden, well tended and empty of meaning.

That night, something stirred on that wall, dark and round. At once, he set an arrow, let it speed, and waited. Something hit the stone.

Another quail, fat, plain and female. By rights, he should call in one of his wise men and read an auspice. He picked the quail up by its feet so that a few loose feathers floated and hovered. The spring air was very clear and smelled of almonds.

Was it a tumor or a son? He knew: It was a tumor. Yet memory mixed with feathers and with moonlight, and he knew that stranger things than sons had happened in his world, even if he'd sooner they had not.

And Merneptah made peace with his fortune and the next day, as instructed, he sent grain and oil to the temple of Seth and asked the god if Bityah was with child.

The answer took this form: Merneptah was conferring with his wise men in the map room, and the Canaanite turned pale and spoke abruptly. "Am I dismissed?"

Merneptah had no quarrel with the man, who had crossed rivers and deserts beyond number and could read many maps. He said, "Why do you think that I would dismiss you?"

"You have called another nomad," the wise man said, and in the doorway stood Moses.

The Pharaoh was so dumbstruck that he was not his own master. The man wore moldy rags; his face was pocked with burn marks; his beard hung in greasy strands. But it was Moses; it could be no other. It was Moses who looked straight through him with the familiar, stunned, unreadable expression. There was a minor priest as well, and he was saying something, but the Pharaoh did not hear a word. Rather, his eyes ate Moses.

Finally, the Pharaoh asked, "Why are you here?"

It was the priest who answered, in smooth Egyptian. "I speak for him. He comes from a true god who works wonders."

"I am a true god," the Pharaoh said. "I work wonders."

The priest said, "There is only one true god!" Then he dropped his little rod on the stone floor where it bounced twice and slithered.

Illusion, then. Fair enough. It could all be an illusion. He could fling back the curtains and let light pass through Moses and turn him to dust and memory. Still, can an illusion stink? And can it stare?

"Throw down your wands!" the Pharaoh called to his wise men, and at once ten green snakes slipped out of their hands. All might have gone well then, but from behind came Bityah.

She leaned between two handmaids, weighed down by her round belly and by gold, walking with tiny, shaking steps. Then she raised her eyes.

"Aie!" She spun through wizards and snakes and she threw herself at the feet of Moses and clamped her hands around his ankles. "You're back! You're back! Aie—love!" Her white hair spread around his filthy feet, and as Moses looked down, his face broke in two, and his mouth opened wider, wider.

"Monster!" Merneptah cried out, leaping forward and taking his wife up under the arms. "Traitor! Murderer!" Dragging Bityah backwards he kicked away snake after snake, and they passed into the mouth of the silver viper of the priest, which turned into a rod as he took it up again, so that when Merneptah threw his wife into the arms of her handmaids, he stood with bare stone between himself and Moses.

The priest asked, "Will you let us serve our god in Sinai, or will you harden your heart?"

"You bring me this man and speak of hardened hearts?" The Pharaoh's voice shook as he struggled towards composure. "I protect Goshen from men without hearts, from the wild tribes of Amaleke, from hunger and thirst and death without burial."

"The true god does not love death," the priest said.

"If he does not love death," Merneptah said, "he cannot know this man."

The two departed from the presence of the Pharaoh on the first day. The wise men called for sacred wood to carve new wands, and the Pharaoh ordered the place where Moses had stood cleaned with lye, meaning to blot it out, yet there remained a circle of uncanny whiteness where the lye had eaten into the stone.

As for Bityah, all that afternoon cries rose from her throat and her hands pulled at nothing. She did not try to tear herself away from Merneptah. She did not try to tear herself away from bed. She wanted silence, but the cries kept coming, and she knew that so long as she cried he would never come back again.

Merneptah whispered, "No more," as he had many times

before. And again, "We are nearing the end of long lives and no more will we have luck or trouble."

Yet all the while, the hard, round belly with his son curled inside of it turned those words false. Bityah pressed both hands against the belly now, and it was as though it lifted her from her husband's hands and into others.

In her chamber, two maidservants were weeping. Bityah watched without understanding. How could anyone weep when her beloved had returned from a long journey? She wanted to tell them he had returned, and she thought she had risen from her bed and walked to the smaller, prettier girl and kissed her on the mouth, but then she knew she had not so much as raised her coverlet.

"My lady, my beauty," the little one called across the room. Her mouth was pink; her slant eyes were like jewels. "When your time comes, let me stand by you."

Bityah thought she had said yes and had given the girl a gold ring from her finger. The girl's hands were empty and her smooth, pale palms spread themselves along her skirt as she turned to her tall friend.

"She's sleeping now."

By and by they would leave; now they have left. Bityah rested her cheek in her long, white hair and waited. By and by she would hear footsteps, heavy as the Pharaoh's. There they were. A rush of something like wind, only sweeter. Bityah looked up at a face that hung above her own face like the moon.

"I knew you would come tonight," Bityah said. And when she spoke to Miriam, Miriam answered.

"Well met, Princess." Her big hands made a cup around Bityah's belly. "Ha! And he rocks in your womb with his big flat feet tucked under, *la la la*."

Bityah sat up and laid hold of Miriam's ears which poked below her head-rag. "Let loose your hair."

"Ow! I told you, Princess. No."

"I want to see it rain."

"You'll see rain enough, of all sorts—ow! Leave go!" Miriam laughed, no maiden's laughter but a wild dark booming that made

Bityah roll backwards and start to laugh herself. Miriam's freed ears vibrated like tambourines. She shook her head and once again Bityah hoped that her head rag would fall free so she could see her hair again.

She had only seen it twice. The first time, she was a young girl, and above a baby in a basket, through the rain, she had seen something sitting in the reeds, a sleek darkness with two hard, glittering eyes. She had moved closer with the basket in her arms and out of the darkness, out of her hair, stepped Miriam. The second time, scant months ago, Bityah, who had spent countless years beneath a curtain, woke one morning to find that curtain's stuff had turned from blood to fine black hair. She raised an arm and rent that curtain, rising towards friendly light.

Behind that hair was a face she knew, the gold earrings, the mouth sticky with dates. In her hand was a flask shaped like a key.

"This opens," she said, and she spilled a drop between the legs of Bityah so that it seeped into her womb.

Then she moved towards the window, singing: "*La la,*" and the key smashed underfoot, and dancing, she was pulled, hair first, out the window, into a rainy sky.

Yet, she returned each day. She made Bityah bind the fragments of that flask into a handkerchief, and now Bityah kept the handkerchief between her breasts. She touched it often; the edges of that broken flask were sharp enough to draw blood. When her time would come, she would know how to use them.

Merneptah did not speak even to the physician about his encounter with Moses. In truth, he was ashamed. He had acted without forethought, like a child who felt betrayed. Taking a broad view, what did Moses matter? If the flight of Moses left a trail of evil consequences, those consequences could just as easily be traced back to his stubborn father or to Bityah, even to himself. Why bear old grudges? This Moses was clearly harmless now. Once he had mistaken the voice of Moses for the voice of his own heart. Now Moses didn't speak at all.

The priest was a different story. His voice Merneptah knew,

and he knew the man's position. That day, he made a point of finding out the name of Aaron's four sons, and at once he had them relieved of their stations. He confiscated the land of Aaron's wife. He considered having wife and sons brought before him, but let matters close.

It was with a cheerful spirit that he took his morning walk beside the wadi. He walked alone, bareheaded, as he had since childhood, carrying only a spear for hunting. His slaves whispered that he gathered water there for magic, and spoke to holy fish. In fact, he gathered nothing and spoke to no one. He only took his sandals in his hand and let his feet drag through the silt and watched the sky.

The sky above the rushes was slate blue. Merneptah drew up first one foot and then the other to replace his sandals, and he turned back to the palace. There stood Aaron, alone.

"Hello," Merneptah said. "Your sons and wife are destitute."

"Hear the word of the true god." Aaron's well-modulated voice trembled. He looked the worse for wear, mud spattered on his gown, most of his neck bands gone. "If you do not let us go to serve him," Aaron said, "he will turn water to blood."

"Will he?" Merneptah smiled and poked his spear into the mud. "What did you say you were to this god?"

"His voice," Aaron said.

Merneptah laughed and Aaron turned so red that for a moment Merneptah felt pity and would have given the poor man anything he asked for had he not, at that moment, caught sight of Moses. He was obscured by rushes and he looked the way he had looked years ago, doggedly expectant. In a fury, Merneptah let his answer fly.

"Turn it to blood," he said, "and I'll taste water. Turn it to blood, but I'll smell water, feel, touch water, hear water rushing. I know what is false from what is true."

"You have closed your heart?" Aaron asked.

Merneptah looked not at Aaron, but at Moses who did not ask his own questions. He said, "I live by truth alone. I do not swear false vows."

So did Merneptah turn his back to the palace with his wet feet slippery in their sandals. Behind him came, thick, unmistakable, the smell of blood.

For three days there was no water in Egypt. The basins were brown with blood. There was blood in the kneading bowls, blood in the bread and blood in the beer. Yet in the palace of Merneptah, all of Egypt knew, the Pharaoh had fresh water. They knew because they saw him bathe and drink.

Never had Merneptah drunk so much as he did in those three days. He called for a jar of water in the morning which he downed with a hunk of brown bread. He called for water always at his feet and at his elbow. Water must moisten his lips as he read his maps and water must wash the stones of the palace. "Water," said Merneptah to all who would listen, "is sacred, the stuff of life. I dedicate these days to the holiness and purity of water."

The servants of the palace kept handkerchiefs over their noses as they baked and stirred and scrubbed with blood. At the end of the third day, every wall and floor of the palace was an even brown, except for a single patch of white in the map room where once a servant scrubbed a circle of lye.

Finally the physician found the nerve to approach Merneptah. He found him sitting, sipping a cup of blood, with his keen yellow eyes moving along the ledger of a book of accounts.

"Look," said the physician. "This is nonsense. There's poison in the water and you're killing yourself. Who would have the throne when you are gone?"

"My son," said the Pharaoh.

The physician ignored his answer and said, "It's clear enough the Hebrews have poisoned the spring where the wadi begins. Purify it. If you want to cover yourself, have your wise men say a prayer or two and wave their wands."

"They have no wands," said the Pharaoh.

The physician rolled his eyes. "Oh, surely they can find a few that haven't crawled away."

Looking at his friend's ironical and sensible face, Merneptah felt so foolish that he spat out the blood in his mouth and said, "You're right." He smiled. His teeth were caked with blood, and he rubbed them clean with his thick fingers and shook his head. "I don't know what possessed me. I'll call that priest here."

"And his brother," said the physician. "That is the one I'd watch for."

Merneptah's throat tightened. "Why?"

After a pause, the physician very tentatively said, "Nomads know things."

"I cannot stand," Merneptah said, "the way all of this blood has made my head ache." Throwing open the shutters of his map room, he took a breath of sour air and vomited into the court below.

The people of Egypt rejoiced when the Pharaoh turned the blood back into water. They drank and drank until they wept, and when some noticed that the Goshen slaves did not drink with them, the rumors were confirmed that every tribe's well had run clear. On this matter, they questioned the god Seth who, in a voice transformed, spoke of ruin for all who crossed the will of Pharaoh.

Merneptah himself seemed like a new man. He sent for Moses and Aaron, calling them not into the map room, but into his great court, for an official audience. This time he did not let himself look at Moses, but motioned Aaron forward with such simplicity that Aaron himself seemed disarmed. He asked Aaron, "What do you want then? You shall have it."

Aaron shivered, as though he had a fever. He raised his absurd silver rod. "Three days in Sinai to serve our god."

"Sinai?" Merneptah asked pleasantly. "The wilderness? Where snakes live?"

"Sinai," said Aaron. The days had not been easy for him. His linen was gray with sweat and dust, and all of his gold was gone. He seemed to have stopped shaving, as there was stubble on his skull.

"A powerful god," Merneptah said. "Powerful gods need temples. Why not build a temple here in Goshen?"

Aaron did not answer. He moved his weight from one foot to the other. The wise men who stood at Pharaoh's throne pressed close to hear, for in that new god's temple they might find a place. All around them rose the rank smell of Moses, yet Merneptah, who had made himself drink blood, thought it no heavy matter to bear the stench without seeing the man.

Merneptah went on. "We have the means to complete a small sanctuary before winter. Of course, a true temple will take years, but a sanctuary, yourself as High Priest, with a tithe of young bulls for sacrifice, with temple slaves—

"Slaves?"

It was not Aaron. Merneptah's chest resounded and at last he knew he had no choice. As surely as his stomach knew blood, his ears knew that voice. Moses had spoken to Aaron.

"Slaves?" he asked again, and he croaked out the word as if it couldn't fit through his throat, and once released, it hovered, and Aaron caught his arm and pulled him back, whispering:

"Brother, if we—"

Merneptah shouted: "Speak for yourself! Ask for something I can give!" He realized he was on his feet, and his eyes were smarting and his heart turned as if it was fastened to a wheel. He shouted: "Do not speak at all! There is nothing I can give you! Nothing!"

But now the two brothers had fled into the dusty sunlight out of which leapt a sudden stream of frogs.

A guard appeared at the Pharaoh's elbow. "What would you have me do?"

"Close the door," Merneptah heard himself say. Then he rose from his seat and kicked great heaps of frogs aside and locked the door with his own hand.

During those days, he walked the palace hallway, room to room, and by the striped light from the shuttered window, he studied lists of gods. Soon, the drone of frogs made reading impossible. Later, a pounding broke the tablets in his hands, so he read papyrus. His scribes repeated tales of every god they knew, but each tale was split in half by a wild kick at the door. Small gnats forced themselves between gaps of wood and clung to Merneptah's face. To flee those gnats, he closed off the north wing and lay in the dark, gathering many thoughts together only to feel them slip away and leave him empty of anything but anger. His bed, clammy with dead gnats, soon fell to pieces, and then he sat on his stone chair with his hands pressed on his knees and felt such wild, white hatred that the walls of his room glowed.

A voice broke through. "Open up, you fool!"

It was the physician, the only man in Egypt with nerve enough to at last demand to see the Pharaoh. The Pharaoh unlatched the door and stood before someone almost unrecognizable. The physician's face was spattered with venom and his eyes poked out from greenish sockets. As he stepped into the room, with him traveled a cloud of flies. He grasped Merneptah by the shoulders and he shouted:

"Are you mad! Are you mad!"

Merneptah shook him off and frowned. "Are you? What would you have me do?"

"Give them what they ask for."

"Them?" The voice of Merneptah rang like ice. "Hebrew slaves? I offered them a temple. What else would you have me give them?"

"If it means this ends, give them everything," the physician pleaded. "Look, they have come three times to see if you will give them what they want."

"Which is?" Merneptah asked.

"Leave for themselves and their flocks—"

"Flocks?" Merneptah pushed the physician out of the way and started down the hall, so he had to trail after him, calling:

"Yes, flocks. Our own cattle are dead, but theirs are thriving. They want their flocks with them when they serve their god. They will take sheep, cattle, and all the gold they can carry."

"Gold?" Merneptah shouted. He stomped towards the open where the walls were black with blood and flies and gnats, and the corners were blue and green with rotting piles of frogs.

The Persian wizard, the most powerful of all, whose long curled beard once was a wonder of the east, staggered towards the Pharaoh on crooked legs and presented a chin eaten half bare with boils and lice. "I fear," he said, "that if you make them stay, their god will eat our gods."

Merneptah pushed him to the ground and stomped up towards the throne. "I know the god," he said at last.

The wise men clustered near, trembling and moaning, eager for wisdom.

"I know the god," Merneptah said. "I know how to meet him, and it is not with gold and oil and grain."

"But his name—" they all brayed out. "His name. We must know his name."

Before the feet of Merneptah bowed all of his scribes, his servants, his musicians, cooks and stewards who spoke in one voice: "For the sake of those who suffer, let them go."

Merneptah laughed. "What do I care if you suffer?"

Then through the prone Egyptians came a cloaked figure holding a staff, and all around him the air was clear of flies. Merneptah felt at his side for a spear, for he knew, at this time as at no other, that the name of the god was Anger and he might, at last, kill Moses.

The hood of the cloak dropped away, and there was a rosy old man who dropped to his knees and cried out: "Lord! Master! God!"

The Pharaoh looked him up and down and frowned. The man's long beard was curled at the tip, and his kohled, yearning eyebrows arched above weak eyes.

"Lord! Master! God!" he said again. "I am Hur, the elder of the tribe of Levi, and I have come many miles to beg, for the sake of slaves who serve you and love you."

The Pharaoh rose from his seat and gazed down in black amazement. "Slaves who love me?"

"More than we love water, sunlight, and life. For who else gives us a home? Who else would protect us from the demons who would make us homeless wanderers?"

With a cough like a laugh, Merneptah took up his spear. "If I ran you through, would you still love me?"

"Oh yes, Lord, Master, God." Hur sputtered out the words.

"And this Moses who has kept you sound while all of Egypt suffers, him you hate?"

"More than thirst, darkness, or death," Hur replied, "for because of these plagues we are so hated in Goshen that we will all find death at the hands of our neighbors."

"And your god?" Merneptah asked him.

"You are our god," Hur said, and he threw himself at Merneptah's feet. Merneptah did not kill Hur, but said rather, "Tell Moses to come here without the priest."

Hur sprang up and shuffled backwards with even, soft steps, and the flies parted around him like fog. Merneptah looked after him, and anger was so mixed with disgust now that his whole body felt like a boil. Turning to the Persian who still lingered by his shoulder, Merneptah said, "Bring me a looking glass."

"Lord," the Persian pleaded. "God and Master."

"Bring it to me," the Pharaoh said again.

The Persian turned and called for a looking glass to be brought to Merneptah, and Merneptah held it to his face and nodded, for the face was one loose boil. It could not be otherwise; there was no beauty in the world, or truth, and no answer, no answer at all.

No beauty, he thought again, and he let the looking glass drop to the floor and then, out loud, said: "Bityah."

What had become of Bityah? Merneptah sucked in a breath, and ran as quickly as he could to her chamber. He slipped on frogs and flies and gnats, and the boils on the soles of his feet sent a wild ache up his loins, yet still he ran, hitting doorway after doorway, forgetting where she lay, calling at last with all his strength, "Bityah! Bityah!" He shouted over cracks that hit the walls and roof top, and his voice broke everything to pieces as he called again: "Bityah!"

He found her in bed, covered by a brown blanket. The physician stood over her, his hands hovering above her belly. Her Hebrew maidservants had left long ago.

"Friend," Merneptah cried out, "How is Bityah?"

The physician looked up at the Pharaoh, and his face was a stranger's. He raised his hands, and as he did the blanket parted, and there was a fluttering of hard, brown wings. "Locusts," he said.

Merneptah feared to take another step. He stared. The locusts cracked and sank from Bityah's head to her feet, and they made a curve around her belly. Finally, Merneptah said, "I have gone mad."

"You are not mad," said the physician. His voice, too, was a stranger's. Then softly, he added, "She is in labor."

Those terrible words made Merneptah suck in a throat full of locusts, and he tried to cry out, but his hacking drove him blindly down the hall, and at last into the small room where he kept his maps. He locked the door.

And the Pharaoh knew he was no longer angry. He was lonely. It was as though that loneliness filled his emptiness to bursting.

Why could he not kill Moses? Because he wanted, more than anything, to be with him again, talking all night about the truth. When Moses shouted about slaves, the word hung in the air and turned like a bird shifting direction, and Merneptah wanted to shout some wild grand statement in reply, only to find, in Moses' cracked voice, a question. And his love for Bityah, what did it matter when he could not speak of it to anyone? Merneptah took his knees in his arms and wept.

There was a small knock. Merneptah did not look up to answer. In spite of locked doors, somehow, there was Moses.

"You called for me?" Moses said.

Merneptah could not rise at once. His knees were useless and his arms lacked the strength even to find the floor. So it was Moses who stepped forward and lifted Merneptah up to place him on a bench of stone.

Again Moses said to Merneptah, "You called for me?"

Through scarred lips, Merneptah said to Moses, "Open the door. I would have air and light."

Moses answered, "There is no light."

"Light," Merneptah said again. He raised his hand towards Moses, though he could not see him, and he said, "These days I have lived in a small dark place which cannot be unlocked."

Moses laid his hand behind Merneptah's head so that it would not rest upon cold stone. "You do not need to talk."

"Once," Merneptah said to Moses, "we pledged friendship in

the name of truth. I know now we made a false pledge."

"That is wrong," said Moses.

Merneptah said, "Speak the truth then. How can I open my heart?"

"Walk," said Moses, and his voice was the quiet voice Merneptah knew, that voice that stopped midway up the throat and softened there. "Along the hallway you will feel between your toes fragments of glass and gold. Gather them and follow."

Merneptah reached again for Moses, but his fingers were too broken and they only hovered. Finally, he said, "You help me up."

Moses bore the Pharaoh from the stone seat, and he opened the door and left him in the hallway in a darkness five shades darker than night, so deep that nothing could be seen or felt, heard, touched or tasted. In such a darkness, pain could not live, so Merneptah found himself able to stand with assistance. He could not see Moses go.

Yet into the hands of Merneptah fell, singly, the fragments. They met each other, and in his mind's eye as he moved from piece to piece those pieces fell together. Who led him from fragment to fragment? Who brings pieces together? Who opens?

He asked, was it always so? Yet he expected no answer and so answered himself: Always, it was so.

The last piece clung to the edge of the gold key. Darkness smoothed into twilight, and against that twilight lay his wife, Bityah, in her third day of labor.

The Pharaoh watched from behind, as her white hair streamed backwards down her frail, golden arms, and she clenched the end of a table. Her mouth opened, and dark thinned just enough to make way for her voice as she cried: "Miriam! Miriam!"

Miriam! Merneptah knew that name. Now between the thighs of Bityah he saw Miriam attending, draped in a cloak, draped in her hair, draped in the scent of dates, but when he rushed to pull her from his wife, the hood fell back. There was his own physician.

"Thank God!" Merneptah shouted, and he cried with pure relief.

"Which god?" the physician asked in his dry voice. "Or do

you know?" It was then the Pharaoh realized that the man who was drawing forth the head of his son was not his physician, but the Angel of Death.

At once, the Pharaoh knew what must be done. He turned from the Angel of Death and spoke not to Moses, but to God.

"So now they cannot turn back," he said. "So they must go to Sinai, for they will never be allowed to stay in Goshen now that you are killing in their name. And now I will tell them to take their flocks and gold and never to return."

From behind, the Angel of Death rose with the Pharaoh's dead son in his arms. His face was just as dry and just as intelligent as the face of the physician, and it was with the physician's voice that he said, "You know they will not go until they're forced."

The Pharaoh smiled, and he clapped the Angel of Death on both shoulders and said, "You speak, and it's with the voice of my own heart! I'll mount a chariot and call my swiftest men, and we won't give them time enough to bake a journey's bread before they're gone."

Through the last rag ends of dark, the Pharaoh mounted a bright chariot, and all of Egypt wondered at his holy anger as he drove the twelve tribes from the wadi for the sake of his dead son. Through the rushes, arrows flew, until at last those tribes were trapped against a deep Red Sea.

Yet closed things open. When Merneptah felt for the gold key, he found that it was gone. He himself was the key, and he drove himself into the open gap of water through which swarmed his enemies, until, over his head, the waves closed up.

Seven

Korah smelled sulfur. He clung with others to a strip of pebbles, and gazed towards a seat dotted with horses and men. "Where are we?" he asked his father.

"We're dead," Izhar replied.

"No we're not. Those men in the water are dead. We're alive. Feel." He placed his father's square, hairy hand on his heart so he could feel it beating.

Izhar drew Korah to his beard and kissed him, weeping. "Son! Look around you!"

Korah turned and saw a hundred thousand strangers milling like sullen ghosts amidst gold piled in carts. From everywhere came the bleating of sheep and goats, a hollow, tidal pulse. Steam hovered and obscured the sun and what lay inland.

"Are all twelve tribes here?" Korah asked his father.

If Izhar answered, it was drowned out by Grandfather Hur's lamentation.

"Oh Evil! Evil! Our god is dead!"

Hur threw himself on the gravel, and Izhar ran to help him to his feet. The other Levites, listless but steady, dipped their hands into that gravel and tossed it over their shoulders by the fistful.

Far off, Aaron waved his rod and called out: "Praise our god! He has triumphed gloriously!"

Yet Aaron's voice was like tin and it carried no farther than some Dannish women who were digging in the sand.

Aaron asked, "Do you search for altar stones?"

It was Hannah who looked up with a dirty face and hard eyes. "We're digging our own graves."

Aaron turned pale and raised his voice. "Find four good stones, and we will bless them with oil and make an altar for the one who parts the waves!"

"I knew you were trouble when I saw you, boss," Hannah said. "I trust in stones. They part heads." She forced her weight forward on the handle of her spade and, with a huff, dislodged the sand.

"We came here to serve the god," said Aaron.

Hannah tossed a clot of wet sand his way and said, "Leave it to the priests."

Aaron wiped the sand from his face. "I am a priest."

"A priest? I thought you were a sea monster!" Hannah said. It was then that Aaron saw the long string of bracken flying from his rod, and he flung it off and frowned down at Hannah who had turned back to her grave-digging as though he were beneath her notice.

Shivering, Aaron climbed to the top of a rock to get some air and clear his head. He thought: it does not matter. Let them shiver, snap and bray. Let them unite only in their eagerness to dig themselves good graves. There is a god who parts the waves, who calls, who knows my brother.

"Moses!" he called, but he could not find him anywhere, only those strangers, and beyond them the still waters speckled with floating horses. The chariots had sunk an age ago. Could Moses have gone to sacrifice alone? The thought stopped Aaron short, and he stumbled back down and found himself among the women of Benjamin who dug graves for their donkeys. He rubbed his stubbled head with both hands; his breath came out raw. When he looked up, there stood in his path a boy holding a severed head by the hair.

Aaron croaked out: "Take that thing away!"

The boy stayed put, and he thrust the head forward and said, "It is for Moses." The boy had a round, ugly face, small-eyed and framed by iron-black fuzz. The head was soaking and Egyptian.

Aaron pulled back. "Moses does not want the head."

"It is for the Lord."

Furious, Aaron said, "Are you a priest, that you would sacrifice?"

The boy turned red and drew himself to his full height which was no higher than Aaron's shoulder. "I am the son of Nun."

"Then go back to Nun! Leave me be!" Aaron gave the boy a kick and sent him back to his own tribe. He left the head behind.

That head stared up at Aaron; its eyes were wide open and its cheeks were bloated with water. Aaron looked away.

His gaze fell inland, to Sinai. It lay beyond the mass of Goshenites, emptied of everything but feces-colored rock and scrub. He had heard about the Sinai all his life; it was where death lived. Already its wind cut into Aaron's flesh and made him feel his bones.

He felt his hands reach through his belt for his knife and his censer; he thought: Seth is a desert god.

Blasphemy! All of the gods are false, save one. He would have hidden in the catacombs, but Moses led him forward into what looked like death and a way had opened. Weak with shame, he steadied himself on crabbed legs and went to search for his brother. Short of breath, he lost his footing more than once on the mounting piles of sand next to the graves the Goshenites were digging.

He would have called out for Moses again, but four big men rushed towards him. He gasped and ducked, and one caught him in his arms and shouted: "Father!"

Aaron shook himself free. Before him stood his four sons. They were so filthy and ragged that it was no surprise he hadn't known them. Abihu's fat face was crusted with bracken, and gravel clung to Nadab's eyelashes. It had been young Ithamar who had embraced him, and now he hugged himself and sobbed.

Abihu, the oldest, told their story. When the Pharaoh forced them from the temple, they sought refuge in the house of Hathora their mother, only to find she had returned to her family estate. They were left to wander Pti-Ramesses where their neighbors suffered plague after plague as those same plagues spared Aaron's sons. They tried to bloody themselves with meat to feign disease, but they were found out during the plague of darkness when an arc of light marked them as Hebrews. So they were hounded out of Pti-Ramesses and forced through tribe after tribe until, at last, Eleazar bargained in slave talk and found them a place in an Ephraimite carriage so they could join the reckless ones who fled Goshen.

Abihu tried to master his voice as he spoke. "I cannot yet

believe— Father, tell me, how can we be Hebrews?"

Aaron set a hand on Abihu's shoulder and said, "We serve a true god."

"We serve Seth," Nadab said with a primness which seemed strange coming from such a filthy boy. "He lives in the holy of holies."

"We serve a god who is not made of gold and stone, but one who is made of power," Aaron said.

It was fox-faced Eleazar who drew close to his father and whispered in slave-talk: "You are this god's voice?"

Aaron pushed him away. "Do not speak of such things."

"Father," said Ithamar, "you've got stubble."

Abihu smacked him. "Honor your father!"

But Eleazar said, "In my satchel is a razor, a cake of oil, and a set of shears."

Slowly, Aaron raised his head, and he saw himself in the eyes of his sons. He shivered and said, "So we will bathe together."

"Where are the servants?" Ithamar asked.

Heartened, Aaron boxed his son's ears and said, "Fewer questions. Fewer questions and more commands!"

They walked thigh-deep into the water, and Abihu and Nadab sang the morning benedictions as father and sons scrubbed and shaved, so that for a time, Aaron forgot about the Sinai.

It was not long after that the tribes felt a wind rattle against their shovels, and they set those shovels down and bowed their heads, remembering the Angel of Death. But it was no angel. It was Moses himself who had passed along the edge of the half-dug graves to the place where the shore ended and the Sinai began. He entered the wilderness without hesitation, in fact with such urgency and conviction that his feet and staff cut into the sand and left a trail.

To Izhar, Hur whispered, "It's the demon of the east!"

But a woman called, "Old nomad, where are you going? There's better ground for good graves here." Moses did not turn to answer; rather he kept going. The tribes closed in. They could not believe that anyone would walk of his own will into the Sinai. They left their shovels by their pits and whispered to each other, "Is that the road to Goshen?"

Korah's face, framed by his smokey hair, turned first towards the trail and then towards his father. "I want to go."

"No, son," said Izhar. "No one goes there."

"What snake bites and leaves no mark?" Korah asked, and his high voice rang out.

Izhar blushed and shook his head. "No riddles now."

"I'm going," Korah said, and he broke away from Izhar and hurried on towards Moses who was receding now. Izhar had no choice but to follow.

Hur caught Izhar's shoulder and tried to hold him back. "Don't let your son make a fool of you."

"I'm already a fool," Izhar replied, and he took Hur's arm. "Come too, father. I'll give you a leg up onto your ass. Maybe he is going to Goshen."

"This is madness."

Yet before Izhar could answer, a hush swept forward, and pushing through the mass of Goshenites was a golden litter such as none had seen before. The litter was borne on the backs of four oiled, shaved priests, and its blue drape was so heavy with gold fringe that it strained against the frame. Briefly, the curtain parted. Inside sat a mighty wizard with a painted face, covered from neck to knee with lapis, carbuncle, emerald, sapphire and red gold.

From the crowd below, it was Raban of Ephraim who called, "Lord Priest, you enter Sinai?"

Aaron motioned for the litter to be set on stone, and only then did he speak. "We will move forward," he said, "for one way closes and another opens."

From his belt, he drew a vial of liquid myrrh, and this he scattered on the stone so that a cloud of sweetness rose, and as the sulfur cleared, so did the heads of the twelve tribes, and they licked the air for joy.

When the priests turned to raise up the litter again on their shoulders, they found themselves dogged by twenty old men begging to take the honor and the burden so no holy feet would touch the

ground. The old men followed the nomad's trail which they knew
could lead only to Goshen.

As the priests passed from the banks of the Red Sea to the
Sinai, they were followed by Goshenites who, homeless now, became Hebrews. Moses himself walked far ahead, a smudge in twilight, less distinct than the deep marks his staff cut into the gravel.
Aaron himself cleared his throat and sat back into a cloud of cush-
ions. It was wonderful to be clean again.

"My brother leads us to the altar. Not long," he said to his
sons, "before you see great wonders."

"Is this god more powerful than Seth?" Nadab asked him.

Aaron replied, "Seth is a stone thing."

Nadab raised a lean hand to his mouth and whispered, "Are
you not afraid we will be struck dead?"

Aaron took a sip of water from a golden gourd and passed
that gourd among his sons. He did not answer.

"Are you not afraid?" Nadab asked again. His face was
covered with a film of perspiration, and the paint around his eyes
ran down his nose.

Aaron gave him a tissue of linen and gold. "Wipe your eyes,
son. Look your best. Let me not see a speck of dirt on your linen or
a line of sweat on your brow."

Yet Abihu asked, "When we reach the altar, how do we
sacrifice? And in what name?" His face was clean and his bearing
blameless so that Aaron did not know how to distract him and was
grateful when the litter suddenly bobbed and swayed and a high
wind blew the curtain forward.

The road ahead was almost black, save for a few cracks
whitened by the moon. The wind sang and so did something else.

"La la la—"

Clearer now, and unmistakable.

"La la la—horse and rider flung into the sea, a man of war is
he—"

"Don't look," said Aaron. "Perhaps it is the wind."

"Amen—Seleh! La la, into the sea!"

Timbrels crashed, and the sour voice swelled around the
company. The Hebrews knew then that Miriam also entered Sinai.

Eight

Nothing was worse than Miriam. She was big as a house and black as a pot. Her big flat feet raised cold and dizziness and death. She sang: "*La la la*—blessed be the man of war! He has triumphed gloriously!"

She and her tribe scattered everywhere, shaking their fingernails, clanging their timbrels, and spreading that song like misfortune. The march was slowed until it barely moved at all. The carts of gold sank in tar pits, and snakes terrified donkeys and made them dump their burdens. The bread was gone now, and the beans were full of sand fleas; salt-meat and figs turned rancid in the sun. Sheep and goats bleated for water, but water was in short supply and there was no more to be found. With mounting thirst, the Hebrews followed the trail of Moses as Miriam's tribe danced cursed circles around even Aaron's litter where she sang through the curtain:

"Hail, hail, my brother of the pretty voice!"

Aaron's sons would look at their father from under their painted eyebrows, and Aaron would not look back. He straightened his lips into a long, hard line and squared his shoulders so the gold rings on his neck clicked and were still.

Nadab asked, "Is she a priestess of this god?"

"She has nothing to do with our god," Aaron said.

"Why are there so many women here and so few young men?" asked Ithamar.

"Because the Hebrews killed their sons," Eleazar snapped at him. "He should have killed you, dolt!"

In those days, Aaron learned to hate his sons, Abihu's bland nobility, as silly in the Sinai as it had been admirable in Goshen, Nadab's pious bleating, Eleazar and Ithamar nipping at each other like two dogs. He wanted to climb out of the blasted blue-draped litter, but then he might face Miriam who could lay curses on his limbs, his eyes, his life, and in whose skirts may well yet lurk his afterbirth. Moreover, he could not leave; it was the litter the tribes followed, and that litter must follow Moses.

Eleazar whispered, "Just treat them like the temple slaves. Promise a little meat and beer and they'll be quiet as mice."

"We are not in the temple, and they are not slaves," Aaron replied. Eleazar would bow his head in deference, but Aaron could see the corner of a smile.

At night, when elegant, mean-mouthed Ephraimites approached with empty water basins, Aaron heard himself promise them wine. Later, when Hur the Levite stumbled towards the magnificence of the litter and begged Aaron to wave his rod and turn Miriam into dust and ashes, Aaron spoke of grapes.

"Sweet clusters, thick and black and fragrant, Amen—Seleh!" In a sweep of burning sandalwood, thirst and witchcraft were confounded.

Then Miriam and her women would pass by again, singing.

"At least make her loose her hair," someone called, "And bring us rain."

Aaron answered, "Our god will provide," but in truth he feared that Miriam would whip her head rag free and bind him with that hair.

He began to fear all women. Hannah, little as she was, made him tremble. She sought him every day, crooning and wheedling as though she'd never called him sea monster, and she laid bribes at his feet, threadbare linens, silver amulets of Hathor the cow and Apis the calf, strings of dusty amber.

"Boss, tell me what he looks like," she would say. "this god. I'll carve him."

Aaron would stop his ears and order the Hebrews forward for fear of losing Moses, yet somehow, in spite of confusion and long delays, Moses was never quite out of sight, though he never seemed to stop moving forward. His trail grew increasingly illogical, traced over the hardest passes where thorn grew or rocks slipped out from underfoot, or through crags where snakes nested. "Our god will preserve us from snakes," Aaron said over and over, but already five little girls from the tribe of Simeon had fallen, and they were left to birds of prey for fear that grave digging would disturb more snakes.

And Miriam danced by singing, "*La la,* coal heads and crackers, crack some rocks for water." Her heavy, red head rag glowed through dust and smoke, and as she reeled her arms up, Aaron felt his whole self reel and tumble.

Boldly, Miriam nagged the Levites who had driven her away so many years before, and Hur seldom left the shelter of a cart heaped with goat skins, for he feared revenge. Izhar pulled that cart over the roughest passes. He had not tasted water for a day now, having given his full store to his father and to Korah.

As for Korah, he walked ahead with his Levite friends and watched Miriam. She tumbled as she danced and kicked up sand and mica.

"Could she be your mother?" Korah asked his friends. The boys didn't think the question worth an answer.

Miriam sang: "Follow, follow, follow—you'll never be thirsty again!"

Jonah chewed the inside of his cheek sullenly, and Ezzi said, "Don't talk about mothers. It's only going to make him cry."

Jonah had spotted Dodi, Zohar's daughter, and he had been so certain that she was his mother that he followed her everywhere and brought her everything he could steal, bags of figs and triangles of hard, white cheese, but Dodi had shooed him away with disgust or, at best, indifference.

"She does look like you," Ezzi admitted. "but she's from Reuben, and she's the daughter of an elder. She can't have anything to do with a bastard Levite once we get back to Goshen."

Jonah sniffled and answered thickly. "But she's my mother!"

"How can you be sure?" Korah asked him.

"I just know."

"I wonder," said Korah, "if we'll know Aaron's god when we see him." He strode ahead, thinking so hard that his legs went loopily astray, and he said, "I think he looks like my father."

"Then he's simple-minded!" Ezzi called, and he dashed off

before Korah could tackle him, though Korah followed close enough
to make swipes at Ezzi's thick, Dannish hair, and they both fell in a
heap of dust and thorns so that for a moment thirst was forgotten.

Then they heard something behind them. Cutting through
stone like a knife through clay was a silver line of water which made
straight for Miriam.

"The well!" Korah shouted.

Miriam herself turned ashen and leapt out of the way, but the
water followed, loosing a little spray as she leapt again and again,
only to find it at her heels. Wavering, Miriam paused, her mouth
turned down in an arch of thoughtful misery.

"So swallow me then," she said to the well.

Rising, the water made to close over her head, and it met a
black fish without fins or scales who dived between its currents and
was gone.

Too stunned to move, the three boys looked at the water.
Korah was the first to find his bearings. Taking a wild gulp of air for
courage, he bolted forward and jumped in. It filled his hair and nose
and eyes, and he leapt out, sleek and shouting. "It's sweet! It's
sweet!"

At once the two boys joined him. They sank into the coolness
that pulled their hair and rags in all directions, and they surfaced to
find the pool had lengthened to hold old men with floating beards,
women whose long gowns hovered along the surface. Aaron's sons
tested the water with tentative hands.

"Probably poison," Eleazar said.

Ithamar pushed his brother aside and dipped his whole head
in so that the others had to pull him out again. Abihu and Nadab
contented themselves with filling their golden cups, and they brought
a chalice to their father. He drank with a sour expression. His eyes
were on the tail of the black fish who still swam away, pulling the
string of water in pursuit.

The well of Miriam was following Miriam through the Sinai.
It would follow her whether she took the form of fish, toad, heron or
woman, and one day it would catch her unawares in her true form
and on that day, Miriam would die. But until the death of Miriam,

Miriam's well would be among them.

Rejoicing, the Hebrews filled their gourds and skins with water, and they were still drinking when they spat their water out and stared.

Before them was a cloud as black as a pot. Thunder rolled up the soles of their feet. They threw themselves in the dirt and wept, for they thought the cloud had been sent by the witch and that they would die. Indeed, fragments of stone struck their heads. The earth gave a buckle, and Aaron clung to the litter, his skull tingling.

The line of storm advanced, swift and ruthless, but as it neared, the thunder turned to laughter and the lightning to swinging chains. It was a mass of men led by a giant with a square black beard who swung his broken chain in an arc and snatched up the first Hebrew at hand, skinny old Reeba. In a thick, cracked voice, he shouted, "Bread!"

"There's no more bread," said Reeba.

"Then women!" the strangers shouted all together, and they cracked their chains in the dust and turned the day to night.

They rushed forward with their zabbs in one hand and their chains in the other, and the Hebrew mothers flew back to cover their daughters with goat skins and throw themselves on top.

The men laughed, and the biggest shouted, "You think that will stop us?"

"This will!" a mother called. She took her bag of half-rancid salt meat and flung it at his head. The other mothers threw all of their meat and cheese and dates at the invaders, crying: "Take it! Eat it all!"

Strings of figs hit the men's knees, and they rolled backwards, wrestling over them as slabs of dried goat ribs rained on their heads. They sank their teeth into whatever came to hand, gnawing it down to pip or bone, and forcing the marrow out with their thumbs. After a while, their wild eyes turned up with satisfaction until they all dozed by Miriam's well with water dripping from their beards.

Thus prone, they proved to be a mongrel crew, some with slanted Hebrew eyes, a smattering of Ethiopians and Cushians, even a few fair-haired Hittites, all lying with their heads on the bellies of their neighbors. The only thing they had in common was a deep cut just above the armpit that had healed to a white scar. Zohar of Reuben approached with his grey beard dragging between his knees, The man with the black beard sat with his back against a stone and a chain bunched in his hand. He did not rise to meet him.

"I believe I know your face," Zohar said. "What is your name and tribe?"

He spat out water and said, "Dathan's my name. And tribe? The tribe of miners!"

Hesitant, in a voice like old leaves, Zohar asked, "Are you the elder of that tribe?"

"Elder!" Rising at last and shaking with laughter, Dathan picked up the end of Zohar's beard and gave it a tug. "I was born in Goshen and my own elder had a beard like yours, old man. It wagged and wagged when I killed my first Egyptian. It wagged when I was caught and sent to my death pounding turquoise from stone."

As Zohar tried to stop his teeth from chattering, Dodi rushed forward, waving her arms until her veils were crooked. "Shoo! Shoo! You're nothing but a pack of bandits! If you don't leave us be, the priest will make the god strike you dead!"

Dathan sharpened his teeth on his lips thoughtfully, then said, "Gods are dung."

The Hebrews listened, keeping their distance in case the earth should swallow Dathan alive, but Aaron approached with his gold cap on his head, flanked by his holy sons. Dathan's eyes moved heavily towards Aaron, and his lips turned up and showed a little reddened gum.

Aaron drew himself tall and faced Dathan, asking, "Who broke your chains?"

"Not some priest," Dathan replied.

"It was the god we will serve in Sinai."

"I served Pharaoh in Sinai," Dathan said, "in his mines, and now we move west and return to Goshen to storm the palace and kill your god in his seat and drink his blood."

Aaron kept his priestly reserve and made his face as still as water before asking again. "Who broke your chains?"

Silence gathered like sweat; everyone waited for an answer, thinking that, at last, they might learn the god's name. But at that moment, Dathan's face transformed. He dropped the chain he had clenched in his hand and stood up, taking a step forward and whispering: "It's you."

The Hebrews followed Dathan's gaze and were dumbstruck, for Dathan was staring up the trail that led to the tiny, receding figure of the nomad.

Dathan bellowed out: "You're the one I saw with the club! You're the walker!"

The figure was smaller than a dust mote; it receded further. Dathan called to his men, "Get up! Get up! It's him! You dogs—stand on your hind legs! Hurry before we lose him!"

Aaron broke in, uncertain. "You follow—"

"Where are you going?" Dathan shouted at Moses, blasting the words across an impossible distance. "Have you been wandering all these years? Two days we've traveled from the mines and didn't we leave a string of guts behind! Guards, overseers! We blacked these broken chains, brother! We blacked them with good blood!"

Far off, light blinked. Without question, Moses had stopped and looked behind him, and in the clear light of Sinai it was almost possible to make out the panic on his face. Then he spun back and fled with such urgency that he was lost in a cloud of sand, and Dathan, dizzy with emotion, stumbled after, calling:

"Where are you going? Where are you going?"

Aaron spoke. "That is not your concern."

Dathan reeled and threw Aaron to the ground. He called, in agony, to Moses. "Why do you let the shaved priest speak for you! Why?"

The other miners wiped their mouths and staggered to their feet, and Abiram took his brother's elbow and whispered in his ear, "Dath, Dath, what's the hurry?"

"I'll tell you want the hurry is!" Dathan shouted. "Our leader's moving on."

"B-but brother, you're the leader," Abiram began. Dathan shook him off and pointed towards the trail of Moses.

"Up! Up you crabs, you rats! Up and follow!"

"But he's heading east, Dath," Abiram said. "And we're bound for Goshen."

"We're bound for where he leads us," Dathan said to his brother, and whipping up his chain, he started down the road, and the miners grumbled, scratched their heads, cursed, and followed.

The Hebrews kept as far from the miners as they could, and as many as were able kept the palms of their hands pressed against the holy litter for protection. Yet that litter followed the same trail as the miners, towards the east.

All of the cheese and meat were gone now, and the Hebrews walked on empty stomachs. Even through the folds of the litter, Aaron could hear them ask each other: Isn't Goshen west? They said west. We're bound east. A new road? The priest knows the way. Yet he follows the nomad. Aaron's head still throbbed where it had struck the ground, and his stomach knotted as he thought: How many days? How long have we walked east? Fifteen days? Twenty? It would be fifteen days more to return. By then the miners would have cut off Aaron's head and borne it back to Goshen.

That night, as his sons slept on beds of quail down and velvet, Aaron left the litter and followed the trail of Moses on his own. He drew on a cloak so that he would not be known and slipped around the encampment of the miners who were still picking bits of dried goat from between their teeth and belching out the last of Goshen's beans. Dathan was telling, again, how he'd seen Moses countless years before, walking off, free as he pleased, from the mouth of the mines.

"We go where he goes."

"But you said gods are dung," one of his comrades called.

"Listen, he's no shaved priest," Dathan answered. "He bears our mark."

"Baa! Who can tell at that distance!"

"I've seen it, I tell you!" Dathan fell back and let his fists rest against stone. "And there's a way to rid us of these tagalongs. You know this country? You know Elim? In a day, I promise, we'll be rid of priests and slaves alike. He knows where death lives. And it's in the palms."

Aaron could bear no more. He forced himself onward, though now he was beyond the edge of the camp and utterly alone. The faint glow of their fire dimmed, and he could make out the trail of Moses almost by feeling the lumps of sand that passed up a ridge or made a sudden turn into a cave that was a likely place for a nest of vipers.

It was in that cave he found Moses. He sat with his chin buried in his knees and his wild beard knotted in his hands. The staff lay at his feet and he seemed barely to breath.

Aaron whispered in Egyptian, "Brother, wake up."

Moses raised his head. "You think I sleep?"

"You're a man," Aaron said.

"Cursed," said Moses.

"Cursed." Aaron's voice broke, and anger overcame him until he wasn't his own master. He steadied himself and crouched beside his brother. "We are in Sinai now. When do we sacrifice?"

"I don't know," Moses said. He seemed to have a hard time getting words out of his mouth, and Aaron took out his golden gourd and gave him a little water.

"How do we serve the god?"

Moses shook his head, and took a little more water.

"Brother," Aaron said, "why are you leading us here?"

"You are free. I am not leading you," said Moses, and Aaron lost patience and took his brother by the shoulders, pushing him back to get a better look at his face.

It was the face he knew, the open mouth, the web of scars, the ragged beard, but something was missing now, some certainty or sense of direction, and the eyes were abstracted, as though he wasn't looking at Aaron at all, but at something Aaron himself could not see. Aaron asked Moses, "Are we going to die here? This is Sinai! Do you want blood on your hands?"

Moses dropped the gourd, and its contents spilled out, dark and flowing. He pulled Aaron abruptly to his chest and heaved and shook until Aaron found it impossible to sustain his anger.

He whispered, "I have had faith and I have followed you."

"I tell you again," said Moses, "I am not leading."

"What are you doing then?" Aaron asked, as gently as he could.

Moses said, "I am running away."

Because he did not know how to answer, Aaron looked out of the mouth of the cave, a distance off, to the miners, to the Hebrews, to all of those who thought that they were bound for Goshen. Finally, he said, "What are you running away from?"

Moses answered, "From all of you."

Aaron could think of nothing more to say. He left his brother in the cave and started back for the camp. As he walked, the moon struck the sandy ridge of Moses' trail and gave off strange glints, armor, the wheels of chariots, and scattered everywhere, stones like round Egyptian eyes. He walked back, all the while wondering how he could have walked blindly, following that trail of consequences, that trail of death. When he returned to his litter, he felt moved to set his hands on the heads of his eldest sons, Abihu and Nadab, and as he did he saw them dead. Anger overwhelmed him, and he thought: So we serve the god by dying? Let us die then! After a while, he slept.

Korah did not sleep. He crept out from his father's arms and walked to the edge of he camp to pass water. He thought: Is lovely Goshen beyond the camp, and will my piss fall on a green land, flowing with milk and honey? Absently, he let his shirt fall back over his zabb and wandered towards the place where his piss had gone. The air was cool and misty and the ruckus of the goats sounded like laughter.

Beside him stepped a strange old man who matched him stride for stride and said, "We have arrived."

Korah's eyes passed over the bare stone of Sinai. Then he looked up at the man. His face was clean-shaven and pleasant. "Are you an elder?" Korah asked.

The man smiled; his teeth were excellent. "I am a Hebrew," he said, "and the Sinai is my home. I turned back once, but now I linger here."

"Are you the god?" Korah asked, for he did not know how he might recognize the god's face, and he had many questions.

The man did not seem to mind questions. He set a clean, long-fingered hand on Korah's shoulder and said, "No, I am not God, but I serve him."

Korah found himself fascinated by the old man's eyes which were set deep and full of light. He kept beside him for a long time without speaking because it was good to walk on such a fine, clear night.

Suddenly, Korah was moved to ask, "Do you like riddles?"

"In point of fact," the man answered, "I do."

"Here's one," Korah said. "What is the god's name? And here's another. When will we be home?"

"As to the first, I do not know," the man replied. "And as to the second, I say again, you are home and you are homeless. You are a Hebrew in Sinai."

"Another then!" Korah's face was flushed now, and blood roared in his ears. "What's made of clay and can't be broken?"

The man shook his head. "Your father must be wondering after you."

Korah felt such reluctance to leave the man that he heard himself say, "Oh, he's simple-minded."

"But you must love him anyway," the man said. He gave Korah a melancholy smile, and he said, "I have two sons and a daughter."

Korah kicked sand and stared through the dust. "Do you know any riddles?"

He answered, "Here's one."

Can you draw out Leviathan with a fishhook
*   or press down his tongue with a cord?*
Can you put a rope in his nose
*   or pierce his jaw with a hook?*
Will he make supplication to you?
Will he speak to you with soft words?

He turned then and walked a distance from Korah through mist and twilight, and where his feet fell there were yellow loaves which smelled of coriander and honey. Yet Korah took no notice of the loaves save as a trail, and he hurried after, but he could find no sign of him by dawn.

Nine

That morning, the Hebrews woke to a cry: "To arms, Israel! To arms!" Peering from their tents, they saw a stubby, fuzzy-headed boy leaping from stone to stone with a spear in his fist, bellowing: "A stranger is in Israel!"

Judean women overtook him before he could reach Aaron's litter, and it took four of them to wrestle him to the ground. Joshua's aunt, Shosha, sat on his chest and said, "Don't bother the priests."

Joshua struggled and chewed his lip bloody, forcing out the words: "Let me go, woman! I have to kill the stranger. He is cursed!"

"And since Nun's death, we're cursed with you, but Pharaoh bless us, Amen—Seleh, we can't kill you," said Aunt Shosha, and they carried him back to Judah where at least he could protect them from the miners.

Dathan had discovered the trail of yellow bread, and he drove his men from tribe to tribe, demanding to know where they had hidden it the day before. They filled their arms with loaf after loaf, and Dathan shouted, "I ought to kill a bitch for every loaf! Filthy hoarders!"

Elders, wives, and daughters told the same tale, that the bread had simply appeared that morning. Dathan belched out a laugh and struck his brother Abiram on the back.

"My brother the priest here waved his zabb in the air and turned stones to bread."

Abiram blushed because standing right there was Dodi, Zohar's daughter. Her puffy face was pink, and her mouth curled down as the miners filled golden basins with the loaves and dragged their booty back to camp.

Some of the young Levites hid behind scrub and watched the miners eat. The boys stuck their fists in their mouths and sucked their knuckles, waiting to see if a crumb would blow in their direction.

Abiram asked Dathan, "What if they were telling the truth about the bread?"

Dathan replied with his mouth full. "Slaves don't tell the truth."

"But if the nomad broke our chains, why wouldn't he give bread to—"

"Those sheep have nothing to do with our leader," Dathan said. "And nothing to do with us. They're with the priest. And they're bound to die anyway. I know this country. Won't be long."

Abiram ground his bread between his broad, blunt teeth and spat in the direction of the heaping basins of loaves. He felt a pulling in his heart which might have been called hunger had he not eaten his fill. He took another loaf and asked, "What do you mean, Dath?"

"Don't stuff yourself," said Dathan. "You'll get slow-witted."

Abiram was already slow-witted, but he turned Dathan's words over in his mind and at last said, "When we reach the palm-trees—"

"Shut your mouth," Dathan said finally. He shrugged his shoulders and at last called to the boys he had seen all along: "Are you sheep or wolves!"

The first with nerve enough to answer was a tall boy with a triangular face and fluffy hair who said, "We're Levites."

"Levites are dung," Dathan said. "We need wolves."

"I know a riddle about a wolf," said the boy. "If you can't answer it, could we have some bread?"

"Why should I give bread to a Levite?" Dathan asked him.

"Because I'm hungry," said the boy.

Dathan turned red, and his black beard bristled as he passed each of the boys a loaf of bread. As he dug into the basin, a stray loaf tumbled out and fell into the scrub. A scout from Amaleke was hidden there. He took up the bread, sniffed it, and rubbed its butt against his chin. Then he ran back to his king.

The king of Amaleke lived in a tent of azure goat skins, and his throne was carved out of a single chunk of turquoise. He was a mighty king: his father had almost taken for a bride the daughter of a Pharaoh and he had his own prophet, the blind Balaam, who was gifted with perfect wisdom. Balaam's beard was a luxuriant gray and his banquet gown, though sandy, still smelled of the incense of Egypt where he had brought peace and blessing for many a year. The king gave Balaam his own tent and his own slave and likewise gave a tent and slave to his she-ass who fattened herself with thorn mash and grew a tidy white beard.

It was Balaam whom the king brought before him when he planned raids on the mines or feared the well-spring was clogged with a curse, and it was Balaam who would tell him the hour when his men should attack. Balaam would raise his whitened eyes and chant:

> *Closed things open.*
> *Blood salts wild oxen.*
> *Blessed be all I bless.*

Balaam would laugh and say, "In Egypt, I would get half the kingdom for such wisdom." So the king gave Balaam half the kingdom.

When the scout rushed back to the king with news of invaders beyond number bound straight for the oasis of Elim, he brought Balaam before him. Balaam led his ass by the reigns into the center of the tent, and her saddle bags were full of bread, goat cheese and water-skins.

"Holy Balaam," the king said, "why are you dressed for a journey?"

"Because by sunset," Balaam answered, "there will be no Amaleke."

The king rose from his throne and said, "But bless me."

"Bless you?" Balaam shook his head. "I cannot say what truth forbids."

"But bless me," the king cried again, and he rose from his throne and reached for the reins of the she-ass. "Stay here beside me,

Holy Balaam, and curse the strangers who would kill your king."

"My king?" Balaam laughed so hard that his beard parted, revealing a belly swollen with goat meat and easy living. He shook all over as he mounted his she-ass and left Amaleke, and the king looked after him as he receded through sun and sand. He had no choice but to gather his men and bid them arm themselves for battle.

"To arms, Israel! To arms!" Joshua called, but he was back in Judah's camp, and from all directions came the cries of "Palms! Palms! Palms!" They had found Elim. With a whoop of joy the Hebrews flew past even Aaron's litter and made for the green smudges in the near distance, the tall palms and their shadows. They streamed in, breathless and weeping, and their legs gave way because they were weak with happiness.

"Palm fruit!" Izhar shouted, tossing a green gourd to Korah who caught it in his shirt and turned in a pool of green light to look the place up and down. All around him, Hebrews had sunk into the soft dull green of summer grass.

Then there was a rustle and a burst of light. The miners had filled up their skins with water and now they were pushing straight though, due east.

"Where are they going?" Korah asked.

Izhar reached out for his son to hug him close. "Oh, Korah, we're saved. We're going to live."

Korah frowned. "Is this Goshen?"

"It must be, for it's where we've ended up. It's where the priest and his god have led us."

The Hebrews wandered through those miraculous palms; they counted seventy. The bounty went to their heads, and they embraced tree after tree, finding tucked here and there new treasures: dates, citron, flowers that gave off a head-swimming aroma. Aaron bid his litter be lowered between four of the highest palms, and there he draped silks and sat on a cushion. To all who approached, he said, "Bring me sheep and bull calves for the sacrifice." To all who brought them, he said, "Bring gold for the altar." It was not long before he was surrounded by so much red, white, and yellow gold and so many young bulls that it would be hours before everything was prepared.

Nadab's face shone. He whispered, "Shall we sacrifice?"

"Yes," Aaron replied.

Eagerly, his sons set to work. They knew just how the altar must rest on the earth and how the knives must be whetted and the incense mixed, and as they busied themselves, Aaron sat between two golden urns where no one could see, and he wept.

Moses was still running away. He did not go to find him because he did not want to say what must be said, and so he spoke to himself in raw Egyptian.

"I will spread incense and draw out the knife, and we will make a sacrifice. I will tell them, I will tell the slaves," he said, feeling his throat fill up at the word, "that we have done what we came here to do. And then the god will kill us."

No answer. Was it Moses he addressed? Who else would answer? He felt heat, remembering the day his rod burst into blossom.

"We are blessed," Aaron said. "This place is blessed." He closed his eyes and felt, between his shoulders, a penetrating pain.

It was the stone of a sling-shot, as Amaleke broke through and forced the Hebrews into the open. Aaron rose with a spinning head and shouted out:

"Blessed! Blessed!" He raised that rod, only to find it slipping from his hand, hot sweat and his own panic mixing with green sunlight until it slithered off into the underbrush, and then he reeled and overturned the urns of gold, shouting: "We're blessed, we're blessed!" like a madman, and then, with a head on fire: "We are not slaves! We are *not* slaves!"

Amaleke came all at once, swinging through palm branches, and around them spun the slippery gold, old men and their daughters. Joshua shouted: "To arms! To arms!" but he was knocked backwards out of the oasis and lost among fleeing goats and sheep.

Moses was walking on a ridge above Elim, not far enough, not fast enough, and as he walked, with the hand that did not hold his staff he kneaded his head to keep from thinking. They were not slaves, but what were they? You freed slaves; that was simple, clear. But what could you do with free people? They would die and trail him or live and trail him; what did it matter? The questions, a thick, droning plague of questions, gathered around Moses. They were like the broad leaves of trees fluttering, or like the wings of locusts cracking, or like the feathers of a coverlet or like a fire that burned and burned without consuming, and if he could only stop asking those questions, he could walk faster.

They didn't know him. They didn't call his name. There was no bond between them. Why didn't they call his name? Surely they knew it. His name had been called for years. Why wasn't it called now? The battle spoke a language that he did not know. It carried to where he walked but he could not understand it, did not know what he was meant to do. Abruptly, the heart of Moses gave a wild pull backward.

They were dying, these strangers. Moses turned and stood with his arms raised, holding his staff in both hands on that high rock above Elim, knowing he was about to leap and join them.

His arms held something.

Chilled, he swung them down. No. They were empty. Slowly he drew them up again and felt a crushing weight.

It was the dead; he could not look to see but knew it was the dead, old men, old women, more women, heaps of them. Their bodies bent the weight of the staff, and it reverberated but did not break. More women now, and five girls dead of snake bite.

"They will break my back," Moses said, but his back did not break, though his burden grew.

There were more now, the Sinai guards gutted by miners, heavy men strangled by chains, water-logged horses, men with blood-clogged throats, and then the dead of Egypt, first-born after first-born, stacked like coal inside the tucks of chariots. Strain and agony ran down the arms of Moses and his sweat steamed off of him like smoke.

The heart of Moses turned in its breast; his shoulders buckled with the force of the turning.

Below, the steam and smoke befuddled Amaleke. They ran

straight into stones which seemed to meet their heads. With light on his face, a dry-voiced Angel of Death swooped them up in his arms and carried them into the arms of Moses who felt his burden mounting by degrees until blood filled his hands and dripped onto the stone around his feet. His arms began to waver.

A hand grasped his left wrist.

"Moses."

He thought he knew the voice and was afraid. Yet the grip was a man's, the hand a hard hand. Moses turned and saw the face of Dathan.

"Why should they live?" Dathan asked Moses.

He could barely get the words out, so full was his concentration as more and more weight bore down on his arms, yet he took his share of the burden and the left hand of Moses did not waver again. Soon after, he found that his right hand, too, was caught up in another hand.

"Why should they live?" Aaron asked in Egyptian. His head was smeared with ash, his breath raw with smoke, his anger absolutely sincere, yet he did not let go of his brother's hand.

The three men stood on that rock for the rest of the day until the battle turned.

This is what Korah saw. His father hid behind a rock and he tried to tuck Korah under the tent cloth where he would not be detected and he whispered, "Sleep."

Yet how could Korah sleep when the air around him rang and shouts tore out, and right by his head something fell with a crunch, and then something else fell on top of it. He wrapped both hands around stones and crawled out, belly-down, along bare dirt.

Above him the world had transformed. People he knew swept past with bloody faces. Shoes made of goat skin stumbled over dark roots, spears, something all twisted together. Then came the smoke. It was as it had been when dark bound Goshen. Korah could not see the stones in his hands, and something shot through him, keener than fear. He sprang to his feet and threw both of his stones, shouting:

"Who are you! Who are you!"

His hair filled with grit and sweat, and his stones spun and flashed through the smoke.

"Who are you!"

That heavy darkness pressed Korah back, but he took a step forward until his feet tangled in something and he fell again. He tried to raise his head, but could not. The heavy stuff binding his limbs did not move.

Then something brushed his chin. Korah raised his eyes a little and saw a pair of black legs. The legs stretched to hips drenched in some black, dripping stuff. Korah choked back a cry. The face was horrible, absolute pitch with eyes like flames and teeth as sharp as pins; knobs of bone moved under the skin of the neck.

Korah stared, his breath stuttering out of him, his singing head still pinned so he could not turn away.

The creature took note of him and addressed him. "Get up."

Under those blazing eyes, Korah opened his mouth but could not speak.

"Get up," he said once more, and he knelt and slipped dead cold hands under Korah's shoulders, hoisting him to his feet. The air was suddenly clear and deathly bright. Korah looked down and saw he had been tangled up in corpses.

Then he looked at the creature face to face, and found he was a boy his own age, a little shorter than himself. Before Korah could speak to him, he leapt away to gather spears. The ground was littered with severed heads, gold, bloodied chain links, teeth, and goats. Korah stood among those heads and spears and gold, and he watched the boy without following.

After they crossed the Red Sea, the tribes had dug their own graves. After the battle of Elim, they walked, looking often over their shoulders at dead who trailed behind them. They searched for Aaron. Families walked together, mothers holding the hands of their daughters, old men carrying bundles of gold and spears.

Those bundles they laid at the feet of Aaron, but Aaron stepped back as from a curse. Dathan too shied away from his miners. Both men made way for Moses. The Hebrews were too weary to feel surprise or suspicion as the nomad came forward. If he was scarred and ragged, what did it matter? They all looked like him now. His face was smeared with pitch and blood, just like their faces. He walked towards them and raised his staff with some effort, as though his arms had been wrenched from their sockets.

He opened his mouth, and gesturing back towards the battlefield, said, in Hebrew, "These are our dead."

That language, neither Egyptian nor slave talk, was strange to them, yet half-familiar. They pressed closer to listen.

"We are done," Moses said again in Hebrew, "with being slaves. We have been freed. But we do not yet know how to serve the one who freed us. We do not know how to live."

It was the first time Moses had addressed them, and the voice was what they might have expected, raw, urgent, not a voice that gave much comfort. Yet what held them there was the way Moses looked at them, like a man just woken from sleep to find before him people who had walked beside him when he dreamed, like a man who wanted hard proof that they were there, actual, alive.

He said, "I learned you would be freed from slavery on a mountain. If we return to that mountain, we may learn what we must do now that we are not slaves. Until then, we must get along as best we can. And we must share our burdens. Each of us has been carrying too much alone."

Moses asked Aaron's sons to turn the blue drape of their litter into a tent and call it the tent of meeting, where they could settle disputes in the open. He asked Dathan to take the gold which they had carried from Goshen and to dig a hole and bury it so they could walk more swiftly to the mountain.

"When we reach that place," said Moses, "we will find the one who answers questions. We will all be priests together."

"Father—" Abihu broke in, reaching for Aaron's shoulder, and in fact sweat sprang from Aaron's forehead at those words, but he kept silent.

Moses turned to Aaron and to Dathan then and took their hands, and he told the Hebrews to return to Elim to bury the dead, but when he looked across that battlefield, he found the dead were gone; where they had fallen, there were loaves of yellow bread. The Hebrews walked back and hesitantly touched those loaves, which smelled of coriander and honey. They handed them to their neighbors, fearing to be the first to eat. After a while, everyone ate the bread. They had no choice. They were hungry.

Ten

Without the gold weighing them down, the Hebrews covered far more ground. Ass backs and carts, empty of treasure, held old men and women and the yellow loaves that appeared in the camp every morning. Miners and Hebrews alike gathered bread; an even portion fell before each tent. It filled them, though it smelled better than it tasted and it melted down to nothing by mid-afternoon. Dodi tired of it almost at once, and she spat a clump of it out of her tent one morning. Her father, Zohar, corrected her. "Daughter, dove, just because we ride with Hebrews does not mean we must take on the manners of a Gaddite. Spit into my handkerchief like a good girl."

"It wasn't a Gaddite taught me how to spit!" Dodi replied, and she giggled in a way that caused Zohar some pain, and carved the loaf into the shape of a lambchop with a little miner's knife.

That knife had come from Abiram, as had a thornwood comb and a polished chain link he had given to her by Miriam's well. She had looked up with her water basin in her hand and tossed her hair out of her veil.

"Shoo! Shoo! How'd you get so big?"

"My mother was big," Abiram had said, and blushing, he had added, "You're big too."

Dodi couldn't force the chain link over her fingers, so she drew it through her hair and pulled the stray ends up with the thornwood comb. Like many of the Goshen women, she had turned brazen, flashing her heavy-lidded eyes, flinging back her head until Abiram's comb flew free. Dodi lost five of those combs. Each time, she teased Abiram until he would carve her a new one. "Deep teeth this time, you bandit!" Then she would sink her own small teeth into his ear, and he would drop the branch of thorn and chase her through the tents until they fell into a giggling heap together.

Hebrews shared close quarters, for company or warmth. No one knew if the neighbor was a noblewoman of Ephraim or a Gaddite or a scabby miner. They wondered how it could have been otherwise.

By night, Moses met with the Hebrews in the blue tent. Once the tent-cloth had been knotted into a compact drape for Aaron's litter. Now it billowed. Dozens of Hebrews pushed in at once, warming themselves at a fire of thorn branches and arguing until dawn.

Miners who had hoarded gold were caught by Dathan and brought to Moses. Old men brought sheep they'd claimed had wandered from their neighbor's flocks. Mothers brought daughters for advice on marriage settlements.

"How much gold can a miner eat? What does it matter whose sheep is whose when we only have backs enough for so much wool? Settlements? A slave is bought and sold. There are no slaves in the Sinai." When Moses spoke, he stepped in close and met the person face to face, bracing his knees against his staff to crouch and get a better look.

"Lord Moses," Zohar said, "the miners are mixing with good Goshen women!"

Moses laughed and asked him, "Mixing what?"

One night, Ezzi the Levite broke through, dragging a surly Hannah behind him. "Please!" Ezzi cried. "Moses, make her admit she's my mother!"

Hannah smirked, dislodged her arm from Ezzi's grip, and said, "I'll do what I please. This boy is nothing to me."

Ezzi grabbed his thick hair in his hands. "Look—same hair, same face!" In fact, Ezzi's face was Hannah's save for a little sheepishness around his eyes.

Moses looked first at one and then the other and at last turned his full attention to Hannah. He asked her, "Why don't you want this boy to be your son?"

"Because," said Hannah, "everyone knows sons belong to the Pharaoh. I've got troubles enough, boss, lugging my tools and my baals through this snake pit without a Levite on my back."

"Why do you carry baals?" Moses asked her.

Hannah shrugged. "They're handy."

"But they're just deadweight, Hannah," Moses said. He laid a hand on her arm, insistent. "Surely a son is worth a thousand baals."

Hannah shook herself free. "Speak for yourself. I don't see you've got any sons!" She turned to go. Moses called after her with a forcefulness that startled all who heard it:

"Some things you can't escape!"

No one knew what Moses meant until a week later when Hannah threw up into Miriam's well and turned towards onlookers with a sour expression, making it known at last that she would bear a child.

Yet when she was alone, Hannah would cup her breasts and look down at her belly, and her sardonic mouth would turn up a little at the edges. She would whisper, so only her she-ass could hear, "And who owns you, boy? Who's your boss, eh?"

Hannah was the first; within three weeks all of the women, even old Reeba, felt their wombs stir and swell. Their ancient fathers and husbands looked at them in wonder and said nothing, averting their eyes from the vigorous miners who marched through the Hebrew camp with bread crumbs on their lips.

"What will they do if they have sons?" Ezzi asked Jonah bitterly. "Chuck them in Miriam's well?"

"Maybe," said Jonah, and he looked both sour and hopeful as his eyes passed over Dodi. She walked on with her round hips swinging. She had forsaken her veil entirely now, and the sun had turned her face pink and had brightened her hair.

Zohar despaired of her. "You're half a witch already."

"Shoo, shoo," Dodi whispered, kissing her old father on the forehead. "Don't you want a grandbaby? A little Zohar to spit up on your little beard?"

"He'll be a little bandit!" Zohar answered. "Ah, he'd be better off if he wasn't born!"

Dodi drew back her hand and struck her father across the face. More stunned than hurt, Zohar stared up at her, and she said,

"That was before, papa. Now it's up to me."

There was an understanding between the women that they could name these children even before they were born, that they would give each other gifts of colored stones or carved thorn branches in thanksgiving. These children would not belong to the Pharaoh, and they would be born when they reached the mountain where their questions would be answered.

One night, three pregnant women pushed their way into the tent of meeting. They were Judeans, rock-hipped, bitter-mouthed hags wearing stones around their necks. Two of them held the arms of a youth, and the third had his ear caught between her fingers.

"Moses," the third one said, "this boy, my nephew Joshua, won't leave us alone. He stares at our stomachs so much I swear that he's a demon."

Joshua turned his small eyes up to Moses and said, "There are sons in there."

"And he stinks!" the woman went on. "And he's always making trouble."

Moses looked for some time at Joshua's face and took note of its roundness and its ugliness. Moses said, "I've seen you before."

"At Elim," Joshua said. He held up a broken spear he had snatched from the hand of an Amalekite.

Moses said nothing then, but his eyes drew themselves deeper into their sockets and his mouth closed. Joshua broke free of his aunt and fell to one knee.

"I serve the Lord," he said.

Moses looked down at him and spoke with hesitation. "We left Lords in Egypt."

Joshua said, "Then I serve you."

When Moses rose to speak to the aunts, they were gone, and Joshua refused to leave the side of Moses. He stood at his elbow, and some who entered the tent of meeting found his stare so disconcerting that they kept their questions brief and Moses got some peace.

At midnight, Joshua disappeared, returning just before dawn with a gritty red face and thorns in the soles of his feet.

"Where have you been?" Moses asked him.

Joshua made a low bow, exposing the thin fuzz on his head, and he raised his spear and replied, "Scouting for strangers, Lord."

"I am not a Lord," Moses said again, and he added, "We are all strangers here in Sinai."

Joshua shook his head. "If we meet a stranger, we must kill him. Strangers are cursed."

This mix of deference and contradiction pleased Moses, though he could not say why. He grew accustomed to the crunch of Joshua's feet on gravel close to his own when they were on the march, and he liked the way the boy brought him his morning loaf.

Moses would raise that yellow loaf and the sun would strike it and release its faint, sweet fragrance. Moses would be thankful for the loaf. He would be thankful for the sun as well. He would be thankful for Joshua who brought him the loaf and who stood some distance off under that sun, looking grim and restless, gnawing his own bread without seeming to taste it. This open, complex thankfulness had something to do with where he was, the Sinai, and something to do with where he was going.

He was, if anything, more of an eyesore than ever, his beard ragged and greasy, the burn scars on his lips extending up his cheeks, mouth slack and bewildered. Yet to many he did not look like the same man. His clear eyes were set in sockets so deep that his gaze seemed to be coming with urgency across a remarkable distance to meet them, and in the way he come in close to them and made sure he could hear what they said, there was an intimacy that made it hard to hold anything back. He walked a little crookedly, so busy listening to whoever walked beside him that he sometimes had to be steered out of the way of rocks and scrub, or off the rim of Miriam's well.

"Mountain—bah!" Hur said. He kept an uneasy seat on the donkey which cantered forward, led by a cheerful Izhar. Hur still kept his eyebrows kohled and his lips dyed, though the paint smeared before noon. "What good will a mountain do us until Miriam is dead?"

"But she's a midwife, and we'll be needing midwives,"

Izhar said. "Besides, we drink at her well."

"Her well? Who told you that? Moses? Moses says a lot of things, boy," Hur called down. "Moses says we'll all be priests."

"And it's true," Izhar replied. "When we reach the mountain."

"You're as simple as sand." Hur's voice vibrated as they gamboled over rocks, and he squinted his eyes against the grit and sunlight. "Where there are priests there are novices, and novices have servants and servants have slaves—"

"Father," Izhar said at last, "you're wearing yourself out. Just hold onto the donkey. I can't lead you and listen to you at the same time."

Hur ignored him. "Then there are the miners. They've ruined our women, which is no surprise since all women are witches. But I say, watch out for your son Korah. They'll make a bandit out of him yet."

In fact, Korah was thick with Dathan now, and Izhar missed his company and admitted some uneasiness. Once Korah returned to Izhar with a wild grin and a big stripe of blood running down his side, and he leapt and held his armpit towards the firelight. "They marked me!"

"Save us!" Izhar shouted. He took the wounded arm and washed the cut with well water, weeping and tearing his beard.

Korah could not make his father stop crying, but the pain shooting through his shoulder gave him such pride that he walked everywhere with his right arm raised high so people could see the wound, and he said to Izhar, "I want to be marked with the mark of every tribe. I want Gad's scarred feet, and I want the donkey-stink of Benjamin. I want Reuben's whiteness and Asher's blackness."

"You can't be everything," said Izhar.

"Why not?" Korah asked him.

When Izhar couldn't answer, Korah wandered through the milling Hebrews. The sun turned Korah's brown skin browner, but his eyes stayed light. It was hard not to take note of him with his scabbed armpit exposed and his triangular face very dark under his fluffy hair.

Dathan would take him on his shoulders in the evening so he

could see the patchwork of the tents, the many fires of red, yellow
and white, and far away the glowing tent of meeting rounded by so
many tiny bonfires that it might have been a moon rounded by stars.

"Look here," Dathan said to Korah. "There's a palace for you,
open at all ends and full of sand!"

"Why do you love Moses so much?" Korah asked him.

Dathan scowled and did not answer at once, shifting Korah
on his shoulders to stretch his back. Then he said, "I had a kid brother
once who asked questions. I answered him with my whip."

"What happened to him?" Korah asked.

"He was killed."

"By an Egyptian?"

"No," Dathan said. "By slaves." Then he crouched to let
Korah down, and he said, "I couldn't kill every slave. There were too
many of them. So I guess I'll have to settle for learning how to live
with them." Shaking his head, he looked again towards the tent of
meeting and Moses. "I don't understand him. He is someone who
knows how to walk away. And he doesn't walk away."

"But why do you love him?" Korah asked again.

"Because I have to," Dathan replied, and then he rattled his
chain links, a faint, half-hearted threat. "No more questions."

Aaron watched the nightly meetings with mounting fear. He
listened to Moses and said to himself: All of the gods are false, save
one, and that god will call to us from Sinai's mountain. Yet every
morning as he rode with his sons in the litter, he could not help but
think of what Moses had said at the edge of Elim. Everyone a priest?
How could that be? And if that could be so, then what was he?

"What are we?" Ithamar asked him, fiddling with his neck
bands. It had been understood that Aaron and his sons would not
part with their gold at Elim.

"We are the servants of a true god," Aaron answered.

In the litter, his sons passed the time reminiscing about life in
Goshen where they'd slept in reed beds and had meat to eat. By now
the cucumbers would be in fruit, entwined with cantaloupes and
watermelons.

"In Goshen," Aaron said, "we served a false god. Now we serve a true god."

"Father," Ithamar asked, "why can't I wear homespun like the other Hebrews?"

Aaron leapt up so quickly that he smacked his head against the beams of the litter. He grabbed Ithamar by the shoulders. "Never forget! You're from a good family! Your mother's bloodline runs back to the gods!"

"But—" Ithamar's tongue stumbled and he turned pink. "I thought—"

"You don't think!" Aaron shouted. A sudden tilt of the litter threw him sideways and he rubbed his head. "Curse this wilderness!"

"Only the gods have the power to curse," Nadab said. "and their chosen priests."

Abihu struck his brother on the mouth. "How dare you contradict father!"

Dryly, Eleazar said, "Father contradicts himself."

Aaron wanted to climb out of the litter, but he could not; the silk curtains were tied from the outside. He sank into himself and finally said, "Unless they suffer all the rites of ordination, they cannot call themselves priests."

Thus comforted, the five were borne for a span of time without coming to blows. When the Hebrews paused for a rest, the old men who bore the litter untied the knots of silk and loosed the curtains, and in the open waste of Sinai, they stepped into the open, and Aaron rubbed his eyes.

Stone wavered under sand the color of dark dung, and a few stunted acacias gave a hand-span's shade.

"Where are we?" Ithamar asked him.

Aaron answered, "In a cursed place."

Blasphemy! Aaron struck his head with his hand. He needed clear air, water, to see his brother. He called for a servant to fetch water from the well, but no one came. Behind him, the litter sat untended in the dust. The carriers had gone away. Their number had diminished in days past. Aaron looked for his sons, but they too had disappeared, so with no one to run his errands, Aaron would have to get his water himself.

He started towards the well. Lately, the women did not draw their water tribe by tribe but mixed and drank together. Slow and laughing, they chewed hunks of the yellow bread and spat over their shoulders.

Aaron found one of his litter bearers drinking from cupped hands. "Here now!" he shouted to the old Benjaminite. "Where have you been?"

The man looked up, squinting against the sun; a stream of water divided his beard. His face looked so common and friendly that Aaron had to remind himself that it was not his place to strike him. "I'll be back to it," the man said.

Aaron almost gasped. He straightened—he was far taller than the man—and spoke with restraint. "If my litter is not soon prepared, we cannot move on."

The man started to answer, but a neighbor, a lean girl from Asher, interrupted. "You've got legs. Plenty older than you are use them."

The Benjaminite seemed to make a half-exasperated gesture to silence the girl, but neither apologized, and when it was plain that Aaron would get nowhere, he turned from them and walked away.

So that day, Aaron claimed his place at the side of Moses and for the first time took to the road on foot. When Moses saw him, his face lit up and he took him in his arms and kissed him. "At my side, as at Elim!"

Moses spoke Hebrew now. Aaron was shocked to hear how easily the language came to him. He whispered in Egyptian: "We need to speak on a pressing matter."

In Hebrew, Moses said, "Go on." By now, they were surrounded by grumbling, laughing Hebrews who did not even seem to notice that the priest walked among them.

Aaron tried Egyptian again. "Privacy is called for, brother."

With visible effort and an edge of annoyance, Moses answered in Egyptian. "What is it, then?"

"What am I?" Aaron asked him.

Oblivious to the language that they did not know, the Hebrews pressed in closer and one began to speak to Moses on a trivial matter, something about sheep or pregnancy. Moses replied, and the two talked in a friendly, meandering way for a while as Aaron walked in silence. Then Moses turned back to him and asked in Egyptian, "What do you want me to say? You are my brother."

"But what am I?" Aaron asked, walking hard enough to feel it, "When we get to the mountain, what will I be?"

"You will be beside me," Moses said. "We will all be there together." Aaron realized Moses had answered him in Hebrew only when the crush of men and women all around him raised a cheer.

Aaron's legs were stiff. He let himself fall behind, watching the back of Moses recede through the backs of ragged, wild Hebrews, and if he left any trail it was buried under their footfalls. Aaron felt someone move in beside him. It was the boy he recognized from the Red Sea. He was forced, by way of forgetting his misery, to start a conversation.

"Son of Nun," he said, "do you think we will get far without obedience?"

Joshua looked up, surprised to see Aaron. He said, "I will not contradict the brother of Moses."

The servility in Joshua's voice was most welcome. "So you agree," Aaron said.

Joshua shifted his spear to his left shoulder and marched on without giving Aaron the comfort of an answer. It was a curse to walk beside that creature whose hideous face showed nothing. Aaron turned away and to himself he muttered in Hebrew, "What am I then?"

Far ahead, Moses laughed, his arm around a woman who had asked him something. His voice carried, raw, happy, affectionate. "We can ask each other questions, but how far will that get us? There's such a thing as loving questions too much."

One day, the Hebrews passed onto a plateau, and thick clouds rolled towards them. At first, they met the clouds with high spirits, hoping for another troop of wild miners to tame, or even a little rain. Yet the clouds closed in and spirits wilted. The air was like a heavy drape that had to be shrugged aside as they walked, and which pressed down at night until they felt beaten down by weariness.

Thunder was faint at first. It made the soles of their feet tingle. Then it lapped at their ankles. One memorable morning it threw them all heels-up to the ground. Moses stood up and turned to them with a puzzled smile. "Go farther. Go on," he said.

The sons and daughters inside the Hebrew women kicked, and the miners helped them onto asses and forced those asses into a cobalt eye of a sky. No one walked happily now, and no one spoke, not even Moses, and in the deep silence between thunderclaps the end of his staff hit the ground with a crack painfully bright.

Aaron and his sons dragged far behind. Aaron's face bore marks of interrupted sleep and worry, and on the third night of the thunder—or the third day—Nadab pulled his father backwards and shouted in a wild mix of Hebrew and Egyptian: "Let me make a sacrifice!"

Aaron shook his head.

"He's angry! He'll kill us! Can you not feel it?"

Another thunderbolt—Aaron flew back, dwindling to nothing in the wake of it. Looking at his sons, he saw that they too were dwarfed and pale, Abihu ghostly silent, Nadab trembling in his mantle, Eleazar scowling under a sheepskin, Ithamar cringing like a slave. Turning his face from his sons, he saw what lay before them and stopped dead.

There was the mountain, an ordinary mountain such as might rise out of an ordinary plateau. It was red-brown, dung-colored, like any Sinai mountain. No fire, no sheer sides, even a clear trail to the summit. Yet every Hebrew stood, deadened with fear. In the silence, the earth hummed, a hum that came from the mingled reverberation of the Hebrews.

Then, a crack; another, frail and sharp. It was the crack of the staff of Moses as he walked on by himself. He walked for a moment without sensing the widening distance between himself and the Hebrews. Then he turned and gestured them forward. No one moved.

When Moses spoke at last, his voice could be heard only

faintly, but they all knew that he'd asked them why they had stopped. Faced with their silence, he took a step back towards them, bracing himself on his staff to lean in closer to read their faces. This time, he forced himself to shout. "We need to go together!"

It was Dathan who answered at last. He looked stunted, standing among his men, and his voice rattled. "If we go up there, we will die."

Moses moved his gaze from Hebrew to Hebrew as though he took each face in his hands and read it, and after a while he lowered his eyes. He said, "No one?"

No answer. Finally Moses sought the eyes of Aaron. They were not easily found, and when he met them at last, he wished he hadn't, for they were dead with self-loathing. Moses spoke again.

"I'll go alone."

As though against a strong current Moses turned away, feeling, as he did, their eyes on him, so that his heart pulled in two directions. He took one step and then another, hoping beyond all reason that he would hear a step behind him, but even that wild hope was made impossible by the humming in his ears.

Something crunched underfoot. Stone? Thorn? Looking down, he saw the carcass of a sheep, picked clean to bone. A film of light fell over the plateau, and Moses saw, scattered everywhere, the bones of sheep, half-buried in red sand, sharp rib cages, snouts, spines. They were the sheep he had abandoned when he went to Goshen.

Then he raised his eyes from the bones of the sheep, stood still. Had he heard something? No, he was not mistaken. Someone was walking towards him. He turned around. There was Joshua with his spear in his hand. Moses watched him approach with a soaring heart. He waited until Joshua had reached him, and then he continued on, matching as best he could his own steps to the steps of Joshua as the two approached the mountain.

At that mountain's base, Joshua said to Moses. "I cannot go farther."

Moses understood. He could not go farther either. Once he had driven himself to this place to find stones to pen in sheep. Now those dead sheep carpeted the mountain's base and for a dizzy moment he could not remember why he had returned. Joshua's face gave no clue. In it, Moses could read only fear and anger.

Joshua said, "I will guard you here."

Moses said, "Who will you guard me from, Joshua?" He did not expect an answer. Turning, he set his heel in the cleft of the rock and once again hoisted himself up into the dark.

Eleven

For weeks, the Hebrews waited in the midst of thunder that swelled like a bubble and burst without warning. Though they lived with that thunder, they did not grow indifferent to it. The ewes dried up and some miscarried, and the women felt their sons and daughters turn in their wombs.

That thunder infected the loaves and well water; they tasted of sulfur. It emboldened the snakes. They roamed the camp at night and slid into the tents, and in the morning, corpses would be found with faint green skin and tooth marks on their cheeks. Just as the Hebrews raised their shovels to dig graves, there would be yet another clap of thunder until the fellowship of the march was beaten to a stupor.

Aaron sat in what was left of his litter with his sons. Filaments of flax and wool had turned the air thick as flesh. He could not bring himself to enter the blue tent and meet with the Hebrews as his brother had done, and so he was left to sit with his rod on his knees and stare through a cleft in the silk cloth at the mountain.

"Father," Abihu said, "I will take my silver trumpet and call all of the tribes together."

"We will not return to Goshen," Aaron said.

"Then we will not," said Abihu, honoring his father. He crossed his fat hands on his knees. His heavy eyelids drooped to shield his eyes.

Aaron said, "We can do nothing without Moses."

"But Moses is not here," Nadab said. He had grown leaner of late, and his eyes had taken on a strange green glaze. It was in Hebrew he spoke. "Moses is on the mountain, where the god lives."

"That is where he is," said Aaron.

"There he speaks with the god," said Nadab.

"That is what he does," said Aaron.

"Father," Ithamar asked in Egyptian, "why are you whispering?" Abihu turned to strike Ithamar for questioning his father, but Aaron caught his hand and answered:

"Son, I am whispering because I am ashamed."

Nadab did not take his eyes from the mountain. He shook slightly, as with anxious laughter, and his stubbling, flax-flecked head looked very big on his shoulders. He moved towards the curtain of the litter and said, "He is on a sapphire throne as clear as glass, and his head reaches heaven. There are twelve pillars holding his arms, and thunder is his footstool, and on his brow are horns of light."

"Shut up!" said Eleazar. He was painting his face before a mirror and did not turn when he spoke, dipping his brush again and again into a pot of kohl.

"Why paint yourself?" Nadab asked him. "Do you think you're in a temple?"

"Shut up!" Abihu said. He pulled Nadab away from the curtain, but Nadab freed himself and went on.

"You think you're a priest? That nomad's the only priest here. He's the only one who meets with the true god!"

"Shut up!" Abihu stamped his foot. It made a muffled thud in the sand, and he stomped it again and again and then babbled in a mix of Egyptian and Hebrew: "You want to follow him up that mountain? He's there laughing, laughing! What are we?"

Aaron answered in a steady voice. "We are Hebrews."

"You're a Hebrew!" Abihu shouted. "I'm a priest!" He threw back the curtain and stormed out. Aaron looked after him, and a drop of sweat fell in his eyes. The air, or something, caught in his throat, and he felt the heat, or his sons, press closer. He heard Nadab's voice.

"If I cannot know this god, I will die."

Another drop of sweat. Aaron rubbed his eyes and felt the world turn red and throbbing.

Ithamar asked, "How long do we have to wait here?"

Eleazar spoke clear Egyptian. "Not much longer."

Around them, no one stirred. It was the heaviest hour of the day when even words had to climb through lips and fight off deep blue air. Therefore, they said no more but stared out at a smudged sky that made Aaron think of the catacombs and Joseph's bones and the time he had looked out his window and thought he had seen his own death look back across a court lit by the moon.

Izhar tied the tent closed. "Father, don't do that," said Korah. "It's so thick in here I could write my name in the air."

"Just sleep, son," said Izhar. There were tears in his eyelashes, and a few dripped down his beard.

Korah pushed his father aside. His eyes were dry and glittering. "You always tell me to sleep. Who can sleep? I'll sleep when I'm dead."

"Don't say that!" Izhar cried. He shook all over, and Korah was ashamed.

"You think he freed us all to kill us?" Korah asked. He had grown scrawny in the past few weeks, and his voice was changing from a boy's to a man's. It was with this new man's voice that he said, "He freed us to make us holy."

"Holy?" Simple Izhar echoed. He raised his arms so his son could enter them, because he knew that Korah was afraid.

But Korah did not go to his father. Rather, the glint between his eyelashes hardened and sparkled. "If we had all gone up together, we could have had all our questions answered, all of them!"

"Son," Izhar said, "come sit by me. Pretend we're back in Goshen, and you're baking bricks and telling riddles."

Korah shook his head, and he parted the cloth of the tent.

Izhar said, "One riddle."

"I need a drink of water," Korah said. "I need to go to the well."

"Bring me something," said Izhar.

"Now there is a riddle," Korah said. "What would you have me bring?" As he spoke, he lifted the flap of the tent, and the dark swamp of the sky blew in and turned his father's wet face black.

"A cup of water," Izhar answered. He gave Korah a copper

cup that had been smelted in Goshen an age ago, and Korah stepped into the open. The cup felt wrong in Korah's hand. He fought the urge to crush it underfoot. As he walked, he had the feeling he could shake and shake his hand and still find the cup clinging.

He walked on. His feet were swift and narrow, wrapped in hard sheepskin thongs. His legs were limber. A burst of thunder rolled up towards him, and in it he heard not death but a voice.

"I will do it," he said.

He walked on past the tents themselves until between himself and the mountain was nothing more than bare rock and the bones of sheep. He drew on all his strength, his singing blood, his curiosity. The cup fell from his hands, and he ran.

Sheep bones caught at his feet, but he ran on, the mountain rolling towards him, wavering, brown and red, and he opened his arms, helpless, and ran on, though he could not breathe. Then his chest snapped.

Fear. A point between his ribs. Impossible to pass. Nothing but fear. Korah hated himself with such fierceness that he wanted to be dead.

He did not want to walk away from the mountain. He looked forward as he walked backward, as though he could stare it down, might hear a voice or see a face or know a name. There were things he could not master, but there was time enough, for he was young and angry and would not always be afraid.

One morning, every Hebrew woke with a start. At first they could not say what woke them. They sat up and sniffed the air.

"What?" Abiram asked Dathan.

"Thunder's gone," Dathan replied. "Get up."

As the two rose to their feet, so did every Hebrew, and they walked outside to a pink sky, a round sun, an ordinary wind. So gentle was that wind that the lightest voice carried across the camp. Everyone heard a little girl call: "He's gone."

A trumpet blasted. It had come from Aaron's litter. The Hebrews hurried, shielding their eyes from the unfamiliar sun, breathless and confused. There stood Abihu wearing a freshly washed shift and a mantle of gold. He blew the trumpet through a cloud of incense rising from the censer in his left hand, and on his head was the white coned cap of priesthood.

Abihu lowered the trumpet and called: "We are redeemed!"

A shiver fluttered backwards like a straw in the breeze. He drew from his belt a priestly wand.

"We will sacrifice to a great god."

His words rode waves of incense, for Nadab joined him, waving a fresh censer, gazing at the sky.

The Hebrews came to themselves as though surfacing from deep waters. Moses had come down! Alive, vibrant with forgiveness, bearing good news, he would appear now and speak to each of them in turn. Relief and weariness almost like grace overcame them then and they drew in closer to catch sight of him.

Again, Abihu blew the trumpet, tuneful and clear, and he said, "You who have gold, bring it here so we might make an altar."

The words brought on confusion, and someone called, "The gold was all buried at Elim."

"Not all."

They turned, and there was Hur the Levite holding a little sack. He'd smeared fresh paint on his grubby face and he stumbled forward and threw the sack at the feet of Abihu. Rings and buckles spilled across his priestly thongs.

As word spread, more and more old men uncovered sacks of gold, some as small as their fists and others so substantial that it was a wonder they had managed to carry them from Elim without detection. Zohar had strung chains under his beard and Raban had braided gold fringe through the black tail of his she-ass. Abihu counted the gold, whispering to Nadab, as around them piled gold cups, gold rings, gold basins, golden caskets filled with turquoise and coins.

Nadab parted the sea of gold, and with wild green sparks in his eyes, he called, "You will see the face of God."

At once, Hannah stumbled through with her dirty brown arms raised and a sly smile on her face. "You'll have no one but me, boss. Mark my words."

The faces of the priests darkened. She was hardly their idea of a god carver, filthy as she was with gravel in her hair and those little piggy eyes, but already she had pulled the softest of the gold aside.

She shouted: "Levites! Levites! You're the kiln stokers! Make a forge and hurry!"

There was something about her sharp voice that made the Levite boys begin without question to gather all their precious hoard of thorn wood and coal into a pile and spark a flame. Ezzi watched Hannah through his windblown hair and he stoked rhythmically, his eyes blinking at the light and heat, sparkles of sweat rolling down his back and a queer trembling in his breast. The flame jumped twice but was tamed easily. At once, gold melted together and a crowd drew as close as they dared to watch Hannah carve their god.

Young bulls were gathered. "Sacrifice!" the old men called. "Sacrifice and blessing!" They skipped through the camp like boys, so pleased to smell the old smells and to make girls cut smooth, dry planks of acacia wood for the god's tabernacle and to choose the shade of azure for the curtains.

Zohar charged at the miners and thwacked at their heads with his judgement rod.

"Bandits!" he shouted. "Now that we are redeemed, you'll get buried alive!"

But Dathan hardly felt the blow. He had thrust his head between his knees and did not look up, even when Abiram pulled at his elbow.

"Dath?"

"Leave me alone."

"I can't." Abiram's voice caught, and he felt tears run into his mouth and wiped them away. "Isn't it a good thing, Dath? Get up. There'll be meat."

"Eat yourself to death then," Dathan said, and Abiram joined the other miners who were leading young bulls and sheep for sacrifice.

The sheep were watered at Miriam's well and it was there that Hur, on fire with happiness, yelled, "Somebody get a net! We have a fish to catch!" He raised his judgement rod, and the miners, who knew Miriam, backed away, but Hur himself turned to grab the fish with his bare hands. He froze.

"She's gone," he said. Red crept up his neck, and his beard bristled. He fell to his knees, scooping out water by the handful. "Help me!" he cried. "Help me find the witch!"

His hands turned bloody to the elbow, and frogs leapt out at him, speaking in women's voices: "Old man, are you on your knees because you worship?"

Hur fell forward into the well, and he surfaced with his beard plastered to his chest, stumbling through the water and cawing out: "I serve the god Pharaoh! Who do you serve?"

The frogs took wing and melted into silver flies with green eyes, and they buzzed out: "*La la la*, Leviathan—"

Scrambling for the bank, Hur smacked his head against a rock, and even as flies congealed to darkness, their voices merged into the harmonies of exiled Levite women.

> *Hathor cow-goddess*
> *Wild oxen*
> *Apis of the pretty horns—*

It was at that moment that Hannah tapped the final swift stroke of a master, heat still streaming through the calf's gold, clutched between pincers, ready to dip into an iron basin filled with water from Miriam's well.

"*La la la*, done then," Hannah sang, smiling and rosy. "Stand back!" With a splash and a sizzle, the god drank up the water and was raised gingerly and set in the acacia tabernacle.

Close by stood Eleazar and Ithamar. They parted the cloth of the litter to make way for the High Priest himself, who wore upon his linen an ephod of blue and a breastplate studded with a grid of gems. Upon the skirts of his gown were blue pomegranates and golden bells. The tribes parted so that Moses might make a sacrifice of thanksgiving before the god and burn the meat in an offering of grace and peace.

But wearing the vestments was not Moses, but Aaron. His face showed nothing. He thought: They will shout now, ask what has become of Moses. He thought: They do not even see my face. I might as well be Moses. He thought: We cannot see each other, face to face. Each thought brought him a step closer to Apis, as through catacombs in the dark.

Dathan leapt into Aaron's path. Squatting and glaring up with bloody eyes, he shouted: "You can't!"

"He's dead!" Aaron said finally. He felt his voice rise from the belly, not like gold and not like the note of a trumpet but like raw pain, and he shouted again so everyone would hear: "He's dead! He's dead!"

"Then we're all dead!" Dathan said, but he was dragged away, and Aaron recovered himself and waited as his sons prepared the sacrifice.

Moses heard nothing, neither the trumpet nor his brother's voice. So all-consuming was the silence that it was like the plague of darkness; nothing else could live inside of it, not light, not wind. He could not even feel his own heart beating. Why had he returned? Did he think he could be called again by force of will? For too many years, he had feared the one who called him. The Hebrews had been right; he would die up there, and die alone.

Yet he remembered: It was all in how he listened. His manhood had come to him when he had learned how to listen with compassion. Anything could call him, in any voice; he would hear it. He would not run away from it. Not now.

That was what so oppressed Moses as he waited. Delay, he could not help it, delay felt like a rebuke. All of the times he had fled from this, and now he had walked into it, after a long struggle, willed it, and would he not be called at all? It was not possible! He felt something familiar stir in him, and knew that it was anger, but he hadn't the strength to fight it. He let it master him and he cracked his staff on the ground, shouting out: "I have come here! Call me! Here I am!"

Moses.

He threw himself down and all his will spilled out of him. What had he done?

I am the Lord your God.

It was the oldest call, the one with teeth, the teeth in his face even as that face was pressed to the earth. It was like his own anger answering, and hearing it, Moses thought: I am dead, I am dead.

I have freed you from bondage. This is how I would have you serve me.

Then Moses asked "How do we serve you?" The question came of itself, and it gave Moses heart. They were not led there to die. He raised his head a little and found the voice, like silence, had crowded out the rest of the world; he could see nothing.

This is the offering which you shall take.

"What shall we offer?" Moses asked, and as he spoke, he felt fear pass a little. It was the right question. He would bring the Hebrews down what they had sought. They would offer themselves up, a blessed offering. A love for everyone below brought on a certainty stronger than anything he had felt before. What had their lives to offer? And then he asked, "What shall we take?"

Gold and silver and brass and blue and purple and scarlet and fine linen and goat's hair and ram's skins—

Moses did not understand. Yet he had some trust in his own bewilderment; it would lead him where he had to go. He wondered how a heart could be golden or a spirit brass. He imagined a city made of the linen or of the hair of goats or the skins of rams. Then he asked, "How should we live?"

Oil for light, spices for anointing oil and for the sweet incense, onyx stones and stones to set for the ephod and for the breastplate. And they shall make an ark of acacia wood.

"They shall make?" The echo, an childhood habit, came out of him unaware; he had lost his composure. He added, "Why must they make these things then?"

Make holy garments for Aaron and these are the garments you shall make.

"Garments?" Moses was on his feet now, so stunned he forgot to be afraid. "Garments for Aaron?"

His ephod shall be blue. Foursquare shall his breastplate be, and double; and set in it four rows of stones.

Moses could not breath. Then, although he knew it was not possible, he shouted: "Aaron! You are Aaron!" But it was not Aaron's voice. If it had been there might have been some sense to this. As it was, his heart spun in mid-air, going nowhere.

And for Aaron's sons make tunics.

"Is this why you freed us from Goshen? You could not free us only to do these things?"

To hallow priests, mingle two rams and one young bull calf with oil and cakes and wash them well and put the bull calf's blood on the horns of the altar and smoke its fat on the altar—

Moses dashed his face into this hands and cried out: "Who are you!"

Engrave my will in stone and carry it to Israel so they might serve me and receive my blessing.

If Moses had a knife for engraving, he would have driven it through his own heart. He looked down and found that he stood on tablets of soft clay such as he had known in Midian, and with his finger he traced out the alphabet of Midian, straight and meticulous. He could not carry this down to them; he would not; he must carry them all up here and together they would ask: How should we live? He must carry them all even if it broke his back. Still, the litany continued, a catalogue of spices, stace and onychia and galbanum and frankincense.

They are holy.

"And what are we?" Moses asked, wanting to read, in anything, an answer he could bring to them.

Make of these spices incense, a perfume seasoned with salt, pure and holy.

"What are we?" Moses asked again. He said, more to himself, "We will not go back to Goshen."

Beat some of the incense very small and put it before the tent of meeting where I will meet with you, and it shall be most holy.

"We are holy!" Moses shouted. He grasped the soft clay tablets to his breast and felt them harden. His voice shimmered with anger, fear, despair. "We are worth more than a thousand baals! We have carried everything together."

Whoever makes like incense will be cut off from his people.

From the soles of his feet, Moses shouted: "We are holy and free!"

He turned from God, and something crunched underfoot like dry, short grass. Why didn't God kill him? Why did he let him turn his face away, full of defiance? He would give anything to die where he stood so he did not have to return and tell the Hebrews why they had been sent into the Sinai. He still felt the force of the words he had shouted, but they fluttered overhead; they were not heard. What was heard then? Who listened?

There was a light breeze on Moses' face now, and it hurt. He felt as though his bones had been burnt down to charcoal, as though he had that frail a hold on life. "We are holy," he whispered, but he could not believe it. He was not holy. He did not know what he was.

Without thinking, he had started down the mountain slope, and he was startled by the sight of Joshua who sat hunched, gnawing on bread. Moses made himself call the boy's name. Joshua sprang up, dropped the bread, and shouted: "My Lord!"

Moses tried to read Joshua's face as he struggled to compose himself.

"My Lord Moses," Joshua said. He stood at strained attention. "You come at a fortunate hour for I have heard from the camp the sound of battle."

Moses accompanied Joshua back to the camp, carrying the hard clay tablets, all the while thinking: I will dash these tablets to the ground, and keep what I heard to myself and no one will know. I will say God commands that we love one another, and we will leave this cursed place. And if I die, I die. And if they die?

He could not let them die. He could already make out the warm fires shifting through the stuff of the tents; he could hear their voices and his heart was pulled in too many directions. Across the camp came rhythmic breathing and sharp cries. He knew the sound, for he had watched a friend led towards such music in the dark.

"There is no battle," Moses said to Joshua. "The women are

in labor."

Joshua's forehead beetled, but he said nothing, rather, sniffing, "Smoke."

"You have a good nose," Moses said.

"Meat," said Joshua. Moses stopped, and the wind blew a burst of incense in his face.

He rushed past the tents where women bore their sons and daughters, striking and striking with his staff, driven towards fire, acacia, burning flesh, and with every blow he felt a fire run through him and a bottomless despair, for it had already happened, the altar, the tabernacle; they had heard; they had obeyed; it made no difference, yet he threw the tablets down and, taking his staff with both hands, struck a final blow that landed with such force that he went down with it and fell on his face.

"Moses!"

He knew the voice. Bits of acacia and broken clay lay all around him, and crouching close was Dathan the miner whose square face was smeared with pitch and who laid a hand on his shoulder.

"Moses, what did he say?" Dathan asked. "How should we live?"

Moses rose without answering, turned around and saw a trail of gold and blood. Two dead men smoked from the shoulders downwards with censers twisted around their necks. Then he saw Aaron and he stared.

Aaron wore an ephod of blue and his breastplate was checkered with gems, precisely as God had described. He opened his mouth to speak but at once was thrown back on his own altar. Moses set the knife of sacrifice to his throat.

Aaron looked up at the face of his brother, and his eyes swam because he felt such sudden, tangled joy. "You're alive," he whispered. His voice vibrated up his neck, and Moses dropped the knife and turned away.

"Take the gold that should have been buried in Elim," Moses said. "Pound it into powder. Mix it with water and force it down the throats of everyone who hoarded it, as it is gold they serve." His voice was dry and did not sound like the voice they knew. It carried over the wreck he had made of the acacia tabernacle to the tents where mothers cleaned their newborn sons and daughters.

"Brother!" Aaron cried out. "You're alive! You're alive!"

Moses only said to Aaron without turning, "You are not permitted to mourn your sons." He walked alone to the blue tent which had been called the tent of meeting. It flapped in the wind, the blue fading to white against the sky.

Joshua called the elders together before the altar, and he stuck the point of his spear between the ribs of Zohar and asked, "Who made the cow?"

"Hannah the god carver!" Zohar said at once. "Spare my life!"

"The Lord alone grants life," Joshua said, and he pulled the head of Zohar back and forced gold down his throat until it flooded through his beard, and he fell in a pool of it, belching and vomiting. He drove all of the old men against the broken altar, pouring into them streams of the gold they had hoarded since Elim. Slowly their blood thickened and their eyes turned up, as gold coated their intestines and drew a net around their lungs. Hur called for his son, and Izhar ran forward and held him close and wept.

Hur whispered through gold-stained teeth, "Bury me in Goshen."

Izhar sniffed, and said, "I'll wash your throat."

"Not with water from that cursed well. No—only swear you'll bury me in Goshen."

"We're not going to Goshen," Izhar whispered back, and it was the first time that he knew this to be so.

"Then may the Pharaoh grant you a short life, Amen Seleh," Hur said, and then he took in his last mouthful of breath, and he died.

Joshua turned to Aaron and his sons, and looked them up and down with his small eyes. Then he turned and hunted for Hannah. He found her in a low tent, suckling a newborn. She frowned up at Joshua.

"Leave me alone," she said. "I've got troubles enough."

"The Lord is mighty," Joshua said. "You have blasphemed him."

"Labor's a blasphemy," Hannah said. "I've been at it since sunrise. Ask my son."

Joshua stared at the newborn whose red head was almost lost in Hannah's breast as he sucked. Joshua's spear turned in his hand.

"You look at him as though you want to gobble him up," said Hannah, "but he's mine."

Joshua said nothing more. He left Hannah with her son and walked away. In tent after tent lay mothers with their newborns, and as Joshua passed, each mother felt a chill seep through the tent cloth, and each rose with her son or daughter and walked into the afternoon.

They walked past their husbands or fathers or grandfathers who lay dead in pools of gold among the split planks of acacia. Reeba bore a daughter on each hip. Dodi held her son before her, and beside her walked Abiram who stroked the fine ends of her hair. Hannah tucked her son into the crook of her arm. Beyond them was the tent where Moses met with God. The other miners and stray Goshenites and Levite boys stood together, as at Elim, without regard for station, tired and sad.

There was no thunder, only the same breeze that had carried the trumpet blast that morning and which blew daylight back like blue cloth.

Moses stood in the tent and waited to die. Even through the cloth he could see the rising moon. Was the moon a god who could bless them? Could he find a god who loved? Moses felt sick at heart because it could not be helped. He still loved God.

He did not know why he loved God. Did he love fear and pain? No, but he loved where fear and pain had led them, into Sinai. Did he love bare rocks and snakes? Did he love thorns? Did he love water springing from rocks, skins from snakes and flowers from thorns?

Moses asked God: "How should we live?"

God answered, *I will be gracious to whom I will be gracious and*

I will show mercy to whom I will show mercy.

Yet what was mercy and what was graciousness? These were questions for a conversation late at night when a young prince might loose an answer like an arrow. Incense was for gods; for homeless wanderers, something else must be holy. Moses asked, "Will you be gracious when there is death?"

What do I care if there is death?

"Yet," Moses persisted, "if we slaughter, if we leave the dead unburied, do you go with us?"

I will bless whom I bless.

"Bless?" Moses threw back the word, an echo and a challenge. "And when there are masters? When there are slaves?"

I will go with you.

"And when there is justice?" Moses asked God. His heart stilled and opened for an answer.

I will show mercy to whom I will show mercy.

Moses did not speak again, for he knew what he would do. He would find clay and a little knife for carving. He wanted to laugh—a laugh of pleasure. It would be weeks before he had them ready, more than weeks, a life's work. Or the work of many lifetimes. God would have his priests and his sacrifice. Justice was not God's business, but his own.

At ease, luminous, Moses addressed God again. "If none of these things matter, why did you choose us? Why choose slaves?"

God answered, *I know you by name.*

"You know my name," Moses said, "but I don't know yours. I don't know your face. I would know you before I begin."

And God said to Moses, *Behold, there is a place by me where you shall stand between two rocks, and while my glory passes by, I will put you in the cleft between them, and I will cover you with my hand until I have passed by. Then I shall take away my hand, and you shall see my back, but my face shall not be seen.*

Moses pushed aside the cloth of the tent and there he found the two rocks through which he could make out the slope of Sinai's mountain. He walked to the rocks, and he pressed his cheek against the cleft. By his eye, the sky turned white as water, and suddenly darkened. Moses blinked.

Before him was the back of an old, stooped man in a robe who moved slowly forward. His feet dragged in the sand.

PART THREE: ISRAEL

One

Some years later, the people of Sinai were numbered, each according to his tribe. Levites carried wax slates from tent to tent, and counted cattle, sheep and sons. The Levites wore white linen and their heads were shaved; they were the servants of the priests.

"How many lambs born?" Hazzan the Levite asked Reeba of Asher.

"Enough, praise God, Amen—Seleh!" Reeba answered, bowing, scraping, hoping Hazzan didn't hear her daughters snickering.

"We'll take the first-born and our tenth," the Levite said, and his mouth burrowed deep into his chin as he scraped his stylus across his tablet, numbering, numbering. He checked Reeba's door post for a tablet of the law and her homespun for blue fringe, and God-bless, everything was in order, and Amen-Seleh, she would live another year.

Of course, there were troubles. The outskirts of the camp might catch on fire, or plague might overtake a tribe or two, but that was Miriam's doing. So long as they obeyed the law of God and gave their due to the priests, they were blessed, blessed, blessed!

Curses belonged to Miriam. At the root of the mountain, they had searched, but they could not find her. She could shift shape as easily as the wind could shift direction. Just as she had taken on Hannah's shape the day she carved the Apis bull, she could become a rock, a snake, a fire, or any woman. After an evil night, a hag would be pulled from her tent and borne to the center of the camp, followed by shouts: "Sing for us, Miriam!" Then they would stone her to death and move on before her curse could follow.

Blessed, blessed was Reeba. She was blessed with daughters, Laila and Sharon, twin girls born at the mountain. If they were a little wild, so were all of the Sinai daughters; it was the will of God. Far better to have daughters than to have sons.

The Levites numbered sons, and those Sinai sons nursed in the wilderness were given to God. What mother hadn't heard the tent cloth flung aside and risen with her arms around her boy?

There would be Joshua. "It is time."

"No. He's not weaned."

"Three years."

The mothers would look at their sons whom they had named even before they were born, those Bens, Ethans and Zachariahs who did not belong to the Pharaoh, and each loosed first one arm and then the other from his waist and would watch him walk away with Joshua.

Joshua trained the boys at arms. Their skin hardened and their eyes hardened until each mother looking on could not find her own son. The boys hung on Joshua and vied for his attention, tossing spears at everything that moved. At nightfall, Joshua thrust his big spear into the sand, and for miles in all directions the mothers could hear the sound of spearheads whet sharp on stones.

Perhaps the boys would find Miriam and kill her at last, and Reeba would be able to sleep through the night without fear that she too would be dragged from her tent and stoned to death. Her daughters laughed and tossed their wild hair.

"Momma, momma!" Laila called, "Where will we get husbands?"

Reeba sighed and smoothed her daughter's hair, though it sprang up again. Laila's grin was snaggled. Her sister, Sharon, had lost all of her teeth, and she lisped.

Sharon asked, "Momma, hash Moshesh a law for mishing teeth?"

"Be happy that you have no teeth, daughter," Reeba whispered. "You don't miss meat."

"I shuck meat," Sharon said.

Sharon and Laila hugged each other, giggling. Reeba herself was silent. It was not good to laugh at priests, nor was it good to laugh at law.

Law forbade meat, save for sacrifice. All fat belonged to

God; common Hebrews made do with the yellow bread. So said the law, in stone, in clay, carved into tallow or thick squares of acacia wood. Laws tumbled from carts, were pinned to door posts, dried in the sun, baked in any handy fire. There was no end to the number of laws and all of them must be followed.

It was Dathan the miner who declaimed law. The years in the Sinai had turned old Dathan baggy, and his beard was tufted with white, but his shoulders still had meat enough to hoist a sack of laws on his backbone as he slouched through the camp looking for trouble.

At first, some asked him: "Why can't Moses judge?"

"God judges now!" Dathan would answer. God was a hard judge. No one could gather thorn scrub without a portion set aside for cripples and orphans. No one could say a hard word against a neighbor without proving that word true. Everyone who broke a law must grant fair compensation: sheep, trinkets, or labor. To quarrel with the law meant hours of wrenching arguments, and those who raised a question might soon exhaust themselves to death.

"If you don't get along, we leave you to the snakes," Dathan said. "That's the Sinai way."

So long as they wandered the Sinai, it must be their way as well. The Hebrews could not camp anywhere for long before the sheep and cattle ate the desert scrub down to the stone, so always they were forced to move on. If they moved on, then they must move together. Better a few should die, so the rest could live.

To remember law, every gown fluttered with a blue thread from the cloth of the tent of meeting where God first gave that law to Moses. Every door post was mounted with law. Law hung from the forearms and the foreheads of the Hebrews so their heads and their hands might turn in a single direction. Dathan said: "Slaves are made of dung, but we are made of law." He weighed out compensation on a set of iron scales. "Something is true or false. Don't trust your hearts, because you don't have any. Trust the weights and measures of law. Trust the scales."

"You mean trust you!" an old Goshenite called. "How do we know you're not an old cheat?"

Dathan shook with laughter until tablets and scrolls

tumbled from his bag. "What could I get from you, old fool? Your copper buckles? Oh, copper's worth a fortune in the Sinai! I'd trade it for a kingdom!"

"It's true. Everything is worthless here," the man replied. "But I remember Goshen."

"You were a slave in Goshen. You lived by a lord and master's will. And now you have no master and no lord," Dathan said. He grinned or grimaced and spread the weights and measures out on stone. "You have God who said: Serve me in Sinai. He doesn't want your gold and he doesn't want your death. He wants you to live!"

It was true; they lived. The laws of God pulled them in one direction, and against all logic, the Sinai did not kill them. They had no choice but to obey Dathan, though sometimes they still asked, "Where is Moses?"

Dathan would bristle as he answered, "Alive, no thanks to you! And if you need reminding, pull the blue fringe and thank God he hasn't just walked off and left you to the mercy of your neighbors. If you want to see him face to face, just follow me."

But even now they could not bring themselves to face Moses, and Moses himself had not appeared since Aaron's ordination when, as God had commanded, he had slit the throat of a young bull, collected the blood in a basin, and smeared it onto the horns of the altar. He had dabbed blood on the tip of Aaron's right earlobe and right thumb and the great toe of Aaron's right foot.

Aaron had turned and lifted his hands toward the congregation, blessing them. Then he entered the tent of meeting. It was not until much later that the onlookers realized that Moses did not enter that tent with him. Moses was not a priest. They did not know what he was.

Some said that he had lost his reason on that mountain and so was confined to the edge of the encampment and held in bonds to hold back his wild anger. Yet it was understood that Moses made the laws, and there was no anger in those laws, rather a dry reason that might have been another form of madness. At times they would remember the old purpose of the tent of meeting, the nights of questions and of arguments, and then a few of them would feel themselves drawn to search for Moses. But then they would remember how they did not walk with him to the mountain, and also they would remember what they read in his face as he dipped his hand into the basin of bull's blood the day of ordination, and they were ashamed.

He must have walked among them when they broke camp, but it was easy to be missed in the crush of tribes. Old women muttered curses and fought for seats on donkeys as their daughters threw stones at sheep. Miners quarreled with their women or with each other. Dathan recruited half a dozen miners to pull the carts on which he heaped tablets of law.

"So now we're oxen. I'd say that's a step down from miner," a Cushite grumbled. His smooth black skin had turned ashen, and most of his teeth were gone. "We can be meat, but we can't eat it."

Dathan gave the cart a heave forward and said, "You think there'd be enough for everyone? You'd be killing each other over it within a week! Better to leave it to God and the priests."

Those priests rode in a litter at the head of the company, followed by their Levite servants. Even their sweat smelled good to eat.

A Persian said, "Let them shave my head and skin my zabb and call out Amen-Seleh, and maybe I'll have some red blood in my veins again."

Dathan tried to grab the Persian's beard, but his grip wasn't what it had been; old age had brought back the pain in his hands. "You want to go back to the mines?"

"I want to go back to Persia," the Persian said. "There's a garden there that has red fruit like paradise."

"Fertilized with the bones of slaves!" Dathan said. "Paradise is dung! We're only free if we live by law!" After a moment he pulled at his fringe of blue and added, "Law and sacrifice."

Sacrifice took place at dawn when the sky was just the color of the tent of meeting and God's presence rested in the tabernacle in its ark of wood and gold. Izhar the Levite stood with his tribesmen, swinging his censer. His head was shaven and his beard a memory.

The blue smoke of galbunum stung his wet, glazed eyes. His naked face was haggard; he sweated off his paint almost as soon as it was applied. His linen was too light; it made him shiver. Blessed, blessed, he thought, but it was awful to stand so close to the holy of holies. It was awful to watch the hungry mouth of God fill with sacrifice. Izhar thought: I must be brave. Levites are the chosen servants of the priests of God. Just as the High Priest approached, Izhar raised his voice with the others to sing praise:

> *Thou art risen, thou art in peace.*
> *Rise thou beautifully in peace.*

Aaron approached. He wore fine azure stuff, and on his head was a great coned hat on which was written "Holy to God." He alone could approach God and live. Izhar sang:

> *It is thou who breaks the prison of clay*
> *to spread on the earth thy powdered gold.*

His face burned. It would not be long. From behind came holy Eleazar and Ithamar with their censers, and Aaron stepped into the tent to God. Afterwards, there would be meat; Izhar could bring a slice home.

But how could he bear all those eyes on him, the envy of the miners and hags who chewed the hateful, hateful yellow bread and saw him pass with pink meat in his hand? How could he bear the words of his own son?

"It might kill me," Korah would say. "After all, it belongs to God." There would be a hard light in his eyes; there always was now.

"But it's our right as Levites."

"You're a Levite. I'm a Hebrew," Korah would say, and Izhar would have to eat the meat alone, though it stuck in his throat. To hear such words from his own Korah! That was the worst of all.

It had begun the day Izhar returned from the priest's tent with his head shaved and his beard bunched in his hand. Korah had been sitting with his back against the tent post and his long colt legs drawn up. He'd looked at his father, and something in his face broke, so he dropped his eyes.

"If you want," Izhar said, "you can have it." The beard was dark and soft, like a mouse, and he pressed it into Korah's hand.

Korah's fingers did not close on the beard, and without raising his eyes, he said, "You look like a fool."

"Well then it suits me, yes?" Izhar began, trying hard to keep from crying. "They always called me simple."

"What do they call you now?" Korah asked his father, and he rose and let the handful of hair drop to the floor. "Do the priests whip you, father? Do they stroke you? Do they feed you what falls off their table?" Question after question poured out of Korah, and finally he took a long, raw breath and struck the tent post with his fist. "Serve who you want to serve. I am no slave."

Then he left the tent. Now Izhar could never be sure if he would find him home. He wandered, swinging his long, awkward arms, thrusting his head forward, kicking back clots of dirt and sand. He might have walked for miles at night, sleeping who knows where. It tore Izhar's heart to think of his son on a bed of thorn and stone.

There was no reasoning with Korah. He had lost all of his old friends. Ezzi and Jonah had been shaved a year ago, and even miners steered clear when they saw him, for he was cursed. Izhar could do nothing but pray that God understood hearts like a father and would bless his son.

Some distance away, Korah smelled the burning sacrifice. His stomach churned. His curly hair was greasy and tangled, and his delicate triangular face, dark with fuzz, was sun-burnt almost beyond recognition. He walked and walked broad circles around the camp, and priestly smoke chased his trail until he gave up, threw himself down in the dust, cracked his hands on his knees, and thought.

His contempt was complete. So was his sorrow. Sometimes he would grip his head with both hands for fear it would fly off his shoulders. He would strut through the tents in the evening with that head pressed in his hands, and with a recklessness he couldn't understand he would hear himself shout at the priest's tent: "You're the blasphemers!"

When Levites approached, Korah recognized his old friends from Goshen, and he folded his arms and dared them.

"Stone me dead. After all," Korah shouted, making his voice deliberately coarse, "don't Moses and Aaron tell you to stone anyone who hates the priests?"

"Go soak your head," Ezzi whispered, looking wan under his face paint. "You used to think before you opened your big trap."

"I used to like riddles," Korah shouted through cupped hands. "I have so many riddles now! What chain is made of clay? When God eats meat, who has greasy fingers? Let's see your fingers, boys!" Tears streamed down his face, and other Levites poked their heads out of their tents, waiting for Korah to be consumed by fire.

It was Dathan who pushed forward. He said, "See here, you puppy—yapping again?"

Korah spat out the words as though possessed. "See here, you lap dog—still chewing the bones Moses throws you?"

"I'll throw you!" Dathan shouted, and he hoisted Korah over his head where Korah stared down, smiling in such a mild and disconcerting manner that Dathan himself froze stock still with the young man in both hands.

"Dathan, elder of the miners," Korah said to him from mid-air, "kill me now. I will not be any more or less unhappy."

Dathan's arms wavered, and he set Korah on the ground and shouted in his face, "Miriam's inside you!"

"So kill me. Bury me," Korah said.

The laughter underneath the words chilled the blood of all who heard them, and they wondered if they would all pay for Korah's madness. Yet no one could bring himself to strike him dead.

They left him to walk on and think too much. The rocks of Sinai, lingering into purple lichen, white thorn flower in the mouths of spotted goats, moonlight on the water of the well, all should have eased his heart. Yet Korah was wary of any ease or beauty. He wanted to keep his anger burning, though it did no good.

He would whisper to himself, "Who is the master?" The

answer would come with a drop of poison inside: "Aaron and Moses are our masters." And what of the master of Aaron and Moses? What of the god who set them free to make them holy?

When had Korah known? The day Aaron was consecrated High Priest, the day Izhar had shaved his beard, the first time Korah had seen the ark. The case of the ark was made of gold and acacia. Incense smoke rolled around it like water, and it bobbed on the shoulders of ten strong, smooth Levites, but Korah's eyes could not leave the dimensions of the box, its top, its sides, its bottom, and at last he had seen it: a clasp and a lock.

Knowledge had struck him blind. He had shouted: "You've locked him up! He's a prisoner!"

Then, too, the boys who had been his friends had laughed and let him be. More and more, Korah thought that he might shout forever and no one would listen even enough to call him a blasphemer.

Thus, Korah was allowed to live, unhappily, with the knowledge that God was being kept prisoner by Moses and Aaron. He dreamed of opening the box and freeing God, as God had freed them from Goshen, but into his chest again came the point of fear he had felt at the base of the mountain, and he did not know how to pass through that fear. He could only press his knees deeper into his chest, with his back against a thorn bush, until blood ran down his shoulders and his anger was lost in pain.

Someone called, "You there."

Korah looked up and shot a glance at the cloaked man who stood before him.

"Are you awake?" The voice was thin, embittered and clear, the face obscured by a hood. "Is this the Hebrew camp?"

Korah answered with equal bitterness. "Twelve tribes live here."

"Just so." The man turned, and Korah felt an ache as he remembered another stranger, a riddle, and a trail of yellow bread, but this man did not produce a loaf. Rather, he pulled forward a boy with black hair and a grubby face who sucked his hand. The man went on. "I have been told that here there are no masters and no slaves."

"So Moses says," said Korah.

"Does he?" The man drew the boy back to him and said, "Keep still, son."

In spite of his foul mood, Korah felt some interest stir. "You are not from Goshen?"

"For some time, I have not been from anywhere," the man replied. "Once, I was from Midian, but now I am a Hebrew."

Korah rose and brushed thorns from his shoulders, looking as closely as he could at the man's face. The voice, he could not read. Finally Korah said, "Take your son and go, for we have a master now."

"A god?" the man asked.

"The High Priest," Korah answered. "And he has an overseer named Moses who holds a whip called Law."

"But how could that be?" The man looked down at his son and up again, and the hood fell back and exposed clipped hair parted in the center, green eyes, and a mouth that sucked back on itself so that every word was edged. He set his hand on the shoulder of his son and said to Korah, "My boy does not talk. He will never talk. His voice poured out one day, and now it is gone."

"What's your name?" Korah asked.

The man shook his head. His chin was narrow and his neck was like a reed.

"They're bound to ask your name," Korah said again.

The man said, "I will tell you my name only if you tell me the name of your god."

Korah's blood stopped in his veins, and then roared through his ears with such force that he had to grasp the man's shoulders.

The man did not shake Korah off, but only said, "So he still doesn't know." His mouth turned up at the ends and his eyes held Korah's own. He said, "No wonder."

Two

The red tent rose above the other tents pitched on the Kibroth plain. The twelve tribes weren't sure whether to tear it down or to keep to their own tents until it went away. It was said that Joshua had seen a man inside, a stranger with a knife. The tribes wavered between fear and wonder, for they had not seen a stranger since the bandits at Elim. Would the knife be found in someone's back? Would he lead an army of giants with red banners? Was it Miriam's work?

In his tent, Dathan held forth on law to a crowd of women, and drew out tablet after tablet. "See here? Same law for us and for strangers. Carved in clay."

"Boss," Hannah said, "do you think that stranger uses his knife to carve clay? Maybe he carves miners."

"You watch your mouth!" Dathan said, showing a little tooth through his beard. "Remember the mountain. I'm not so sure you're not Miriam."

Since Joshua had taken her son, Hannah did not much care for life, so she said, "If I'm Miriam, how come no one's stoned me yet?"

"Your skin's too thick for stoning," Dathan said. In fact, Hannah would have been stoned years ago, but she was saved by a general respect for her thousand baals which still hung from the walls of her tent, rattling in the slightest breeze like bones.

"How do you know Miriam's not you, boss?" Hannah asked Dathan. "She'll travel up your nostrils and eat you from the inside out and save your lungs for a bellows."

The women cackled. It seemed impossible the mob could fear a single stranger with a knife. Dathan looked at them, shaggy, unveiled, ragged, diseased creatures, the mothers of Sinai. Without husbands, without fathers, without sons, they did not know who to love and who to obey, and so they teetered between perverse humility and recklessness.

The miners bore the brunt of their confusion. Abiram would return from Dodi's tent with a lemon-sized lump on his head where she had broken crockery. The Gaddite women welcomed callers like good angels, but in the morning they wept and moaned until their men returned to their own camp looking as spent as ghosts.

Law, Dathan thought, was given by God to teach us to be balanced as scales, to have balanced natures. The weights and measures of our quarrels are balanced against our need to beat back death. But what becomes of law when no one fears death? What if the fear must have another face?

Abruptly the women in Dathan's tent fell silent, lowered their eyes, and made way for Joshua. No one liked to stand too near.

He walked straight to Dathan, bowed his head, and said, "I have a use for the stranger. He could be a scout."

At such times, Joshua looked almost comical to Dathan, with his enormous mouth and his round head spiked all over with bristling black hair. Always Joshua set his spear butt-first in the dirt, and his eyes stared out from either end of the point.

Dathan flicked that point with his thumb. "What would you scout for, ape?"

"For blessedness," Joshua replied.

Dathan did not trust Joshua. He didn't like his looks and he didn't like his boys and he didn't like the way he talked, as if someone had stuck a trumpet up his ass. But it was Joshua who had walked with Moses to the mountain. To remember that day made Dathan back off, and he said, at last, in a flat voice, "Suit yourself."

Joshua mustered his boy-troop. They walked silently, for their feet were bound with skins. They did not raise sand or dust. Though Joshua was full-grown, his boys already stood head and shoulders above him, and they had so much thick, hard flesh to them that some believed they shared the Levite's meat. Joshua denied the accusation in this manner: "If you eat the Lord's bread with a pure heart, it will sustain you."

Such talk did not make Joshua well-loved, and more than a

few who watched the troop approach the red tent hoped that it would swallow the boys and their leader without a trace. The silly Sinai daughters trailed behind them, flinging stones and singing,

> *Follow the ape who blasts hot air!*
> *Sharpen your zabbs on his black hair!*

The mothers would pull them back for fear the lost brothers would strike their sisters dead. "Besides," they would say, "among those boys will be the fathers of your children, and who wants to start a courtship with a curse?"

Still, no one could imagine the boys taking wives. They were in love with Joshua. Joshua himself, one of the few men in Sinai of age to father children, would not so much as allow the shadow of a woman to cross his tent.

"I have no use for women," he would say.

"They have a use for you," Hannah would answer.

And Dodi, who had grown flabby and gray, would do her best to thrust her old hips forward and call out: "Maybe if you'd have a pack of your own sons, you'd stop stealing ours."

The Sinai daughters would giggle, for they knew Dodi had a son who did not follow Joshua. His name was Jonah. As for Hannah, if she so much as heard Ezzi's name she would spit against a curse and touch the baal tucked between her breasts. "That kiln-stoking bastard almost got me killed! I had a son and now he's gone. I've got troubles enough."

The mothers agreed. They had sons once; now they were gone. The water babies might be Levite servants now and might have meat and gold, but they were poor risks, for who knew when Pharaoh would change his mind and claim them. They were hardly prospects for their daughters. When Reeba found Sharon whispering to Ezzi, she almost drowned her in the well. Jonah was known to attract girls to his bed with little scraps of sheep-meat, and any daughter found with mutton on her breath was beaten until her mother broke the switch. What would these girls have been in Goshen with a proper Lord? Who could ever know?

"At least Joshua would tame them," Reeba often said. As Joshua marched towards the red tent, the mothers followed.

Joshua pulled up the flap of the tent, and said, "In the name of the Lord!" Nothing came out but close air, edged with iron. He tried again. "Reveal yourself."

At last, the stranger stepped matter of factly from the tent and said, in an even, alto voice, "Not likely."

It was Reeba who drew her hand to her mouth and said, "That's a woman!"

Joshua took a step back, clearly shaken. His spear dropped from his hand and he looked, suddenly, like a frightened boy.

"No use for women, eh?" Hannah muttered. She shook her head and felt very pleased, though she couldn't have said why. The others pressed closer to see, and the woman suffered their gaze without taking her eyes from Joshua who snatched up his spear and tried to regain his composure.

He said to her, "The Lord has cursed Midian and all of her inhabitants and the whole of Edom and also Moab and the whole of—"

"Son of Nun," the woman said, "suit yourself." She turned, and on her long, straight legs, walked back into her tent.

The mothers pushed inside after her, curiosity overcoming any fear, whispering to each other and eyeing the stranger with wonder tempered by suspicion. It was Hannah who asked, "Where are you from?"

"A cursed place," said the woman.

"What's your name?"

"A woman's name."

"Do you always answer in riddles?"

"I speak as I please," the woman answered, "and my son does not speak at all."

"Oh—oh—you have a son!" Dodi shoved the mothers aside and found the small boy curled up in a corner, but he was a great disappointment, a stunted youth picking at rocks and gazing blankly at the red cloth of the tent.

Reeba asked, "Pardon, but why is your tent red?"

"Because," the woman answered, "red dye is common."

Frustrated, the mothers finally stomped off and let her be, but Reeba, Dodi and Hannah found themselves at the banks of Miriam's well, and there they talked in low voices. So Joshua wanted a scout? What would they scout? Could they be close to settled land?

"Husbands for our daughters," Reeba whispered. There was a raw edge to her voice, for lately Sharon had been very pale, and she had suspicions.

Hannah scouted above the peaks of the tents and settled back on her haunches with a faint smile. All three reflections shivered in the water of the well. "What I could use right now," Hannah said, "is a cheek full of spit weed and a belly full of meat." The thought that close at hand might be spit weed, meat, cheese, beer, and vineyards turned the women's heads.

"Shoo—if all the girls out there are like that stranger," Dodi added, "they'll be anxious enough for good mothers and wives!"

Reeba made Dodi lower her voice, and the three huddled close before Reeba whispered to Hannah, "You will talk to your son."

"Sure, boss," said Hannah. "You try to find him in that boy-troop."

"No," Reeba said. Her voice was so faint that it might not have been there at all, but her words were distinct. "Your son."

Hannah's face turned ashen, and she sprang to her feet and would have run away, but Reeba's wiry grip held her fast. Dodi had begun to slink off, but she too found her ankle caught in Reeba's fist. Reeba was impossibly old now, her bones held in place only by a web of tight, black wrinkles, but her strength remained considerable, and caught hand and foot, Dodi and Hannah had no choice but to listen.

"Your sons are chosen by God. They're holy servants. And they could talk to Ithamar the priest and he could make a grace offering and ask God to grant us a place in some settled country."

"Shoo—shoo—we're to stay here and serve in Sinai. Every-one knows that." Dodi reached out and plucked at her blue fringe. "Besides, they aren't ours. They're Pharaoh's."

Reeba said, "Pharaoh lies under the sea."

"Then they belong to someone else."

Gathering up her face like a fist, Reeba said, "There is a law:
Honor your mother. If you claim the boys they'll give you anything
you ask for. They'll make God find us a home where grapes grow."

"There's no such place," said Hannah.

Reeba added, "They'll give you meat."

It might have been the encounter with that stranger, the sun
winking off the well, or even the rattle in Reeba's voice, but the word
meat took on its own life. No one spoke for a moment, and it
suspended there and swelled. It was as though it struck them for the
first time that the Levites did have meat: lamb, goat, ox roasting over
thorn fires, perfuming the camp, floating above the well. They
women remembered meat. The meat filled black stew pots, and the
foam around the rim was flecked with garlic. They felt themselves
sink into that foam; it closed around them as they fell.

"Well," Dodi began, "just to ask a little favor."

Reeba said, "God has blessed us. We are only following the
law."

Dodi and Hannah looked at each other. Before they could
think twice, they were ten strides from Miriam's well, led by the
force of the will of Reeba towards the place anyone with sense did
not approach, the Levite tent.

Hannah said, "We'll just say, 'Give us meat and we'll be your
mothers.' No nonsense."

Dodi nodded, but her face was flushed. By now, the source of
Reeba's request was half-forgotten and neither woman fully knew
why they wanted to claim their sons. They felt as though they walked
against a force that sharpened to a point between their breasts, and
they did not like the look of the sky. The clouds were low, darkening
the acacia trees and bringing on an awkward silence until they could
hear their own unsteady footsteps in the gravel.

Hannah sniffed their air. "Bad news."

Distinctly, something hit the ground. The sheep penned
nearby raised their heads and bleated.

"That can't be hail," Hannah said.

"It's not!" Dodi dodged something; it was a quail.

The quail had dropped feet-first from the clouds, head tucked under wing. Another glanced off a tent post, a third off a rock. Tent after tent opened as mothers and their daughters looked out to see.

Dodi waved her arms. "Praise God! Praise God!"

Hannah tried to hurry Dodi forward. "Don't sing! You want them to think you're Miriam?"

"Praise! Amen—Seleh!" Dodi shouted, and she whipped up two fat quail in her hands and fell to weeping as around her dozens more slapped against the ground. "They're ours! They're ours to keep! They're ours because we've been so good! They're our sons!" And it was almost as though she had claimed as sons the quail that rained down thick now, piling against the sides of tents and underfoot, and Dodi would have danced for hours and wept herself sick had Hannah not pulled her off.

"Let's get inside. You don't want to be knocked senseless!"

She dragged Dodi towards the Levite tent to grant their end of the bargain.

The tent of the priest's servants was white and open-sided so the Levite youths could take the golden vessels in and out without disturbing Ithamar's naps. It was Ithamar who had been commanded by God to train Levites, but for the most part, he lay on a big pink cushion and let himself by shaved by servants, every once in a while running his finger along the edge of a censer to make sure it was clean.

The youths were left to wander off and take a tumble with a willing Sinai daughter or to play knucklebones. Ezzi and Jonah had finished a game and didn't have the spirit to begin another. They were alone in the tent, and each was thinking of Korah, though neither had the nerve to say his name. Sometimes all that had to happen was that some Levite would tell a riddle, and Jonah would burst into tears.

"You cry too much," Ezzi said. "Grow up."

"But I am grown up," Jonah would insist. Shaved, his head looked more doughy than ever, and greasy smoke from the sacrifices had turned his complexion spotty. Sometimes Ezzi would let him win a game of knucklebones just to clear the dogged sorrow from his face, but it never worked for long.

That day Ezzi had decided to keep winning until Jonah stopped being his friend, which would have made matters simpler. Then he raised his eyes from the game board and dropped the piece. There stood Hannah and Dodi with wild eyes and feathers in their hair. Hannah held a dead quail by the legs and she said, in a flat voice, "No funny business. We're here to tell you we're your mothers."

Ezzi nodded, bewildered, and before he could think of what to say, Jonah suddenly rushed at Dodi and threw his arms around her neck.

"Oh, you're here! You're here!"

Dodi turned red, and she looked at Hannah helplessly, but Hannah seemed to decide that Jonah was none of her business. She addressed Ezzi.

"Now there's a lot of fresh meat out there. You were quick enough to stoke a fire once. Let's see you do it twice."

"I don't understand, mother," Ezzi said.

"Neither do I, but here's the truth. I'm an old woman and I don't care." Hannah threw her quail on the floor at Ezzi's feet. "Be quick before I change my mind."

Ezzi and Jonah gathered thorn and acacia and started a crackling fire so hot that they had to shield their eyes. It was Reeba of Asher who marched the mothers through a gray sea of dead quail, and there was nothing wild about her and nothing humble. Rather, she strode firmly, staring ahead and speaking with authority.

"We are blessed by God," Reeba said, "with sons and daughters."

The daughters barked and whooped, tearing out feathers by the handful until they were buried to the neck, and they tumbled out with down all through their hair. Sharon tossed a naked carcass to her mother Reeba, and Laila poked five more through with a branch and let her mother grill them until the sky was brown with scent.

The miners smelled the meat and pushed forward. Dathan called after them, "Keep back! Keep back! It's not blessed by the priests!" It did no good. The savor pulled them forward like a chain. The women beat them off.

"This is ours, given by God," Reeba said. "No one will take what is ours again!"

Once the miners had been young and ruthless. Now they were old men. They could not pass the wall of fire and women. They sank into the dust and begged like dogs.

Dodi laughed. "What do you beg for, pups?" She held the mightiest skewer in her hands, and she drew it from the fire so gravy dripped a brown line across stone and ash. Laughing, she slipped the quail free. Its crisp skin could barely contain its flesh, and Dodi popped it in her mouth and swallowed it whole.

The other mothers followed suit until they shoved their daughters back into the piles of quail down. The skin slipped under their fingers.

"Mother!" Ezzi cried to Hannah. "Don't! Don't! You'll choke!" He grasped her by the waist, and she shook free and shoved another quail into her mouth.

Jonah was too slow to catch Dodi, who had swallowed two, red-hot. Her cheeks turned crimson, and her forehead blazed. "Stop! Oh, mother! Stop!"

No one could stop the mothers, for there was no end to their hunger and no end to the quail. The miners first stopped begging and then stopped watching and then slowly backed away. The daughters burrowed themselves into the mountains of quail down and shivered. After a while, the fire died. Ezzi's arms ached with stoking, and he stopped at last and stepped back, noting that it was suddenly very quiet.

Jonah was the only other one left standing. A drip of gravy ran from his forehead to his cheek, and he touched it and made to touch his mouth. Ezzi caught his hand.

"It's poison," he said.

Jonah met Ezzi's eyes and both at once looked down. The plain was covered with the bodies of old women. They lay face down, their grey or white hair spread amidst thin bones, and their arms, smeared with quail entrails, green and cold.

"Who poisoned the quail?" Jonah asked.

Ezzi shook his head and started to walk away, but Jonah caught his shoulder.

"Who did it! Who poisoned the quail!"

"Why do you ask me?" Ezzi screamed back. "I'm not a priest!"

"Was it Miriam?"

"It wasn't Miriam," said Ezzi, and though he couldn't say why, he knew it more certainly than he'd ever known anything in his life. "It was God."

"But we obey God. We follow law and make sacrifice."

Ezzi turned towards the Levite tents where they stored the golden censers and the frankincense, the holy stace and onychia and galbanum. He said, "The priests make sacrifice."

"But it makes no sense. It makes no sense. I don't understand. I don't—"

Ezzi shoved Jonah back, shouting, "We're not priests! It's not supposed to make sense to us! If we'd gone with Moses to the mountain, then we'd understand!" He put his hand over his mouth and thought: Korah. He had to find Korah. To Jonah, he said, "Let's take a walk."

"Now?" Jonah shook his head. "I can't leave my mother."

"She's left you. You want to stay here until she rots?"

"It's our fault," Jonah said.

"Talk about not making sense. Now let's go before we both go mad."

The two walked off, and from the piles of white and gray feathers at last the daughters surfaced. They did not speak, but slipped, demure and silent, towards the dead. Their faces were down-white, their eyes fluttering and gray. With small spoons they moved sand and began to bury their mothers.

Korah was sitting with his back against a tent post, and he didn't seem surprised when Ezzi parted the red cloth and drew in a trembling Jonah.

"You were right," Ezzi said to Korah.

Korah now wore a small, soft beard, and he pulled at it a moment before he asked, "About what?"

"About everything!" Ezzi answered. He looked the tent up and down. It was twilight and too dark to see much more than the strange woman hunched over, whetting something on a stone. "Is this your home now?"

"I don't have a home," Korah said. "I'm a Hebrew."

"Stop the riddles! This is no time for riddles!" Ezzi took Korah by the shoulders and made him stand, and he shouted straight into this face, "We're lost! We're all going to die here!"

"No," said Korah, and his voice was quiet. "We're going to live here."

"But we've lost our chance. Everything's gone wrong. We're not blessed! Never were!"

Korah let go of his beard, and he set one hand on either of Ezzi's trembling shoulders, and he said to him, "Every one of us is holy, every one of the congregation, and God is among us."

It was clear that he had changed. No more the outbursts and the fits of rage. There was a depth in his eyes would have been terrible had it not been rimmed by his familiar lashes. It was Jonah who pressed close and asked, "What happened?"

"What happened?" Korah looked Jonah up and down and laughed. "You do look foolish without your hair. You've got a melon of a head."

The words passed over Jonah who whispered, "What's happened to you?"

Korah said, "Both of you, how would you like both hair and beard?"

"You're asking us to cross the law of God," said Ezzi, and he grew uneasy. The scraping from the corner quickened as the stranger whet her knife.

Korah asked him, "How would you like to be priests?"

Ezzi went cold. Jonah drew his hand to his mouth. Neither could find it in them to answer. It was evening now, and through the red cloth of the tent streamed enough moonlight to set a red cast on Korah's face and beard as he went on.

"You say you aren't blessed? I say we are. And all we have to do is pass through the rites of ordination."

"But— but—" Jonah stumbled out, "you said we could have hair and beards and—"

"That is of no importance. There are plenty of men who shave, but they're not priests," said Korah. "There's only one thing that marks a priest, and that all men must go through if they want to be priests."

The woman sparked flint then and lit a brazier full of coal so that Ezzi and Jonah clearly saw the tent's sparse furnishings, a basket full of snake skins, a copper basin filled with water, the son who slept under a pile of streaked gray wool. The woman turned a questioning face towards the two Levites and then set her knife into the brazier so that it turned black, then red, then white. With a set of pincers, she cast it in the basin.

Korah asked them again, "Would you be slaves or priests?"

"Will it hurt, Korah?" Jonah asked. "Don't tell a riddle. Just tell me: will it hurt?"

"There's no harm in riddles," Korah said, "as long as you're not afraid of answers, Jonah."

There was a tenderness in the way Korah addressed Jonah by name which made him feel light and fearless despite the deeply frightening face of the woman who now held the knife.

Korah concluded. "Yes, it hurts, Jonah. But then it's over. And you know you can bear anything. That's why you're able to face God."

Jonah glanced once at Ezzi, who still held back, though he watched his friend steadily. Then he crouched, took the hand of Korah, closed his eyes, and waited.

Three

"It was Miriam," the Cushite whispered. The fuzz on his head and chin had gone white, and his ashen hands shook a little as he gathered yellow bread. "Miriam killed them all."

"No," Dathan replied. "It was God. Because they ate the meat which was forbidden by law."

"But are we cursed if we crave what any blooded man would crave?"

"Yes," said Dathan.

The miners hunched over, chewing and chewing, but their throats were like knots because each of them had known some of the women who lay dead. Abiram could still feel Dodi's belly underneath his cheek; she had smelled like home. Suddenly, he stood up and shouted, "I'm tired, Dath. I want to die!"

Dathan pulled him down. "There's a law that says you can't!"

"Law is dung!" Abiram shouted.

"So are you," said Dathan. "But, brother, you just happen to be dung protected by the law of God, so I'm not going to let you die."

Abiram slumped and listlessly gnawed the bread. Behind them, the stones of Kadesh piled into a cliff that gave some shade. It was easier just to sit and obey, here at the edge of the world.

They had moved to Kadesh from Kibroth after the women were buried, and it was as cursed and unlikely a place as the roots of Sinai's mountain. Despair weighed down the miners so they could not even find the will to pick a quarrel.

Unexpectedly, the Cushite sat up. He said, "They got her."

Dathan scrambled to his feet, and from a distance he saw two of Joshua's boys with a pike across their shoulders. Slung across that pike was something dark and heavy.

"They've poked the black fish through—throat to snatch!"

The Cushite clapped his hands. "Amen—Seleh. They've killed Miriam!"

Indeed, the black mass stained the pike crimson, and even at a distance gave off the musky stench that each miner remembered. Even as Dathan felt sharp pleasure at the thought of Miriam dead, he hoisted up his stack of laws. "Was she stoned properly?"

"Oh, what's the difference," Abiram muttered.

Dathan threw him a sharp look and wiped the bread crumbs from his lips. He heaved the sack of laws further up his shoulder and started towards the boys.

When they saw the old miner heading in their direction, they stopped and stared at him. On the pike was not Miriam but a bunch of grapes. The grapes were purple, as heavy as heads, clustered thickly on a tree trunk of a stem.

Dathan set the sack down and said, "Where did you get those?"

They looked at each other as though deciding if they ought to speak at all. Then the one closest to Dathan answered, "Canaan."

When Dathan heard that word, his stomach turned to ice, though he could not have said why. He wanted to tell them that the grapes could never be divided evenly and that they would bring trouble, theft and quarreling. He wanted to tell them to return them to Canaan or to mash them underfoot. Yet to say all of these things would have meant lingering under those two pairs of wolf eyes, so he turned and walked back to his comrades. The musk of the fruit clung to his hair and skin.

Abiram looked his brother up and down and said, "There's trouble."

"No," Dathan said. "But there will be soon if we don't move on."

"Move on? We just got here. Why—?"

"I say move on!" Dathan shouted, and every ounce of blood pulled him towards the cart where he could pile the laws of Moses and shout: Move on! Move on! It was no good to stay in this place where the air sang and where the absence of the old women was like a lump in every miner's throat. The Sinai daughters were living ghosts who only came out of their tents to gather bread, draw water, or lead their tithe of sheep and young bulls to Levi for sacrifice.

As ever, at the morning sacrifice, Ithamar and Eleazar stood beside their father under a cloak of fragrance, but the smoke had a bite now. It was rumored that the urns of holy wood from Goshen were almost empty. The Levites who swung the censers were few in number, and most did not swing them high. They let them droop from their hands as their faces turned inward, thoughtful and distracted.

Why distracted? At first, nights of talking. While the priests slept, the youths would slip away, and under a clear sky, they would listen to Korah the Hebrew who sat with his long legs spread before him and his face transformed.

Jonah and Ezzi sat to his left and right. Already their hair had grown back, and faint beards darkened their cheeks. Korah's own beard, soft and smokey, curled up into his hair.

"As long as you shave," he said, "you're boys."

"But what of God's law?" they would ask him.

"Did you receive the law from God or Moses?" Korah asked.

Such wicked questions were backed by a middle-of-the-night silence where the world turned on an axis of voice and turned back again, free and giddy.

"God is no barber, no butcher and no jeweler. What has God to do with shaven heads and sacrifice and gold?"

He spoke with such authority that soon many Levite youths stopped shaving, and they began to pose questions to Ithamar.

One boy, whose chin was riddled with stubble, woke Ithamar from his nap one afternoon and asked, "Lord Priest, why do we wear a fringe of blue?"

Ithamar raised his head and rubbed his eyes, grateful the question was so easily answered. "To remember law."

And the boy opened his cloak and showed Ithamar a whole blue garment and said, "I've made a coat of law. Am I a blasphemer?"

Another, jutting out the beginnings of a beard, strutted from tent to tent, declaring, "What if I make a house of clay inscribed with law? Do I still need a fragment on my doorpost?"

At night, Korah said, "Law is from the mouth of God. How could it be confined to clay? How could it be heard by two brothers alone? All of us are holy!"

No one could understand the change in Korah. By day, he walked across Kadesh with his Levite troop loping behind him. Some said that milk flowed from his footsteps and honey from his tongue. No one could think of any other reason why so many followed him, even as they themselves dogged his heels to hear themselves called holy.

Dathan even found a few of his own miners clustered around Jonah. "See here! Don't get yourselves in trouble!" Dathan said. He glared at Jonah whose lank beard grew only in patches. "You're greasy as ever, Levite."

"And you're blessed," Jonah replied.

Dathan's lip curled. "Don't tell me what I am. I've seen things you can't imagine. You've never been through more than a bad night's sleep."

Jonah raised his robes to show the miners that he had been sanctified.

Dathan whispered through a clenched throat. "You did that to yourself?"

"I chose," said Jonah. "You can too."

The miners stared at what they had only known in legend, what took place in the sacred rooms of temples, a mark which could not be erased, deeper even than their own. They felt fear, and the fear melted into wonder and the wonder into keen interest. They raised their eyes to see the face of a priest. That face was spotty, eyes red from lack of sleep. It was not painted or even very clean. Yet, unmistakably, the face was holy.

"It hurt," said Jonah. "But it stops hurting later, and then we can face God and have our questions answered."

Abiram pushed closer. "All our questions?"

Dathan pulled him back. "What would you ask, you fool! About Dodi? I told you already—"

"Shut up!" Abiram shouted. "Let go of me!"

"I won't let go. I tell you, law—"

Abiram swung free and faced his brother. "Tell me why we killed those men in Goshen! Tell me why Hoge died!"

Before Dathan could answer, Abiram broke into a run for the red tent.

"Blasphemer!" Dathan shouted. He threw Jonah to the ground. "They only want the meat! They do it for the meat! And the meat's poisoned!"

Then he ran off to catch Abiram, but he lost him in the push of miners heading for the tent. There they were circumcised by the woman, and their feet were stained with blood. Afterwards, they passed through pain and fever such as they had never known, worse than the marking in the mines, and from that pain they surfaced, and everything was different.

So Korah's troop was first called the Levite Blasphemers and then the Circumcised Ones and finally the Priests. The red tent rattled with comings and goings. The priestly tent looked empty and dim, and no one bothered to polish the gold.

Aaron had not noticed that the gold was tarnished. His eyes were dimmer than they had been in Goshen. It was not surprising that he did not see the cause of Ithamar's distress when he rushed into the tent in tears. Then he caught the stench. Ithamar's mantle was spattered with dung. His hands flew towards Aaron's shoulders.

"Father! Father! You don't know what they say!"

"Nor do I care," said Aaron. "Get off me, boy. You stink!"

"They say—they say—" Ithamar babbled, "they say you don't know God's name, that you go into the blue tent and do nothing."

Aaron's hands braced his knees. Slowly, he rose from his stool and he said, "They are—"

"I know—I know—"

"Stop blathering!" Aaron shouted. He took up his rod and with a sweep of his arm drove his son away. "They will all be consumed by fire!"

Ithamar rubbed his eyes and blearily looked for servants

who would take the filthy mantle from his shoulders, but there were no servants.

Aaron said, "Call your brother."

"But like this? I can't go—"

"Find Eleazar, who has more sense in his little finger than you have in your thick head!"

For fear of Aaron, Ithamar rushed out, dung-stained and cowering.

As the years passed, Aaron had found himself more and more dependent on Eleazar. Eleazar had raised many wearisome and unpleasant duties from Aaron's shoulders and always seemed to know when a first-born sheep was ready to be claimed or where twin heifers were hidden or when a miner had his eye on meat.

Even now, it seemed Eleazar was well ahead of Aaron. He entered the tent, sat across from his father, and at once got to the point at hand. "No one can live like this for long. Going here, going there, how can they know left from right? How can a wanderer be obedient?"

"Because our God is true," Aaron replied. "And he blessed us on the mountain and ordained myself and my sons as priests."

"The mountain," said Eleazar, "is far away. Order can't weather a long march, father. We both know." Then he pushed his seat closer and whispered, "I have spoken to Joshua."

Aaron frowned. He did not like to hear Joshua's name. It brought to mind an old shame. "The ape has no respect for priests."

"But hear me out," said Eleazar. "There is a land not far from here. Good land." Eleazar slipped his hand into a linen pouch and drew out a handkerchief stained red at the base. He unwrapped a grape which filled the whole palm of his hand. "Did you ever see such a fruit, even in Seth's vineyard?"

"Do not speak of Seth," Aaron said at once. His head swam with the musk of the grape and it kept him from thinking clearly.

Eleazar set Abihu's old silver trumpet into Aaron's hand. "Call Israel to battle and they will forget rebellion. In Canaan you will be a High Priest in God's temple."

Aaron pulled away and struggled to his feet. "I am High

Priest and the whole of Sinai is God's temple."

Eleazar smiled. "Remember Elim."

"I remember holding my brother's hand!" Aaron shouted now, so blind with rage and confusion that he couldn't see his son before him. "I remember what we bore together to the feet of God!"

"Remember," Eleazar repeated in his low, sweet voice. "the months after Elim when Moses called the whole of the congregation holy. What were we then?"

"That was before God's blessing," Aaron said. "Now each knows his place."

"Do they?" Eleazar bowed and set the single grape on his empty seat, and he left his father. Aaron stood alone for a long time. The open flap of the tent let in a breeze and it rustled and raised a little dust. If Aaron closed his eyes he might have been in his old room in Seth's temple on one of those dry strange nights when bare lemon trees rattled.

He knew his place. He was the High Priest who stood before God and knew him. He bore God's blessing back to Sinai. What was his place?

He thought of the day he had been ordained, when his face dripped with the calf's blood and he stepped into the tent of meeting only to find Moses was not beside him. Stunned, terrified, nevertheless he felt his spirit suspended by a thread of wonder. He was the priest. Not Moses, but Aaron, the slave boy, the brother left behind. He mastered himself and took a step towards the tabernacle as he had been commanded. He readied himself to face God.

Yet when he opened the tabernacle, he saw nothing more than a box made of wood and gold. A few sand fleas hopped on its rim and left indentations on a film of dust.

Aaron blinked. The box was still there. He raised his priestly wand; his breastplate shifted a little and he pushed it back in place again. He must not fall short, must observe even the smallest ritual.

God was silent.

Aaron wanted to call: Speak to me! If he had, the Hebrews who surrounded the tent of meeting would have heard. They would have known. Again, he faced the holy of holies, and he dropped to his knees and whispered in Egyptian. "You have chosen me for your priest. I am ordained according to your word. Bless me."

No answer.

"You speak to Moses," Aaron said, suddenly agitated. So disordered was his spirit that he thought he had leapt up and wrenched the ark from its tabernacle and dashed it until the gold and acacia flew in all directions, but he found himself instead back on the ground with his head crushed against his breastplate, sobbing with such restraint that his cries carried no farther than his throat.

Since then, Aaron had entered the tent of meeting when appropriate and left with a knowing smile. No one could question that he had been chosen to know God. Everyone near the tent felt such deep panic that their blood froze as they watched their High Priest part the cloth and step inside, and they knew he was blessed because he left that tent alive.

In Goshen, he had learned to live in despair, and he had not lived so very badly before he had met Moses. He supposed the calm life he had led could be rebuilt, stupidly, out of lie after lie, laid like clay bricks together. He could build a temple out of lies. Yet this was more likely when he did not believe there was truth in the world, when he had not known God.

Aaron looked at the grape on the footstool, purple and translucent, and saw in it a dark fertility of lies, but also richness, sweetness, a life that was possible, not the impossibility they all faced now and that he seemed to have to bear alone.

He was still looking at the grape when two Levite servants entered to prepare him for the evening's sacrifice. They were sad youths, lonely for their friends who had long ago gone over to Korah's camp. They looked ashamed. Aaron wondered if all that kept them servants was a fear of the knife which would make them priests. Aaron took care to walk with particular dignity. On his feet were the sandals of holiness and on his face the smile he had constructed year by year: strength tempered with awe, a smile like a rod which might at any moment burst into flower.

He generally did not even notice who stood watching, yet that day he could not help but sense a mob. When had they begun to jeer? Since Kadesh? Since Kibroth? Since ordination? Cat-calls roared past the Levites and overwhelmed their psalms. Scrappy, fuzz-faced youths flung curses. Yet beyond them, Aaron knew, others were silent and fearful of the power that lay within the tent of meeting. Even Korah and his troop must sense that power.

Still, as Aaron pushed aside the blue cloth, he felt eyes on him, and he knew. They did not fear. They watched. As he opened the tabernacle and closed his eyes to transform himself into the figure of a priest who had met God, he could hear voices.

"What does he do in there?"

"Nothing."

For the first time since Aaron had been ordained, he could make out the faint, dark oblongs of their ears against the very cloth of the tent. Their breath rasped. They were waiting. He waited too, though he did not know for what. His found himself taking from his belt Abihu's silver trumpet. What followed made no sense, yet all the same he drew the trumpet to his mouth and through it came a low, flat voice:

You are not pleasing in my sight.

Aaron felt the trumpet drop away, but his numb hand found the mouthpiece, and he said more.

You have blasphemed. You have broken my commandments. I will bring fire and death as I have brought them on the plains of Kibroth. Cease your rebellious wandering.

Aaron thought: I am already dead. There was no blood in his body and he could not even feel the metal mouthpiece between his lips, yet the voice kept coming, not his own voice. Whose voice?

Go into the land of Canaan, a green land which I have given to you, for your God is the Lord of Gods and so must Israel be the Lord of Nations.

With a great crack, the tent beam fell, and Aaron stood in the open air with the trumpet in his mouth. The ark, too, was exposed. Before them, with a corner of azure cloth bunched in his hand, stood Korah.

He addressed Aaron directly. "Are you God?"

Aaron's eyes flicked back and forth for Levites who would drag Korah away, yet every Levite had dropped his censer and now stood staring at Aaron with baleful eyes.

Korah asked again, "Are you God that you speak in God's voice?"

Aaron replied, "I am High Priest."

Korah said to Aaron, "You take too much on yourself." He pointed to the ark. "Open the box, so we can speak to God as priests together."

Aaron's voice shook. "You choose death?"

"We choose not to be slaves," Korah said. "Open the box so there are no prisoners or slaves among us."

Even those who stood with Korah trembled then, for inside that ark was God. Their hearts raced and their knees turned to water, and it was just at that moment that someone rushed over and stumbled, face first, over the heap of fallen blue cloth. They did not know, until he reached out and gripped Aaron's hand to pull himself to his feet, that it was Moses.

No one could remember when they had last seen him; he had changed. Rising, he looked diminished, stooped. Brown clay had worked its way into the network of scars that covered most of his face. He was breathing heavily; the fall had winded him. He said to Korah, in a wild, sad voice, "What have you done?"

Korah looked resolute, faced with the two old men. "You do not serve God," he said, "but yourself and your brother."

"You know how to serve God?" Moses said to Korah. His voice rasped, and the words came out in wild bursts. "You think you know?"

"No," said Korah. "That is why you must open the box. So we can question God as priests together."

"You take too much on yourself," Moses said to Korah, looking at him closely, and, for an instant, in that gaze was something of the man the Hebrews had known after Elim who would crouch a little and lean on his staff to meet someone face to face. Korah did not drop his eyes; he looked directly at Moses, and nothing in his own expression softened. Finally, Moses said, "In the morning you and your company will stand as priests before God. God will make a choice."

Moses stepped back, almost falling on the tangle of azure cloth again. He and Aaron were both lost in a shadow that crept over the tent; night was falling. Korah's companions surrounded him, waiting to hear what he would answer, but he said nothing. His eyes were on the ark.

That night, Dathan found Moses sitting outside of Aaron's tent. He swung towards him wild-eyed and sweating, and he wiped his forehead with throbbing hands and cried out: "Make a law!"

Moses looked up at him. "I don't make law. God makes law."

"I'll knead the clay," said Dathan. "and you'll carve the words and then I'll take the tablet to the tribes and tell them: This Canaan is no good!"

Moses' eyebrows fluttered a little. He said, "I don't make laws. Law belongs to God."

"And God would have temples and kings?"

"After tomorrow," Moses said, "you will know what God wants."

"Tomorrow!" Dathan spat. "Two sets of skinned priests. They're all fools. Korah was a smart kid once, but he needs fresh air. He's bored. All that talk about holiness, holiness. That's one thing. But this Canaan! Canaan means the end of everything. Once we have land we have owners, we have gold. We both know."

"What do we know?" Moses asked. He sounded tired.

Dathan struck the tent post with his fist. "You know that if we have Canaan we'll have Lords again. We'll be like everyone else. We'll have masters and slaves. You don't want that."

"What I want makes no difference," said Moses.

Dathan grabbed Moses' shoulder and gave him a friendly shake. "Don't say that. It makes all the difference. If it weren't for you, we'd all be dead."

Moses tried to free himself. "Aaron is God's priest. Do you stand with Aaron or Korah?"

Dathan's grip tightened. "If it weren't for you, we'd be sheep or wolves. We'd be scared all the time, and either we'd eat shit or cut our neighbor's throats. But you led us to Sinai. And you led us to law."

With a sharp tug, Moses loosed his shoulder. "God's law."

Dathan read his face. "You know better."

Moses only asked again, "Do you stand with Aaron or with Korah?"

"We walked away from Pharaoh's law. We walked away from death. We'll walk away again," Dathan said, and he gestured eastward with a shaking hand. "We'll write the Law of Feet. Get up. We'll go together. We'll leave these sheep and wolves to Canaan where they'll kill each other."

"And what about your brother?" Moses asked him.

Dathan went on as though he hadn't heard. "We wouldn't look back. Just the way you didn't look back when you left the mines that day. You were marked, but you just got up and walked away, like a free man."

Moses raked his dirty hands through his beard and said to Dathan, "I have a brother and he took my hand at Elim. You also took my hand, Dathan. Why did you take my hand?"

"Because I love you," Dathan said to Moses. "Because—"

"Because you are not free," said Moses. "You cannot walk away without looking back."

"You're lying!" Dathan shouted, and he bolted out into the open air and was lost in a cloud of sand, but Moses knew he would not get far before his heart pulled in the opposite direction and he returned to his brother.

When the red tent emptied that night, Korah sat with his back warming near the brazier. He hugged his knees, thinking again and again of the locked ark. He wondered if the lock could be broken by force. Could he break it with the woman's knife?

"I need your knife," he said to the woman who sat weaving snake skins into a black ephod.

"More men to turn into priests?" she asked. Her voice was still bitter, and her months with Korah had done nothing to soften her face or her heart. It was that very hardness which allowed her to take the zabb of a man in her hand and, heedless of pain, draw him through fear to holiness.

"No," said Korah. "I have a box to open."

The woman frowned, and she bowed her head and dug her hand between her breasts. When she spread her fingers, in her palm there was a key.

Korah's mouth spread in a line and opened slowly. "Where did you find that?"

"On the shore of the Red Sea," said the woman. "It lay between two pebbles. I took it, though I do not know why." She gave Korah the key and said, "It is made of gold. A soft metal. It may break in the lock before it turns."

Korah closed his hand around the key and set that hand against his lips, and for the rest of the night, he moved his mouth over the ridges of the key, and he had many strange dreams.

The woman left him there and woke her son, and the two stepped out to take a walk. They stood for a moment in front of the tent, filling their lungs with frosty air. The sky was clear, and stars spread in a range of colors from one border of cliff to the other above mist drawn out of scrub and thorn. She pulled her son close and let her hand linger in his black hair.

A man stepped from the mist. His long face was clean-shaven, white and old, and he trailed loaves of yellow bread. Walking towards the woman, he said:

> I will question you and you will declare to me.
> Shall a fault finder contend with the almighty?
> Have you entered into the springs of the sea
> or walked in the recesses of the deep?
> Have the gates of death been revealed to you
> or have you seen the gates of deep darkness?
> Have you comprehended the expanse of the earth?

The woman answered, "Yes."

"You're lying," said the man.

The woman drew her lips together for a moment. She took her son's hand and walked away.

Four

This is what Korah dreamed. He stood in the center of a field. The field was red with barley, and he said out loud: This is not Sinai. Then: This is not Goshen. He could not think where the field could lie, nor could he understand how he had managed to, himself, become an ear of barley standing on a stem. Around him, ears rustled, bowing their heads to the earth. Korah wanted to shout: Do not bow to me! Yet he was barley and had lost his voice. Thus he was forced to rustle and to rustle, and he rustled himself from the stem until his head flew off, rose up, and sparkled like a star.

Into the heavens he floated, and around him stars bowed down, pointmost, the crescent moon among them. Again, Korah tried to cry out but found stars had no voices and so could only burn and burn and hope his heat would drive the bowing stars away. Yet in burning, he fell from heaven and found himself on the top of a mountain where goats chewed thorn.

What would you have me do?

Korah threw himself face down on stone, his heart skinned as with the stroke of a knife, but there was a small hand on his shoulder, and looking up, he saw the woman's son.

The boy's face was as dull as ever, but there was a maliciousness in his green eyes, and when he opened his mouth, out came the voice:

I am God's first priest. Who are you?

"A Hebrew," Korah answered. Scrambling up, he looked down at the boy and added, "I too have been consecrated."

So you are ready to meet God face to face?

"I am ready to let God go," said Korah. He felt with his dream hand for the key and found it clasped between his thumb and forefinger.

The boy looked up at Korah, and his mass of black hair slipped from his forehead and revealed straight black eyebrows. *Tell me, Izhar's son, about life in Goshen. Is it all they say? Did Israel's tribes live without trouble? Did they not lack for meat? Did they know where their parents were buried? Did their homes have old foundations? I have spent my life in wandering, and such wonders seem impossible.*

Korah replied, "They know where their fathers are buried, but not their sons."

Bah. Sons. Who cares for sons? There will always be enough sons. If some die, it does not matter.

Shivering, Korah backed away and said, "You too are someone's son, child."

Korah has a father who loves him, said the boy. And he raised his lean, brown arms and everything dissolved into red which proved to be the cloth of the tent, riddled with sunlight.

It was late morning. Korah sprang up and the key dropped from his hand. As he scrambled for it, he noticed that the woman and her son were gone. They had left the snake-skin ephod and a pair of boots.

In the tent of Aaron, Moses sat, deadened by a hard night. Aaron himself was frantically tying his ephod, scrubbing tarnish from gold, trying to lose his worry in anxious fumbling, though above it all a note of terror sang.

Moses asked, "Where are your sons?"

"Finding Levites!" Aaron snapped. His head, shaved in haste, bled in three places, and the blood rolled down his cheek. He wiped the blood with his dirty scrub cloth, threw it to the floor, and turned to his brother. "I must know."

"What do you have to know?" Moses asked Aaron in a voice that told him nothing.

"Get up," Aaron said to Moses. "I want to see your face."

Moses reluctantly hoisted himself to his feet and let his head rest against his staff. Aaron took that head in his hands and stared at it with such force that the air crackled.

He asked Moses, "Will I die today?"

Moses closed his eyes. "Don't ask me that," he said.

"Who else do I ask? Who else!" Aaron pushed him away and rubbed his own head in his hands. "I can't ask...can't ask...anyone."

Moses shuffled towards his brother, dizzy and sluggish. The air was sour with the sweat of the two old men; the tent had been closed all night long. Moses said, "You are the priest."

Aaron did not look up, but said, in a hard Egyptian whisper, "What are you?"

"I tell you!" Moses shouted now in a broken voice, "I have no hand—"

"You're still running away," Aaron said.

Moses felt a white heat overtake him, and he drew back his staff to strike, but his heart turned, and he threw the staff on the ground and took his brother in his arms.

Under the heavy linen and gold, Aaron shook and sobbed, whispering, "Why is he silent? Why doesn't he speak to me? If he would say a word, my name—"

"You are ordained," Moses whispered again and again, trying to still his brother's trembling. "You are ordained, ordained at God's word, and you serve God. You are the one who serves God."

Aaron looked up. "In silence?"

"That is how it is done," Moses said.

"Why should I believe you?" Aaron asked, pulling away a little.

"Brother," said Moses, "a silent God has no quarrel with you. Do you want to quarrel with God?"

"No, no," Aaron said, his voice steadier now. He wiped away dried blood and tears. "I do not know if you are saying this only to comfort me. I do not always please God. I know. The quails—"

"Not on your account," said Moses.

"Whose then?" Aaron asked him.

Moses said, "Mine, maybe." He did not say more. He turned to open the flap of the tent so they could complete their preparations in the daylight, and Moses himself knotted the twined ephod with its belt of linen and buckled the beautiful breastplate, and in silence, Aaron tried to find peace but could not.

He said to Moses. "I was not permitted to mourn my sons."

Moses tied Aaron's sandals and looked up. "It is difficult to be a good father."

"Some days," Aaron said, "I think about our father."

"I knew him," said Moses. "He spoke to me."

A shadow passed across Aaron's face as he said, "He spoke to you? What sort of man was he?"

"He took on too much," Moses said. He drew the second sandal from the box of vestments and tied it onto Aaron's foot. He did not speak again.

From either end of Kadesh came the two camps. Korah walked from the red tent with two hundred and fifty priests, a rag-tag band of shaggy youths and miners swinging by their chains censers made of iron water basins. They had filled the bowls of the censers with dry thorn that crackled as it burned. Abiram's face flickered through white sparks. Dathan walked beside him. Korah himself was not who he had been the day before. He looked frail under his loose-knit snake-skin ephod. The boots made his steps small, and the hand which did not hold a censer was balled up, white-knuckled and shaking, as though he were about to throw a punch.

Eleazar and Ithamar had managed to gather only the most elderly of the Levite servants, among them Izhar who had been all but dragged from his tent where he had gone into mourning for a son already dead. The servants had been covered with as many treasures as their frames could carry: onyx, turquoise, lapis, and topaz mounted in red gold, white gold, yellow gold. Aaron himself stood before the door of his tent, sad and unsteady. His silver rod of priesthood was in his hand, and Moses grasped his elbow.

Between the two was the place where the azure tent had stood, which now held the bare ark. A night's dust had dulled the gold work; it looked like a dirty box. Observers stood at a distance, the surviving Goshenites, a handful of Sinai girls, and most numerous and powerful, Joshua's boy-troop who ringed the servants of Aaron with a dark, still, watchful presence.

Moses stepped away from Aaron and moved towards the ark. His face was lost in the competing smokes of the censers. His voice was faint but clear.

"You want to know how to serve God. God will give an answer. If Korah and his fellows die a common death, then maybe Aaron is not God's ordained. But if God makes a new death for them and the earth swallows them up and closes over them alive, then you will know God has ordained Aaron alone and that Korah and his followers despise God."

A few stray Hebrews who had wandered behind Korah slipped away, but Korah broke the silence and called out: "Let God answer in his own voice!"

"What will come to pass," said Moses, "will be God's voice."

Now Korah stepped forward, and his censer cracked against the ground. "Open the ark so we can tell God that we love him. Open it so we can know his name!"

Moses did not answer. The smoke around Korah parted so that the flat blue of the sky shone through and the world itself had turned into the tent of meeting, and Korah stepped through the clear air towards the place where God lived, and he thrust forward his fisted hand.

As his fingers opened, so did the earth. It opened before him, spread like fingers, catching up everyone who stood with him and throwing them down into a place without a bottom. They cried out and flung their censers in a wild attempt to catch the edge, but those censers flew from their hands, raining thorn sparks in all directions, and the hairy limbs of miners, the smooth limbs of Levite youths, spun, flickered, and were gone.

Maddened, the Hebrews fled so recklessly that they tumbled over ridges and cracked their skulls, and the living stumbled over the dead in the rush to leave the place where a new death had been made for Korah, for fear the Lord would close the earth over their heads.

This is what Aaron saw. Smoke clogged his throat, and he breathed only sometimes. His ears were full of swinging golden bells. If death would seek him, it would not have long to travel. If life came to him, it would not stay for long.

When Moses spoke, Aaron could not hear him. When fire swallowed Korah, some words blew back to Aaron from the pit.

"He will let me free him!"

Aaron's rod was still in his hand. His ephod was smeared and his breastplate had come loose at the shoulder. Before him was a pit closing over two hundred and fifty living men, and beyond that a plain of the dead; a plague of death swept towards him.

He stood between the living and the dead, and raising his rod, he drew up a surge of dry heat. Then silence. Aaron knew. He had heard God's voice at last. He was not blessed, not blessed at all.

Aaron said out loud: "Brother, I want to know."

Moses was at his side now, with a blackened face and eyes turned inside out.

Aaron said, "I want to know God's name."

Moses turned away. The quiet air emptied of smoke and made every word ring like a drop of metal. From far off, at first faint:

"*La la la*— I know a name."

Aaron turned white. He grasped Moses as he struggled to keep his balance, and Moses flicked his head back and forth to find the source of the song.

Dancing among the dead was Miriam herself, in her own form, great, black and old. She laughed and loosed her hair; her wrinkles filled with raindrops. In her raised arms she held something.

"Many names I know—you know a name—*la la!*"

"Oh Lord," Aaron whispered deep in his throat. "preserve us from the witch."

But Moses seemed less frightened than drawn forward, and slowly he loosed Aaron's arm and, with shuffling steps, moved towards his sister. He passed with care around the bodies of the dead and the scattered iron censers. Snuffed thorn smoked through the rainfall, and the earth was slippery and bright. The staff of Moses cracked as he raised a free hand for balance.

"*La la la*— I know many names— Amen-Seleh— many a name

you know."

"Sister!" Moses shouted. "No riddles now! The truth! I won't harm you!"

Miriam only laughed and thrust forward what she bore through rain and thorn smoke. The face came into focus. Clipped black hair. Straight eyebrows. A long neck like a reed. The voice of Moses caught.

"You know a name—a name is known to you—" Miriam sang again. Then, from behind, crept the bright line of Miriam's well which had sought Miriam for long years, and finding her disarmed and singing, it swooped behind her heels, swallowed, and in a flash of spray, drank her at last.

From far off came Aaron's voice. "Brother! What name?"

Moses did not answer. He only looked through abrupt sunlight at the place where Miriam, Zipporah, and the well had been. It was bare and dry.

Five

At first they were reluctant to bury the dead. After all, was it wise to pay respect to those brought low by the hand of the Lord? Israel would have sooner moved on, but it was Moses who took his staff and began to dig in the sand. They dug through that afternoon and night, until they hit bare rock.

Over each grave, the name of the dead was spoken, and it was at dawn that one of Joshua's troop found the body of a boy he did not know. He took the corpse to Joshua, who knew everyone.

Joshua gave the corpse a glance. "He is not from any tribe," he said. "Bury him under the name Stranger."

It was so. The sand was piled over Stranger as it was piled over the others, and by midday the troop of Joshua had completed their task and sat among the graves, gnawing their yellow bread.

Priests were forbidden to touch the dead, so Aaron, Eleazar and Ithamar kept to their tent. They heard Moses direct the Levite servants:

"Take up the fallen iron censers and pound them flat, for they are holy."

The old Levites shivered, and one said, "The false priests held those things. If we touch them we will die."

"They are holy," Moses said again, and for fear the earth would swallow them alive, the Levites gathered the censers. Thorn ash still clung to their bases and rose in clouds as they were pounded into flat breastplates. The Levites pounded without spirit.

Only Izhar whacked and whacked, smashing each censer with two strokes into a flat, dull plate. He stripped off his linen so his back, with its off-white whip-scars and its knots of muscle, was bare to the sun, and he thrust out his beardless chin and cried out: "Give me another! Give me another!" until he flattened seventy that day.

When the tasks of Israel were complete, Moses brought the survivors to the edge of Kadesh. As Aaron stood before his litter, he looked out over a sea of heavily veiled girls and young men bearing spears, all of the children born in Sinai. Who was left from Goshen now? A handful of old men like himself and Moses, his two sons, and Joshua, who stood foremost with the Amalekite spear in his hand.

Moses said, "We go to Meribah."

How many times had they broken camp to wander? Aaron could not say. Yet now there was none of the old grumbling, the chatter of the women who would mutter: "Where? As if we don't have enough trouble where we are!" or the miners who would call out: "Do you mean our legs to be ground down to stumps?" Dathan was not there to shake the laws from his sack of homespun into his cart and shout: "Move, you dogs! Shake off those fleas and move it!" There was not even the sound of goats and sheep.

There were only hard faces. Aaron could not look at those faces for long. He turned and sought Moses, and the face of Moses was horribly flat, as though it had been pounded in a single blow.

"We go to Meribah," Moses said, "and then to the borders of Edom. You ask for no more signs?"

Joshua stepped forward and said, "We serve the Lord."

At Joshua's words, the rod in Aaron's hand burst into flower. Aaron drew it back and the blossoms scattered and gave way to ripe almonds. Aaron wanted to shake that rod from his hand. It was perverse. They were not in a garden. They were in the Sinai where almonds never blossomed and fruit never ripened. Yet even as Aaron wavered, Eleazar took the rod and raised it above the heads of Israel.

"Know this!" Eleazar called. "We serve the Lord of Gods!"

Under the banner of the fruited branch, they left the graves of Kadesh and walked some distance before sunset, that they might camp the night far from that cursed place.

It was not until morning that a few of Joshua's boys approached their leader and said, "The well is gone."

Joshua turned and shielded his eyes with his hand. Nothing.

Before them was no sign of an oasis, not so much as an acacia tree. He nodded and said, "The Lord will provide."

Indeed, behind their heels was holy bread. Indeed, within their veins ran chosen blood. How could they doubt the word of Joshua, beloved of Moses, hero of Elim, who, as they were born, secured for them blessing at the foot of the Lord's mountain? They marched under his banner and whetted the points of their spears on his whetstone.

So they too said, "The Lord will provide."

Word came to the Levites that Miriam's well was gone, and with it any hope of water. Yet how could they grumble if grumbling brought down death? Most of them walked bearing the plates they had pounded, and their shoulders ached under the awful, blasphemous weight, but they could not take them off for fear of the Lord. The iron made them all the hotter, and already their water gourds were empty.

Inside the priest's litter, Eleazar said to Aaron, "Why don't you just get the nomad to strike a rock?"

Aaron shook his head, and more than his head shook, for he had caught a slight, persistent fever.

"The Lord will provide," Eleazar whispered in Egyptian. "Strike at night. He'll know where. And at night we make a sacrifice and say it came from—"

"I don't know where it comes from," Aaron said.

Ithamar shook himself from a doze and muttered, "It comes from the Lord, Amen-Seleh." Then he went back to sleep.

Eleazar glanced at his brother and gave his father a conspiratorial smile. "I don't know if the Sinai has turned him from a fool into a madman."

"And what has it done to me?" Aaron asked him. The heavy litter curtains compressed the scent of almonds, and the aroma was so overbearing that at last Aaron could not stand it. He worked at the curtain's knot until it broke and he stumbled from that moving litter into the open.

He hit the dust face first, and he rubbed his head; the Levites who bore the litter stopped and looked down.

"Lord Priest," one asked him, "would you have us raise you to your seat again?"

Aaron looked at the man. He was at least his own age, and the seven other men who bore the litter were no younger. In Goshen, by now, they would have beards curling down to their knees, and they would have retired from kiln-stoking to a life of sleep and shade. Maybe their granddaughters would have brought them cucumbers to eat. Maybe they would have sucked out the marrow and looked out of the shadows with the seeds between their teeth.

"I will walk," Aaron said.

Turning, the Levite motioned the others, and they bore the litter on.

Where were the granddaughters now? They were in the rear of the company, wordless and veiled, bearing as many burdens as a Goshen ass. Sharon was hugely pregnant and set both hands below her stomach and walked a little slower than the rest. Faint dust followed her, but no water.

Aaron made himself stand and force one foot before the other, and his determination pushed him past the litter and beyond a tabernacle grown so dull with sand that it was almost black. After a time, he found himself beside Moses.

Moses did not look happy to see him. He only said, "You're a fool to leave your litter."

Aaron covered his bare head with his hand against the sunlight, and staffless and rodless, he stumbled to keep pace. "I couldn't breath in there," he said.

"And so?" Moses said, without turning his head.

Aaron said, "I want to meet my death where you can see me."

Moses stopped walking, and for a moment Aaron thought he had been staggered by his words, but he was only looking for a way along a cliff. Once he found it, he walked on past Aaron without looking back.

Aaron called out: "You heard me!"

Moses tramped forward, receding in the dust as though there was no one behind him at all.

"You heard me!" Aaron called in Hebrew, not even caring

that everyone could hear. "I'm dying, Moses! Boys can live for a few days without water, but not an old man!"

Moses turned at last. He waited until Aaron was close enough to hear him, and he said, "I am an old man too."

"I'm not you," Aaron said. "This is not my native land."

The face of Moses was gray above his beard. "I have no native land, Aaron. I have no home."

Under the flat iron of Moses' face burned fire, and in it Aaron read such despair and rage that he felt his thirst congeal to fear, and he fell back and kept a distance so he would not have to look into that face again.

At twilight, Israel reached Meribah. It was a stone plateau. The tongues of the cattle hung dry, and a few sheep moved listlessly towards some rumor of grass though their throats were too parched to work anything down. The Levites shrugged off their iron armor and felt the Angel of Death pass over them, brushing close enough to make them hug themselves and stare at the moon. Joshua's boys licked their dry lips with dry tongues.

One asked Joshua, "How far are we from Edom?"

Joshua replied, "Not far."

"So we conquer them and take their water?"

Joshua shook his head.

The boy was twelve years old, already two handspans taller than Joshua, and he could handle a spear better than a warrior of Goshen or a bandit of Amaleke.

"Your son will conquer with you," Joshua said to him. "And your grandson."

"As you say." The boy bowed his head.

"Already," Joshua said, "the Lord has provided us with sons."

For in the camp of the women, Sharon had gone into labor, though she did not make a sound. There was something chilling in the silence, as dry air filled with nothing, as the faces of the other girls revealed nothing, as Sharon emerged with a son who did not weep.

The boy-troop kept a distance. For all their love of blood, they felt sick and dizzy at the thought of what lay between a woman's legs, and though none confided the fear to Joshua, Joshua himself said, "Wait until the son is weaned."

"Captain," one asked Joshua, "how are sons made?"

"They are provided by the Lord," Joshua said, "as he will provide us with water."

At dawn, they gave thanks with a sacrifice of all the sheep and bull calves that had died during the night, bled by Eleazar and Ithamar and burnt in a grace offering. Aaron had grown too weak to hold the sacrificial knife, and he refused to be closed in his tent. He lay in the open air with his head on a stone.

Moses sat on a rock some distance away with his staff over his knees. He listened for complaints, for murmurs, for anything but silence. The sun traveled first up his toes and then over his knees and then across his chest, and it was when it lay in a thick line across his shoulders that he rose from the rock and walked to the place where his brother lay dying.

Aaron's head was stubbled and his upper lip was flecked with hairs like froth. His eyes were closed, but Moses could tell by the pulse below the lids that he was still alive and listening.

Moses said, "Joshua tells them that God will give us water."

Aaron's voice traveled up as on a thread, so faint that Moses could not think whether the words were in slave talk, Hebrew, Egyptian, or some other language that they spoke in common. He said, "You are afraid."

Moses knelt down, and he parted the lips of Aaron so he could say more.

"You are afraid God blessed the ape." The words trailed off, not because Aaron was dead but because there was no moisture to smooth the voice along. Moses forced himself to his feet and walked away from Aaron into the open.

He walked past the tents of Israel. Silence, as the elderly Levites prepared yet more dead sheep and cattle for the altar and polished gold with handfuls of hot sand. Silence, as Joshua's boys crouched with their eyes turned towards Canaan and waited for the

Lord to give them water. Moses felt his spine tighten as he walked past the veiled girls who gathered around the tent where Sharon nursed her newborn son. He walked until he came to a rock.

The rock was porous and cleft. Moses hoisted back his staff and felt, as he did, his shoulders spread and his heart divide to breaking point, and then with all of his strength, he struck.

Water crashed on his knees. Pushed back, he fell in the path of a broad spring that spread across hot stone, plastering his rags to his body and pulling his hair and limbs in all directions, and he wept because he was still angry. He wanted to strike that rock again and again until it was pulp, though he would break his staff or break his back in trying, though it might swallow him alive.

But Moses was doomed to live for a long time. The Israelites drew him from the water, gathered him in their arms, and carried him away. Still, the anger of Moses was not gone. He shouted: "You are cursed! You are cursed!" but they did not answer, and he knew that he was shouting not in Hebrew, but Egyptian. His stutter had returned, as had his gape, so as they rushed him to the tabernacle he wrestled himself out of their grip and stood, the picture of bewilderment, calling out: "Cur-cursh! Cursh! Cu-urse!" The curse could never find the Israelites.

Nor could the water find Aaron. He had died without Moses beside him, on a rock surrounded by a ring of flowing water. Around the island of a rock where Aaron died floated a bulrush basket, heavy-laden. No one dared touch the basket as it made a stately circle, and it was not an Israelite but a goat who started pulling at the woven bulrushes and overturned its contents into the water.

It was an afterbirth suffused in gold, glowing and fragrant. It floated for a moment, light streaming through it as though it were preserved in honey. Then it began to sink, leaving a ghost of honey-gold on the surface of the water before even that seemed like a trick of sunlight, something they could not be sure they saw at all.

Aaron was buried a week later with great ceremony at Meribah. The night of Aaron's burial, one of the boys said to Joshua, "There is the sound of battle in the camp."

Joshua shook his head and only said, "Keep away."

"But listen!"

Suddenly the night tore in half with a shriek. It was the cry of an eight-day-old son being circumcised. Joshua rose from his seat and stood before a span of silky water. He said, "Keep away from the women's tents. It has nothing to do with us. Just let them be." If he did not look pleased when he took his seat again, neither did he look displeased. Rather, he looked towards Canaan which lay eastward, and his small eyes focused to points of light. He turned his spear in his hand.

As for Moses, he watched years pass, dumb with anger, living on bread and hatred. Sometimes he would hear a voice.

You are holy.

Against good sense, his heart would clog his throat.

Bless yourself, for you are holy and he is not.

"Joshua is not holy?" Moses would find the strength to whisper. The fact that he whispered would tell him that he feared Joshua now.

Not Joshua.

Moses knew the voice was not God's. Still, his ears turned up to listen, and his hands would grasp his staff so he could rise and speak.

He would not go, Moses, Korah said. *He would not leave his prison. He would sooner stay there, locked away, and let you bear the blame. Don't trust him.*

And rising, Moses said, "I have no choice."

Six

Once there lived in Heshbon a young prince beloved of his mother and father, and his name was Arnon. Most prized was Arnon for his beauty, his well-formed limbs, and his black, bright eyes, and, moreover, upon his cheek was a birthmark like a grain of amber resting on a length of silk.

Prince Arnon liked to dress in the guise of a porter and walk through Heshbon's market so he might mix with his subjects and learn to be a worthy king. He took no servants with him, but carried on his back a porter's basket heaped with the fruits of Heshbon: pomegranates, lemons, apricots and green and purple figs. All who saw him marveled at his light step and his silken cheek and his narrow waist, and every woman who watched him pass wished in her heart that he would bear those ripe figs to her chamber.

One day Arnon set down his basket and sat at the threshold of a garden, and the gate of the garden opened, and there stood a lady in a light veil who said: "Porter, I would have you bear me back dainties of all kinds, pastries swimming in honey, almond cakes, saffron rolls filled with preserves and glazed with rose water, and, moreover, the finest purple figs in all of Heshbon."

A breeze passed from the west and blew the lady's light veil from her face, and a single glance ravished Arnon's heart. He took the gold ring from his finger, and said to the lady: "Here is a pledge that I will return with all you desire before the sun has set."

Arnon searched market after market, yet each merchant's figs were either green and bitter, or black and dry. By the day's end, Arnon was near despair, when suddenly he stepped into a thick, damp fragrance. He saw that he had come upon the back gate of the very garden where he had begun, and beyond that gate grew clusters of grapes and figs.

Yet before that gate stood a terrible jinn who said to Arnon: "This is my garden, and every fig within belongs to me. I alone can sate my lady's craving for figs, for my figs are fresh and my figs are purple and my figs are bursting with seed.

Arnon said, "Your figs are very marvelous, but not so marvelous as the tale of Balaam and his Ass."

"By my zabb!" the great jinn cried. "I would hear this tale! And if it is as marvelous as you say, you will choose figs as you please, but if it falls short, your life will be forfeit."

So Prince Arnon began:

Know, oh auspicious and mighty one, that Beor, King of Moab, was seduced by a jinn who bore him two sons. The first was named Balak, and he was as beautiful as the day is bright, and on his chin was a birthmark like a grain of amber. The second son, Balaam, was born blind, but truth spoke through him, and he was truth's beloved, so that all whom he blessed were blessed and all whom he cursed were cursed.

It happened that when both boys approached manhood, the king called them before him and said, "I would have Balak be king after me, but I would know what might become of blind Balaam."

Balak said, "Oh father, I would place half the kingdom into Balaam's hands, that he might bless us."

King Beor kicked over his seat and shouted: "You would place a blind man beside yourself? Neither of you are fit to follow me! You and your brother will be pulled in two directions, you, Balak, east to China, and you, Balaam, west to Goshen, that you may die in the wilderness of Sinai."

Balaam, who had mighty powers, drew up his small hands to hold his prophecy, and thus recited:

> Woe to you, O Moab!
> > You are undone, O people of Chemosh!
> He has made his sons fugitives
> > and his daughters captives!

So did Balaam curse his father. Before setting out on their journeys, the two boys wept and clasped each other. Balak said to Balaam: "Take the white she-ass which was given to us by our mother the jinn, for she knows all the road between Moab and Goshen and is surpassing wise."

Balak bade his servants take from the stable a milk-white ass with intelligent blue eyes, and ears as sharp and pink as petals. The she-ass lowered herself to the ground, so Balaam could climb onto her back. Moreover, Balak tossed across the saddle a double bag strung with raw gold and heavy with provisions.

"This too is a gift from our mother," said Balak. "It is filled with the bread of fellowship, and can not be emptied."

Balaam thanked his brother for his help and fled Moab, and over many years he had countless adventures which do not concern us here. Yet let us say that indeed the white ass knew the road to Goshen, and from thence to Midian and Elim and from thence back to Moab, and a firm friendship formed between master and she-ass, for she was Balaam's eyes.

Prince Balak lived a long time in China and married the king of China's seven daughters, seven girls like young moons, more beautiful than any women in the world save Bityah the Light of Goshen. When Prince Balak heard that his father had fallen, just as Balaam had foretold, he took his wives and sons and traveled over mountain and sea to claim the throne for himself and his brother. The people of Moab were so charmed by Balak's slim waist and his black eye and his seven wives and seventy sons that they welcomed him at once.

"Yet who is this brother, for whom you hold half the kingdom?" they asked him.

"He is the one who blesses," Balak answered.

The Moabites wondered how they could be more blessed than they were with Balak as their king, and they anxiously watched the roads for Balaam and his ass.

Now it was in those days that Israel conquered in the Negab, setting fire to cities, throwing kings from thrones, and sparing not even the grasses of the plains. King Balak prepared his many sons for

battle, and each day he watched for his brother, so he might bless
Moab, and Moab might be blessed.

It happened that Balaam had just returned to Moab and was
watering his she-ass by the river Peleth, and there a messenger found
him and begged him to return to his brother's court and bless Moab.

Balaam said, "I cannot say what truth will forbid."

"Yet he holds half the kingdom for you," said the messenger.
"He says your blessing and your curse have the power to turn a
battle, and that you have perfect wisdom."

"All of that is so," said Balaam.

That night leave came to him, saying: *Go to your brother*. And
Balaam saddled his she-ass, and she lowered herself to the
ground so he could mount her. The stirrups of the princely saddle
were worn dull and smooth, for Balaam had traveled to earth's end
and back since he had last met his brother.

The road below the ass's bonny feet was straight and clear,
yet he had not traveled an hour before the ass reeled into a vineyard.

Balaam whispered: "Walk on, my beauty. Well you know the
way." But she did not move. He drew out his switch, which he had
seldom used before, and he tickled her ear. She reared and knocked
the saddle sideways. Angered, Balaam struck in earnest, and the ass
bore down against the vineyard wall and pinned Balaam's left foot
against the stone with a sickening crunch. A shot of pain made
Balaam strike the ass's head so hard that he broke the switch, and he
shouted: "Move! Move! Move!" The ass paid him no heed, but rather
lowered herself to the grass and sat.

The blood of Balaam mixed with stone and grass. His foot
was pulp. Pain and anger filled his bones and he drew up his fist to
strike the ass again, but before that fist came down, the Lord opened
the mouth of the ass, and she spoke, saying:

"What have I done to you, that you struck me three times?"

Balaam answered, "You mock me! I wish I had a sword so I
could kill you!"

"Am I not your ass?" she said, "that you have ridden on your
whole life long? And was it a common thing for me to cause you
harm?"

And when the words had passed her lips, Balaam's blindness fell away, and his eyes were opened, and he saw before him an angel holding a sword.

The angel spoke to Balaam: "You did wrong to strike the ass, for had she passed beyond this point, I would have surely killed you and left her alive."

Balaam's eyes stung, and they took in every shadow on the vineyard wall, and every feather on the angel's wings. He said, "I did not know death stood in my way. I had leave to go."

Go, said the Lord, *though death stands in your way, and speak only the words I speak to you.*

The ass rose from the vineyard grass, and Balaam rode past the place where his death had revealed itself, on to the court of his brother, and as he traveled, he could not question what might come to pass but knew only that to any who had eyes, truth was wayward and must be served without hope of wisdom or of love. And Balaam said:

> *Who is this that hides counsel without knowledge?*
> *Therefore I have uttered what I did not understand,*
> *things too wonderful for me,*
> *which I did not know.*

> *"Hear and I will speak:*
> *I will question you and you declare to me."*
> *I had heard of you by the hearing of the ear*
> *but now my eyes see you; therefore I despise myself*
> *and repent in dust and ashes.*

When King Balak heard that his brother was coming, he was so anxious to meet him that he rode past the gates of his palace on the fleetest of his horses, shouting: "Brother! Beloved! Well met, for Israel is no more than a day's march from here, and you must curse them!"

King Balak leapt from his horse, and Balaam's ass lowered herself to the ground so that Balaam could dismount and meet his brother. King Balak saw that Balaam's blindness had passed away, and he rejoiced.

But Balaam said, "I came to you, but can only speak those words the Lord sets in my mouth."

King Balak said, "Surely your tongue will turn them to our favor. Look! At the palace gates my many sons sacrifice oxen so the smoke may carry your curse onto Israel."

"You might prepare seven altars," Balaam said, "and on each altar sacrifice a young bull and a ram, and still I can only speak what the Lord sets in my mouth."

And the Lord laid words on Balaam's tongue. He turned his empty hands up to hold his prophecy.

> *Balak bids me: Curse Israel.*
> *How can I curse whom God has not cursed?*
> *From the tops of rocks I see him*
> *and from hills behold him.*
> *Who has counted the dust of Israel,*
> *or numbered their stock?*
> *Let me die the death of the righteous!*
> *Might my end be like his!*

King Balak flung his arms around the shoulders of his brother and cried, "What have you done? I asked you to curse our enemies and you have blessed them altogether!"

Balaam answered, "I only say what the Lord has put in my mouth."

Now all heard the mustering of Israel as they approached Moab's border. King Balak said to his brother, "As you are no longer blind, go with me now to a place where you can see Israel and know what they will do to your people."

King Balak led his brother to a high place, where the view spanned the plains of Zophim. There marched Israel. Their heads were like a shining cloud, and behind their footfalls lay dead without number, burnt grass, and the ruins of Sihon, Medeba and Ar. Balaam spoke over Israel a parable:

God is not a man that He could lie,
*   neither the son of man that he should repent.*
Behold, I am bidden to bless,
and what he has blessed I can not call back.
God, who has brought them out of Egypt
is like the lofty horns of a wild ox.
Behold: Israel rises like a lioness
and lifts himself up like a lion
who does not rest until he's eaten of the prey
*   and drunk the blood of the slain.*

King Balak wept, and he fell to the earth before his brother and begged: "Say no more. Neither bless nor curse them."

Yet Balaam only raised his hands and replied, "I neither bless nor curse, but only speak the word the Lord sets in my mouth."

"Then turn at least to Moab, so a blessing can fall on your own people!" Balak cried, and he raised his brother up and mounted him on his own horse and rode to Peor which overlooked the whole of Moab, with its flat roof-tops, red barley, and white vineyard walls.

Yet before King Balak could stop him, Balaam turned back to face Israel. He looked at them, bronze-colored men with black eyes, bearing captured bows and spears, youths close behind, leather slings ready in their hands, their pockets full of sharpened stones, veiled women with sons slung on their shoulders, daughters leading red cattle and yellow sheep, Levites swinging censers like catapults so the Lord could ride above war on a cloud of holiness.

So Balaam loosed the word of the Lord from his tongue and took up his parable:

The saying of Balaam the son of Beor
The saying of a man whose eyes are open
*   fallen down, yet with opened eyes;*

How goodly are your tents, O Jacob
Your dwelling places, O Israel.

As valleys stretched out,
As gardens by the riverside,
And his kingdom shall be exalted.

God who has brought him forth out of Egypt
        is for him like the lofty horns of a wild ox;
He shall eat up the nations that are his adversaries
        and shall break their bones to pieces,
            and pierce them through with his arrows.

Blessed be all who bless you
        and cursed be all who curse you.

King Balak struck his hands together and he bellowed out: "Flee Moab! I would have given you half the kingdom, but fear now for your life, Balaam! Do you seek your own death?"

"I need not seek it," Balaam said, "for it has found me, and it will not be by your hand."

Balak called his seventy sons to strike his brother dead, only to find those sons gone. The two brothers stood on the height of Peor alone. Only the horse and white ass stood beside them, their moist breath the lone smoke of divination, their flanks bright in the sun.

Balaam said, "I cannot be silenced, but I will go on, and tell you what this people will do to Moab in the end of days."

The saying of Balaam the son of Beor
The saying of the man whose eyes are opened;
who sees visions of the almighty,
        fallen down, but with open eye.

I see him—but not now.
I behold him—but not near.
A scepter shall rise out of Israel;
It will crush the forehead of Moab.
Though your dwelling be firm

Though your nest set in a rock
you shall be wasted.

After Balaam finished his prophecy, he mounted his white she-ass and left his brother. King Balak mounted his horse, and he too went on his way.

When it was clear that Prince Arnon had concluded his tale, the jinn said: "Indeed that is very marvelous, but rather lacking, for what became of the seven daughters of the King of China, and what of the wonderful white ass who spoke to Balaam, and what of Balaam's foot, smashed to pulp, as I will smash your own head in a few moments?"

Arnon smiled at the Jinn and only said, "My head and my death do not belong to you, but to Israel, who already blast their trumpets at the gate of Heshbon, and the lady in the garden, whom you will not give to me, will soon be dead, and so will you, mighty jinn.

"Jinn do not die!" the mighty one roared, and he made himself as high as the gate, and blasted fire through his yellow teeth until the leaves spreading across the fig vines withered.

"No," Arnon replied, "but they are forgotten. It will be as though you are trapped in a corked lamp, and tossed into a well without a bottom, and no one will draw you out, neither pretty prince nor lady."

When the jinn saw that Arnon was unafraid, he brought himself down to the height of a man, and his teeth grew white and tiny as a kitten's. "Prince," the jinn said, "I will give you figs if you will tell me a tale which will cheer my heart."

Arnon quickly agreed, but before he could begin, a trumpet sounded, and Israel set fire to the walls of Heshbon.

Seven

In the end, they left Moses on Mount Nebo. Before him was a young ox bound for sacrifice, already bled by priests and set on a nest of burning coal.

"He will not enter Canaan with us," Joshua had said. He laid his head beneath the hands of Moses for a blessing. What did Israel have to do with him? They were blessed, blessed with fearlessness, with hearts that never pulled in two directions.

"He blesses whom he blesses," Moses had said to Joshua.

"And in his name," Joshua had said, "we conquer."

Nation after nation had fallen, kings, queens, priests and prophets, Og the King of Bashen and all of his household, threescore cities of Argob emptied and smoking, and the giants called the Zamzummim, and Edom, and Arnon of Heshbon, and Sihon, Heshbon's king, and Balaam son of Beor, and all of Giliad.

Moses watched Israel cross the Jordan, and as he waited to die, he asked again, "What do they have to do with me?"

The young ox roasted. Bled dry, it did not take long for the fire to meet its flesh and bubble through its skin. Moses turned his face away.

From somewhere: *Eat the ox.*

Moses did not answer.

Eat it and live, Moses.

The stench thickened. Moses thrust his head in his hands.

Eat the meat.

"I will not!" Moses shouted now. He hoisted himself up, though his knees were useless to him, and hot air clenched his skin. Very faintly, he asked, "Why should I live?"

Then he knew. He could eat and gain strength enough to climb down Nebo, and he would meet Israel on the west bank of that

Jordan river, would stand before them and would speak.

What would he say? If they were blessed, how could he face them? If they were cursed, how could he save them? It was not in his hands. Yet how could it not be in his hands? How could he let them go?

The ox's muzzle turned a little in the fire. Its eyes were open, popped with heat blisters, and its black neck throbbed. Shivering, Moses said again, "I cannot. Leave me alone."

You pity the ox but not Canaan? You pity the ox but not Israel? The ox is dead, Moses.

"What can I do for Canaan? Leave me alone, Korah!"

You think I'm Korah?

"Who are you then?" The throat of Moses clenched, and his nose ran into his beard.

You don't know me?

"You are not God," Moses said. "It isn't simple. I cannot save them. Leave me alone to die."

Tell me, Moses. Don't you know my voice?

Moses held his ears closed with his hands, and then he whispered: "Merneptah."

Ever the voice of your own heart.

Through smoke, Moses watched the calf vibrate, and his stomach gave a pinch and a pull. He shouted, "Never the voice of my heart!"

Your own heart commands, Moses. Your own heart.

"I do what God commands!" Moses said. And as he spoke he felt compelled to thrust his hands through burning coal and grasp the sacrifice. He would draw it from the altar. He would piece it together, fill the bloodless neck with his heart's blood, and bear it across his shoulders into Sinai.

He would move slowly, for the mountain pass was steep. But then the ox would bellow and the Sinai stone would answer. Surely he would burn from the neck downwards. Burning, he would carry the ox so far into the Sinai that nobody could follow, or separate their mingled bones, or know their names.

Afterword

The passages from the books of Exodus, Numbers and Job are from the Revised Standard Version. Note that this novel is scripturally accurate only in coincidence with my imagination.

> "...for all of the congregation is holy, every one of them, and the Lord is among them..."
>
> Numbers, 16:3

Amen, Seleh!

Carbondale, Illinois, 1990/Philadelphia, 1997

Simone Zelitch received her MFA from the University of Michigan where her first novel, *The Confession of Jack Straw*, in manuscript, won the Hopwood Award for Major Fiction. She began her second novel, *Louisa*, while teaching creative writing at Southern Illinois University at Carbondale, and continued to research it as a Peace Corps volunteer in Hungary. *Louisa* won the 2000 Samuel L. Goldberg Prize for Jewish Fiction. Ms. Zelitch teaches at Community College of Philadelphia. *Moses in Sinai* is her third novel.